Sunshine casts

DOUBLE VISION:
A Vista de Lirio Mystery

Successful realtor Julia Brooks moves to the quirky neighborhood of Vista de Lirio in the California desert and meets a riotous cast of eccentric characters. But her semiretirement is spoiled when she finds the body of the neighborhood lothario dead in the kitchen of her brand-new listing. Even more complicated? She also meets his ghost.

DOUBLE VISION is all new paranormal women's fiction and the first book in the *Vista de Lirio Mysteries* from USA Today Bestseller, Elizabeth Hunter, author of the Glimmer Lake series, the Elemental Mysteries, and the Irin Chronicles.

Praise for Elizabeth Hunter

DOUBLE VISION is a gem of a book that showcases how important female friendship is, even under the strangest of circumstances. Delightfully weird and definitely magical, it's the kind of book you want to grab when you are feeling the need for a quick and cozy escape.

— CAT BOWEN, ROMPER.COM

Elizabeth Hunter's books are delicious and addicting, like the best kind of chocolate. She hooked me from the first page, and her stories just keep getting better and better. Paranormal romance fans won't want to miss this exciting author!

— THEA HARRISON, NYT BESTSELLING AUTHOR

Developing compelling and unforgettable characters is a real Hunter strength.... Another amazing novel by a master storyteller!

— RT MAGAZINE

The bottom line: if you're not reading Elizabeth Hunter's novels, you should be!

— A TALE OF MANY BOOK REVIEWS

This book more than lived up to the expectations I had, in fact it blew them out of the water.

Elizabeth Hunter actually makes me look forward to growing older, especially if comes with these awesomely fun psychic perks. Her new paranormal women's fiction series is a truly fun, entertaining read!

If you can describe this book with one word, you'd use the word "enchanting". There is something about it, cosy, mysterious, secret, atmospheric and hidden that just kept pulling my strings.

Double Vision

A VISTA DE LIRIO MYSTERY

ELIZABETH HUNTER

Cover Designer: Karen Dimmick/Arcane Covers
Content Editor: Amy Cissell
Line Editor: Anne Victory/Victory Editing
Proofreader: Linda/Victory Editing

For more information, please visit ElizabethHunterWrites.com

Recurve Press, LLC
PO Box 4034
Visalia, CA 93278
USA

Chapter One

There was something magical about nights in the desert. Julia Brooks stepped out of the guesthouse on her ex-husband's estate, marveling at the lights and music that filled the evening. She walked up the brick path, circling the back patio of the Spanish estate in Palm Springs and toward the sounds of revelry centered around the pool.

She'd heard the guests at Dean and Sergio's monthly dinner party from inside the guesthouse—it wasn't her first time—but nothing could prepare you for the onslaught of eccentricity and friendly chaos that awaited guests at Sunday Dinner.

It was her first party as a new resident of Vista de Lirio, the wealthy and exclusive corner of Palm Springs where Dean, her ex-husband and business partner, had lived for twenty years.

Julia spotted an elegant woman in a vintage emerald gown from the corner of her eye. The woman walked soundlessly across the grass, stopped to give Julia a curious look, then continued toward the deeper shadows of the garden.

"Hey, gorgeous!"

She turned toward the sound of the familiar voice and saw

Dean waving her over to a table covered in wineglasses, champagne flutes, and myriad bottles of bubbly and other libations.

She spun around. "I came prepared."

"You look fantastic." He leaned down, kissed her cheek, and handed her a glass of champagne all in one smooth motion. "I see you got the memo."

Julia looked down at the rich blue caftan that nearly swept the ground, then around the glittering azure pool. "This is my first caftan, Dean."

"You're in Palm Springs now, darling. It won't be your last." Dean was six foot tall with silver-grey hair and a jaw that seemed to get more sculpted the older he got. "Trust me, you're going to love it here. You already fit right in."

She knew the rich cerulean color of her silk caftan set off her blond hair and clear blue eyes, but she couldn't escape the feeling that she was walking around in public with a bedsheet thrown over her bra and panties.

Julia wasn't in Orange County anymore.

She sipped her champagne for courage. "I think we should wander."

Dean motioned toward the crowd. "Sounds like a plan." He pointed at the table. "Just come back to the bar and help yourself when you need a refill, or grab a waiter if you can catch one."

They strolled through the bunches of people dancing near the band. There was always live music at Sergio's parties, and that night it was a group that was currently covering Gogol Bordello's "Start Wearing Purple." She saw a couple dressed straight out of the forties dancing in the shadows, but she couldn't see their faces.

Weird. And wonderful. That was Dean and Sergio's parties in a nutshell.

Thankfully, Julia was not the only woman in a caftan. The partiers wore a mix of fashion, but except for the couple in the shadows, it was all very casual. "You do know that if I was the only one in a bathrobe, I was prepared to kill you."

"Are you kidding?" He looked down at his own clothes, a pair of linen pants and a loose white button-down shirt. "I'm the most formally dressed person here. Well... I am now that my children have retired for the evening. The girls are much more formal than me."

Julia smiled. "I'm sure they think all this adult insanity is completely uncool."

Dean sipped a glass of gold whiskey, his favorite. "They're thirteen now. They think everything their fathers do is uncool."

"To be fair, I'm pretty sure only half these people will keep their clothes on all night, and the wildest ones are old enough to be their grandparents." Julia craned her neck and saw a tanned couple in bathing suits—who had to be in their seventies—sneaking behind a hedge. "I kind of get why they want to exit stage teenager. What are they up to?"

"Aurelia and Juliana are on a classic-horror-movie kick right now. I think they're watching the *Creature from the Black Lagoon* with Analu." He looked at Julia very seriously. "They have informed us that they are too old to have a nanny, so they now call Analu their respected companion."

"Your children are delightfully weird."

"Thank you. Good thing I dumped *you*."

Julia laughed out loud. "It was a solid plan."

Dean wasn't only her ex-husband, he was her best friend, and he knew she'd never wanted kids. They'd gotten together in college when settling down with babies didn't seem important to either of them and had split in their late twenties when Dean realized it was. In the middle of that, they'd started the beginnings of what became one of the most successful real estate companies in Southern California.

They liked each other too much to split the business, so Julia had taken the Los Angeles territory while Dean moved to Palm Springs with his future husband, promptly settled into weird domestic bliss, and had a couple of kids, a string of golden retrievers, and one rescue alpaca named Paco.

She swept her eyes over the green lawn of the gated estate and the half-naked people running around. "Remind me why I moved out here?"

Dean put his arm around her. "To spend time with family and friends. And because you missed our monthly explosion of sophistication and elegance."

"Right." Julia smothered a laugh as the band started into another cover. "I am never going to remember all these people."

"The overall vibe is intended to overwhelm. Don't worry, we'll wait a few months before we quiz you." He waved at a woman flying by. "Hey, Lily! Good to see you."

"Neighbor?"

"She used to be. Just moved across town." Dean waved at an older man. "Morty, looks like you got some sun."

He yelled back, "I just flew back from Cabo. It was fantastic."

They crossed the patio, and Dean introduced her to more people she wasn't going to remember.

"I think the entire city is at this party." Julia finished her glass of champagne and reached for another off a passing tray. "I thought you said it was quiet here."

"For twenty-nine to thirty days of the month, it is." Dean set his drink on a table where it was whisked away by another uniformed waiter. "Loosen up, Jules!" He squeezed her waist. "And don't forget the reason you moved here was to relax and spend time with the people who really matter in your life."

She looked at Dean. "You mean Sergio?"

He shrugged. "Obviously Sergio."

Julia couldn't hide her smile when she caught a glimpse of

the host and orchestrator of the monthly madness, who was holding court in a sunken firepit and telling a story that had everyone in stitches.

Dean's husband was what Julia would fondly describe as a people collector. He was born into a ridiculously wealthy Brazilian family, his mother was a celebrated actress, his father a musician, and Sergio had grown up on an estate in Los Angeles, surrounded by the gifted, the rich, and the bizarre.

And anyone who caught his eye as vaguely interesting, he invited to Sunday Dinner.

Julia watched Sergio keep his guests enthralled, a young woman in black net gloves and a chic black bob on one side and an older woman on the other, elegantly clad in a crimson caftan, a gold turban, and large black sunglasses that covered half her face.

Their host was wearing all black to set off his dark hair and eyes. The man might be in his late forties, but he still oozed sex appeal.

Julia elbowed Dean. "Your husband is hot."

Dean smiled. "I know."

"But there's something wrong with this picture."

Dean frowned. "The bevy of women surrounding him? That's actually pretty normal."

"No." She laughed. "No one here has phones."

"Oh! Sergio outlawed them a few years ago." Dean caught Sergio waving at them. "Come on. We're being summoned."

Julia whispered, "How does he manage to keep all the phones away? Is that even legal these days?"

"He bought a velvet bag that Jim carries around. Everyone has to put their phone in it until they leave or he won't serve them a drink."

"Like... a key party?"

Dean pursed his lips. "You know... a few switched phones

over the years have led to more than one divorce. You may be on to something there."

They wound through legs and stepped down into the firepit area, only to have Sergio rise to his feet and spread his arms. "My darling ex-wife!"

"And my favorite home-wrecker!"

Julia grinned when Sergio swept her into a dramatic embrace, dipping her as she struggled to keep her champagne from spilling. Just as quickly, he set her on her feet and her glass nearly went flying. A friendly hand reached up and steadied it.

Julia was dizzy when she saw who'd caught her arm. It was the cool woman with the black bob and net gloves who'd been sitting next to Sergio. "Thanks. I'm only allowed two, so I'd hate to spill it."

"No problem." The woman raised a perfectly plucked eyebrow. "Favorite home-wrecker?"

"Old joke." Sergio plopped back on the sectional that surrounded the fire and threw his arm around the dark-haired woman. "Julia and Dean had been split up for years when we met."

Julia cocked her head. "I do think you got him on the rebound, but since you've been together twenty years and we were married for three, I think it worked out."

"Damn right it has." Sergio leaned forward and grabbed his drink. "Julia Brooks, meet Evelyn Landa, aka EV Lane, the illustrious comedienne, noted ventriloquist, and famous cockblocker. You're welcome." He waved a hand. "You both met fabulous people tonight."

Julia nearly snorted her bubbly.

"You know what?" Evelyn wasn't amused. "One time, Sergio. One time I interrupted you and Dean, and you have never let me forget it."

"He's horrible about grudges," Julia said. "I once had to

cancel a brunch because my sister was in a car accident and he didn't speak to me for a month."

"Typical."

"What can I say?" Sergio was nonplussed. "I'm a Scorpio."

Sergio promptly ignored both of them and began whispering to the older woman wearing the sunglasses on his left.

Evelyn muttered, "You are *such* a Scorpio." She held out her hand. "Call me Evy. I go by my initials for bookings because retirement homes can't tell if I'm a man or a woman. I get more gigs that way."

Julia was instantly fascinated. "So you really are a comedian?"

Evy nodded. "I'd love to say that most of my money comes from that, but Geoff is way more popular than me."

"Geoff?"

"He's her dummy!" Sergio interjected as he waved at someone across the firepit. "Phillipe! Come sit next to Genevieve while I get us more drinks."

Then he leaped up and was gone while an older man came and sat next to the elegant woman on Evy's left; they immediately began a conversation in animated French.

Julia shook her head. "There's nothing like Sunday Dinner."

"It's the best, right?" Evy sat back and kicked her feet up near the glowing blue flames of the firepit. "You either meet the worst people or the best people here. How have we never met? I know I've heard your name. Are you local?"

Julia sat back and let out a breath. "Just barely. I just moved to Palm Springs a couple of weeks ago because I'm kind of semi-retiring?" She grimaced. "I can't decide if this is going to work, and retiring sounds so damn old."

Evy laughed. "That sounds *rich*. I, on the other hand, am going to work until I die at the rate I'm going."

Julia forced a smile. "We'll see if it takes. I'm only fifty-one, but Dean is convinced that I was burning out in Orange County."

"Oh, you're his business partner!" Evy stopped herself. "And the ex-wife. I get it now."

"Yes, we've been partners nearly twenty-five years."

Evy sat back with a smile. "Lot has changed in LA, huh?"

"So much." She shrugged. "A lot of it felt like riding a wave. We got very lucky."

"And now you're going to sell houses in Palm Springs?"

Julia nodded. "The idea is for both Dean and me to kind of cut back while our associates take the lead on the footwork in the city. He's going to do more commercial stuff here while I do more of the residential." She sipped her drink and scanned the party, which showed no sign of calming down. "This is a funny town."

"Funny is a generous way of putting it." Evy had to raise her voice as the band got louder. "This is the best neighborhood though. Vista de Lirio has a little bit of everything. Big Spanish estates like this, little midcentury cottages, and everything in between."

"All very high priced though."

"Well, *now* it is, yeah." Evy pointed to the aged couple that had emerged from behind the tree. "But see Elaine and Morty? She was a bookkeeper and he was a public defender. So it's not all rich people. They've probably been in Palm Springs for forty years now."

Julia nodded. "On sun damage alone, I'm going to assume you're right."

"They're hilarious. I think they've been divorced three times."

"From each other?"

Evy nodded. "They just keep getting remarried. It seems to work." She pointed to another couple. "See Perfectly Preserved and Pool Boy over there?"

Julia craned her neck to see the stunning blond woman Dean had greeted earlier. She was probably in her fifties and was sitting next to a much younger man. They were lounging by the pool, and he was hand-feeding her grapes.

"Wow." Julia blinked.

"I know."

"Life goals?"

"I guess that depends on how much you like scandal."

Chapter Two

J ulia poured another glass of champagne for herself at the bar after she handed Evy her margarita. "This is local gossip?"

"The only kind I partake in." Evy swung around and pointed a finger at the pair by the pool. "Her name is Lily Putnam. She and her husband are in the middle of a very messy divorce, and that is literally her pool boy. Justin something."

"Seriously?" Julia smiled. "You know, you hear the cliché, but I don't know if I've ever actually met anyone who ran away with the pool boy."

Evy held up a hand. "Wait, no. He used to be the pool boy. Now he's saying he's her private chef. I'm pretty sure he used to work as a massage therapist at one of the nicer spas in town."

"I'd say this was a better job." Julia couldn't stop looking at the young man. Then she felt a little dirty—he was young enough to be her son. Then she reminded herself that she never wanted kids, so that must mean she could look her fill. "That man is underwear-model good-looking. In real life. You don't see that too often, even in LA."

Evy lifted her glass. "That he is. And Lily is no ugly stepsister. She is making May-December work for her."

Her eyes moved away from Justin and Lily to fall on a woman who'd been sitting across from her and Evy at the firepit. She was roughly Julia's age with Asian features and long dark hair in a neat center part, holding a martini and sipping it at regular intervals, clearly intrigued by the chaotic goings-on but also a little removed. An observer, not a participant.

Julia was guessing that, whoever she was, it was definitely her first Sunday Dinner.

"Hey." She nudged Evy. "Do you know her? I haven't seen her talking to anyone at the party."

Evy cocked her head. "I think Sergio said she was new. His dermatologist?" She snapped her fingers. "No, his dentist."

"We should go say hi." Julia put the champagne bottle back in the ice bucket. "How much do you want to bet Sergio knew she was fresh in town and said, 'Hey, why don't you come over to my house for Sunday Dinner?' And instead of the cozy family meal she was probably picturing, she showed up to this." It was exactly the kind of thing her friend would find hilarious.

By the look on Evy's face, she was thinking exactly the same thing.

"Yep." She picked up her glass. "We should go say hi."

Julia and Evy walked over to the woman, who looked up at them with a curious expression.

"Hi!" Julia held out her hand. "I'm Julia Brooks and this is EV Lane. We thought you looked like you... needed company."

The woman blinked and raised a hand in greeting. "Oh! I'm flattered, but I'm not a lesbian." She smiled politely. "And I'm not really into being a third. Like I said though, very flattered."

Evy's eyebrows went up. "If you thought that, then we're flattered too, I guess?" She sat down next to the woman. "We thought you looked new to the Sunday Dinner madness. We weren't propositioning you."

The other woman blinked. "Oh." Her cheeks turned a little red. "I'm sorry, this entire evening is not what I expected, so I wasn't sure what—"

"Completely understandable." Julia sat across from them on the edge of the firepit, enjoying the warmth against her back. Desert nights could be chilly, and she was pretty much still wearing a bedsheet. "So let me guess, you're new in Palm Springs and you met Sergio and he said, 'Why don't you come over for Sunday dinner with my husband and me?'"

Her eyes lit up. "Yes!"

"And then you arrived to a debauched combination of a toga party and a bohemian carnival?"

The woman smiled. "Honestly, I walked in and was positive I was in the wrong place until I saw Sergio." She held out her hand. "I'm Vivian Wei. He told me I could tell everyone that I'm his dentist."

"Are you his dentist?"

"Yes! Not a story. Though I could hardly work on his teeth because he was making me laugh so much."

"He's like that," Julia said. "And you should be flattered. Sergio only invites interesting people to Sunday Dinner."

Vivian said, "I'm not sure about that, but I definitely feel more adventurous after tonight." She frowned and pointed over her shoulder. "Did I see an *alpaca* roaming around?"

"That's Paco," Julia said.

Evy shuddered a little. "He's not friendly."

"Just avoid him and he'll avoid you." Julia was quick to reassure her. "But he will kick you if you try to pet him. He pretty much only likes Sergio and Dean's daughters."

"Oh."

"So you're a dentist?" Evy snapped her fingers. "Dr. Wei! I think you're my aunt Marie's dentist too! Marie Landa."

"Marie Landa?" Vivian grabbed her purse from her side and dug through it. "I don't..."

'You're giving her a root canal later this week," Evy said. 'I'm hoping she'll stop complaining after that, but I have my doubts."Julia turned to Evy. 'So are you *from* Palm Springs? Do you have a big family?"

'I grew up here, but most of my family moved away. It's pretty much me and my aunt who are still local. I live with her; she's a hoot."

A younger couple wearing only swimsuits ran past them, jumped over a toppled walker, and then ran toward the pool, shrieking as they dove.

Vivian narrowed her eyes, watching them. 'I can't decide if I'm too old or too young to be at this party."

'Neither and both," Evy said. 'Vista de Lirio is pretty unusual. There are about equal parts retired middle-class folks, successful entertainment people, and rich, lazy trust-funders. It keeps things interesting."

'Dean is rich," Julia said. 'And Sergio has a trust fund. So they fit in both ways."

Vivian nodded but didn't say anything.

Julia continued. 'Honestly though? I ask myself the same thing all the time. And I used to be married to Sergio's husband."

'You used to—"

'Oh!" Evy slapped Vivian's knee. 'Look who showed up for the drama."

Julia turned and looked in the direction Evy's eyes were pointed.

A handsome man with wavy steel-grey hair and a closely cropped beard had wandered over to Julia's new role model, Lily Putnam, who was still being fed grapes by her personal chef. The man's hands hung loosely in his pockets, and he looked amused.

Evy sat up straight. 'That's Michael O'Connor."

More than a few people were watching the exchange. Half the party was discreetly following the interactions between Lily,

Justin, and the newcomer, including the odd characters lingering at the edge of the garden.

"Michael O'Connor, the director?" Vivian asked.

"Oh!" Julia recognized the name. "I've heard of him, but I never put a face to the name. That's not Lily's ex-husband, is it?"

"Is that man feeding grapes to that woman?" Vivian squinted. "I thought it was her son... but on second thought, I really hope I'm wrong."

"Mick is a director—not that knowing him has done *me* any good over the years 'cause he mostly does dramas and the big expensive explosion stuff—but he's also best friends with Richard Putnam, Lily's ex. He used to stay over at Lily and Richard's house all the time when he wasn't working, and there were all kinds of rumors."

"About?" Vivian looked confused.

"Oh, if he and Lily had a thing. Or if he and Richard had a thing." Evy waved a hand. "He's been friendly with Dean for years, so I know it's just talk."

"Hmm." Vivian craned her neck to look. "Looks like it's not all that dramatic after all."

Michael drifted away just as quickly as he'd wandered over, leaving Julia with the impression that the man was definitely not impressed with Lily's new boyfriend.

Vivian and Evy had fallen into a conversation about Vivian's move from Chicago, leaving Julia to sit back and play the observer again. There was the woman in the green gown she'd noticed on her walk over to the party, but she'd met up with a curvaceous blonde in a white retro bathing suit and a pair of high heels.

Marilyn Monroe impersonator? At Sunday Dinner, it was completely possible.

The pair caught Julia watching them, so she raised her champagne glass to them. The woman in green frowned a little, and the two drifted away.

"Hello, my darling." Sergio dragged a chair next to hers. "Tell me, are you finally ready to cast your lot with the Vista de Lirio menagerie?"

She smiled at him. "And give in to my inner retired starlet?"

He glanced down. "You have the muumuu for it."

She slapped his arm and he laughed.

"I don't know about this whole 'cutting back' thing," she admitted. "I *like* work. I know Dean was worried about all the stress, but—"

"Julia." The playfulness had left Sergio's voice. "You had a heart attack. At barely fifty-one, you had a fucking heart attack."

Oh. Right.

Okay, there was that one little...

Tiny.

Thing.

She took a deep breath and let it out slowly. "Technically, I think it's called a cardiac *event*." She looked at Sergio and forced a smile. "An event. Doesn't that sound more festive?"

"A cardiac event is a *heart attack*." He wasn't amused. "So this is how it's going to go since you are my family and I don't let my family kill themselves with work." Sergio put his arm around her shoulders. "You're going to have a fabulous time tonight and drink a very mild amount of that very expensive French champagne. Then you're going to sleep well and Jim is going to make you a healthy breakfast in the morning. And then, according to Dean, you are showing *one* house."

"One?" One was nothing. "I'm not an invalid."

"One." He bumped his shoulder into hers. "Lucky for you, it's in the neighborhood and it's the second nicest place. After mine, of course. It's very big and glamorous and the commission would probably fund a small South American island nation, okay?"

"Fine." She put her head on his shoulder. She *was* feeling

tired, and she didn't want another Sergio lecture about her little event three months before. "I will show one house."

The doctor had told her that her life needed to change, and she accepted that.

She did.

Of course she did.

Julia just wasn't sure that moving a hundred miles to the desert and into a veritable garden of eccentrics was going to be all that great for her well-being. Then again, life back at her house in Laguna Beach had gotten weird too. Weird and stressful. Stressful and fake. She hardly knew any of her neighbors anymore, and those she knew, she didn't like much.

She saw shadows flitting in the corner of her eye, but she decided to close them and focus on the solid weight of a friend's shoulder, the chatter of interesting companions, and the warmth of the fire.

She was here now. Vista de Lirio would be her fresh start.

Tomorrow would come soon enough.

FOR MOST OF HER ADULT LIFE, JULIA HAD SLEPT SIX hours a day. She was up at dawn and working until midnight. Meetings and parties late at night didn't help, and she was ruthless about waking early to keep fit so she could present a very specific image to her clients.

It was her life. Her job. Sleep took a back seat every time.

But since her heart had decided to throw a temper tantrum, whether she liked it or not, Julia was sleeping a solid eight hours a night, which was why she didn't rouse until nearly nine o'clock the next morning.

She threw on a lightweight robe and opened her door to be greeted by a riot of birdsong, glaring sunshine, and the smell of coffee and fresh bread.

"Morning, sunshine." Dean was reading a newspaper on the patio, a cup of coffee in front of him along with half a glass of fresh orange juice.

"Hey." She padded over with bare feet and slipped into a comfortable wicker chair. "How late did it go?"

"I finally went to sleep at two," Dean said. "Up at seven—unfortunately, I had meetings this morning."

"Is Sergio still sleeping?"

"Oh no." Dean waved a hand. "He got up with the girls, packed their lunches, got them off to school. He's helping a friend with a gallery opening that's set for next week. He'll probably come home for lunch."

Julia was tired just thinking about it. "Where does he get so much energy?"

"Twenty-two years together and I still have no idea. Meth? Unicorn blood? He'd say good genes; his mother is the same." Dean set down his newspaper. "How did you sleep?"

"Very well." She stretched, gently tugging her arms back to stretch her chest muscles. "Sergio lectured me again last night."

Dean raised an eyebrow, but he said nothing.

"I was informed that I am showing one house today and that's it."

"You were on complete medical leave in Orange County," Dean pointed out. "Starting back slowly makes sense."

"It's been three months. I think I can handle more than a single house."

"Three months is not that long."

"I feel fine." Which was true. Physically, Julia felt fine. She was taking her medication. She was incorporating yoga and gentle exercise instead of five-times-weekly boot camp on the beach. Needing more sleep was probably a good thing. As for the distrust she felt for her own body, that wasn't Dean's business. "Tell me about the house."

"You met one of the former owners last night." Dean acquiesced to the change of subject. "Lily Putnam?"

"You mean my new hero?"

Dean smiled. "I have to admit that Justin is very nice to look at."

"She's what? Fifty-something? And she's got that one feeding her grapes? That's more than looks, Dean. That's skill. I want her to teach me her secrets."

"Do you really want a twenty-year-old boyfriend? Be honest; I can find one for you."

"No, not really." She waved a hand. "I'd have to teach him everything. No, thank you."

Dean's smile was rueful. "Lily's appeal might have a little bit to do with trips to the south of France and a yacht in Newport too."

"Details." Julia turned toward the house when Jim emerged. "Look at him! Now *that* is a man." The older man approached the table with a cup of steaming-hot coffee. "The most gorgeous man in all the land, Dean. Don't you think?"

Jim smiled. "I'll tell the missus you think so, Miss Julia. Breakfast?" Jim might sound like an Italian gangster, but he'd been Sergio's valet for forty years.

Had she mentioned that Sergio was really, *really* rich?

"A little bit of anything you have around for breakfast would be great, Jimmy. An omelet, crepes maybe—?"

"How about some oatmeal and fresh fruit?"

Julia narrowed her eyes at Dean. "I see someone received the memo about Julia's new boring diet."

"What?" Dean pointed at his plate. "That's what I had too. Sergio put both of us on a diet as soon as we heard about your heart thing."

She sighed. "Oatmeal and fruit would be great."

Jim disappeared, and Dean picked up his newspaper again. "Sixty-one."

"Jim?"

"No, Lily Putnam. She's sixty-one."

"That's some excellent plastic surgery."

"I'm sure it was. Richard only paid for the best."

Julia's attention was caught by a streak of gold in the corner of her eye. One of the dogs was racing around the yard while Paco stood in the center of the lawn, munching on something, a bright green feather boa draped around his neck.

"Someone put a feather boa on Paco," Julia said. "Was the money all Richard's?"

"No." Dean lowered his paper and squinted at the alpaca. "She was an actress. Lily Rose was her stage name. Did theater for years. Had a major role on a soap for ages and then some commercials. Had a very decent career, but Richard's from old money on the East Coast. She brought the fun social life, he brought the cash. Eventually he got into film production and financing, but the introductions were all her."

"Interesting."

The dog was circling the alpaca, barking at the suspicious feather boa while Paco continued munching with zen-like calm, his floppy hair shielding his eyes from the morning sun.

"So neither one of them wanted the house?"

"Oh no, they *both* wanted it," Dean said. "A lot. It was a huge fight. Casa de Lirio, they call it. House of the Lilies. It was the first house built in the neighborhood and has the best view of the mountains."

"But neither one wanted to buy the other out?"

"They both tried, but in the end, neither Richard nor Lily wanted the other one to have it if they couldn't. It's actually spelled out in the divorce that neither one can put an offer in on the property for at least ten years."

"That's insane."

"That's rich people divorcing."

"What if there's something about the house?" Julia wiggled

her eyebrows. "Some secret they don't want anyone knowing. A body buried in the garden?"

Dean shrugged. "Who really knows what goes on between two people, you know? Walls can't really talk."

The golden retriever had caught the end of the feather boa, but the previously aloof Paco turned with unexpected alacrity and aimed a kick dangerously close to the retriever's back end. The dog gave an indignant yelp, let go of the boa, and crouched on the grass, letting out one disappointed bark.

"I have the keys," Dean said. "The house is only three blocks from here if you want to walk over after breakfast."

"Sounds good." She turned back to the table. "Is anyone going to try to get that feather boa off the alpaca?"

"Unless Paco takes it off" —Dean lifted his coffee— "the feather boa stays."

JULIA DRESSED IN A PAIR OF GREY LINEN PANTS, A bright yellow tank, and a white button-down to visit her first official listing in Palm Springs. She walked the three short blocks with the keys in her hand, her notebook and a tablet computer stored in her tote.

It was early spring in the desert, which meant that the few flowers that bloomed in the harsh landscape were showing off, including a brilliant slope of mariposa lilies that gave the neighborhood its name.

Casa de Lirio sat at the end of an upward slope, a historic Spanish estate that had been built in the first wave of Palm Springs development that drew the rich and famous to the desert city the 1920s and 1930s. The sprawling Spanish revival home was surrounded by a high white wall with wrought iron trellises and bright red bougainvillea.

Julia opened the mission-style wooden door next to the

driveway gate and entered the compound where she immediately noted the updated landscaping with large shaded areas, sculptural desert plants, and drought-tolerant blooms.

Someone had paid a lot of attention to the landscaping.

The brick path led from the driveway up to the arched entryway of the first enclosed patio in front of the main house. She knew there was a guesthouse and a pool house on the three-acre property as well.

She felt a prickling sensation on the back of her neck when she opened the wood and wrought iron door. She froze in the entryway, suddenly certain someone was inside.

"Hello?"

Nothing.

She took her phone out of her pocket and dialed Dean. It rang twice and he picked up.

"Having trouble getting in?"

"No." She flipped on the lights and marveled at the intricate Spanish tile in the entryway. There was a fireplace, and a low sofa and coffee table had already been staged. "Is anyone else supposed to be here? The house stager or something?"

"No." Dean sounded cautious. "Is there someone there? Sheila should have been finished last week."

"I don't know." There was nothing Julia could put her finger on. She hadn't heard anything; there was just an itch at the back of her mind. "I don't see anything out of place. I haven't heard anything... exactly." She walked to the left of the entryway, following a narrow hallway where a butler's pantry and a powder room broke off. There were swinging double doors that led to the kitchen, and light seeped in from the edges, creating an eerie outline.

"Why don't I just stay on the line while you do the first walkthrough?" Dean suggested. "You know how old houses can be."

"It wouldn't be the first time I've freaked myself out." Julia pushed through the kitchen doors and smelled a distinct copper scent. Maybe the cleaners had just polished the vintage farm-house sink she'd seen in the pictures. "Dean, I think I may have been..."

She walked past the kitchen island, and the blood rushed from her head.

Julia's arm fell to her side even as Dean's voice continued on the phone. Her brain couldn't make sense of the image that assaulted her eyes.

Justin the pool boy, personal chef, and boyfriend of the previous owner was lying on the earthen-hued Saltillo tile. An angry wound marred the back of his head, and dark red blood spread out under his body; his head was frozen at an odd angle, and his eyes stared lifelessly into the distance.

Julia heard a scream before she could catch a breath, and her eyes swung to the left.

Standing over the body was Justin, his image wavering in the streaming light from the windows, his eyes fixed on the broken body sprawled across the kitchen floor.

"What the hell is happening?" he shouted, staring at the ground. He looked at Julia. "And who the hell are you?"

Chapter Three

J ulia closed her eyes. Opened them. Closed them again. Opened.

Nope, it was still there.

Justin—whatever version of Justin that remained talking—was snapping his fingers. "I know you. Were you at the spa? I know I've seen you…" He frowned. "Did we… you know?"

Julia's brain was frozen. "I don't understand." Her eyes kept darting from the dead body on the floor to the apparition. "What… I mean how…?"

"Julia?" A tiny voice caught her attention, and she realized Dean was calling her name from the forgotten phone in her right hand.

"Oh shit." She lifted it to her ear. "Call 911. Or… oh God, I think he's dead. What if he's not dead?" She looked at the ghost. "He must be dead. Do I need to—? No, he's got to be dead."

Dean shouted through the phone. *Tell me what is going on are you okay?*

"I'm fine!" She looked at the image of Justin that was pacing back and forth over his body. "I mean, I think I am?" *Just having a nervous breakdown.*

"Jim is calling the police right now. You're at Casa de Lirio? What is happening? Did someone attack you?"

"No! And yes. I mean yes, I'm at the house." And so was Justin. Two Justins in fact. One that was very pale and very dead. And one that was definitely... not really Justin but also definitely Justin. Or some version of him.

What. The hell. Was happening?

That was it. The near-death experience had finally caught up with her and she was losing it. "There is a *body* here, Dean. I walked in the kitchen and there's a dead body here." She saw the pool of dark, nearly black blood staining the floor. "I think he's been dead a while. We may have to replace the tile."

Justin stopped pacing, and his mouth dropped open. "The fucking tile? Are you for real right now?"

Julia winced. "I'm sorry—I don't know where my brain is. Obviously the tile isn't important."

Dean reassured her. "Don't worry about it. I cannot even imagine that kind of shock. Are you sure you're okay? Is it someone who broke in? I found a squatter in a property one time whom we discovered had a massive stroke and—"

"It's not a squatter; it's Justin."

"How do you know my name?" Justin was sitting on the counter next to her, and she nearly lost it again. She hadn't seen him move to the counter, but there he was. "I know I know you."

"Justin?" Dean asked.

"Remember the guy with Lily?" Julia said. "The pool boy— I mean the chef! It's him. I think he's still wearing the same clothes as last night, but I'm not sure because he didn't have a shirt last night and he is wearing one now."

"Ohhhhhh." Justin nodded. "You're Sergio's ex. You know?

I would not have tagged him as bi. Dean yes, but not... Oh, maybe you're Dean's ex."

"Will you shut up!" Julia hissed.

"Is there someone else there?" Dean's voice rose. "Julia, I want you to get out of there right now. Go to the street and wait for the police!"

"Yes." She clutched her purse and held it to her body like it was armor as she fled the kitchen. "I don't know why I was standing there."

"Where are we going?" Justin spoke behind her. "Hey! I was not finished in there with my body, okay? Will you turn around?"

"Dean, I'll call you when the police get here."

"Are you sure? Why don't I stay—?"

Julia hung up the phone and spun on the apparition following her. "What are you doing?"

"I don't know!" Justin spread ghostly arms and Julia instinctually stepped back. "Oh my God, I'm not going to hurt you. I don't..." He frowned. "Do you think I could?" He made a fist and tried to punch a vase sitting in a nook in the hallway. His fist went right through. "Yeah, I didn't think so."

"You're dead!" She pointed her finger at him. "Go back to your body! Or... go into the light. Or something. But I do not want to see you again."

"Oh, I'm sorry." The sarcasm was palpable. "Am I not following 'being dead' protocols to your liking? Lady, do you think I've done this before?"

Julia closed her eyes and pressed her fingers to her temples. "This isn't real. I'm hallucinating. This is... a bad reaction to my blood pressure medication or something. This isn't real."

"Yeah, I keep telling myself that too, but I'm still dead," Justin muttered. "I didn't even understand what was going on until you showed up." He cocked his head. "Do you think everyone can see me or just you?"

'Stop talking!" Julia spun and marched toward the door again. She walked outside, leaving the front door open, and walked to a low concrete wall surrounding a decorative interior courtyard at the front of the house.

She sat on the wall and closed her eyes, focusing on grounding herself like her therapist had taught her.

Five things you can see. She slowly opened her eyes and looked at the garden. A flowerpot with a red geranium. A birdbath. The sofa in the conversation pit. A sepia-toned chiminea fireplace. The canna lilies in pots by the front door.

Four things you can touch. Julia closed her eyes and fingered the rough seam of her linen pants. Rubbed her fingers over the cotton-cuffed shirt. Squeezed the strap on her leather handbag. Touched the rough plaster under her fingertips as she leaned on the wall.

Three things you can hear. The wind rustling the palms that lined the driveway. A pair of blue jays arguing by the orange tree.

'Um... HELLO? I'm still here, lady."

Julia's eyes flew open and Justin, even more see-through in the bright sunlight, was standing right in front of her face. 'Are you kidding me?" she yelled at him. 'I am not your person. Go away!"

'You're the only person around as far as I'm concerned." He put his hands on his hips. 'Do you think I like this situation any more than you do? You need to figure out who killed me."

'No, I don't!" She frowned. 'Wait, you don't know?"

'I don't even remember coming over here last night. I don't know why I would have; I hate this house. Lily loved it, but I—" He cut himself off, and a stricken look overtook his face. 'I died before Lily. Oh fuck. That wasn't supposed to happen."

A stab of pity hit Julia's heart for the first time. 'I'm sure she's going to be devastated, but she has a lot of friends—"

'Fuck devastated! This was not how the deal was supposed

to go!" His sculpted lips twisted. "She's probably going to live another twenty years, and you know what? I was fine with that. I was going to put in my time. She wasn't a bad lay. She was still a beautiful woman. There was enough money to hire help. But then I was supposed to get mine."

Julia's lip curled. "Oh, you're gross."

"Like you don't know a dozen trophy wives who have the same thing with old men? I wasn't going to cheat on her. I wasn't going to treat her badly. She knew the score, but this?" He tried to kick the wall, but his foot passed right though. "This is very fucked up!"

"The fact that Lily outlived you is the fucked-up part? Not the you-*dying* part?"

"Okay, both of them are fucked up." He was thinking, and it was obvious it took some effort. "Why would anyone kill me? People *love* me."

Julia couldn't seem to stop seeing the man, so she decided to just go with it. Who knows? Maybe delusions were where it was at. Sergio kept pushing magic mushrooms as a way to change her outlook on life. This was much more intense.

"I don't know. Maybe you saw something dangerous? Maybe you came here for a good reason, but there was a burglar or something."

"Who's going to rob an empty house? There wasn't anything here but the staging furniture, and we all know how cheap that shit is."

"Excuse me? Dean and I happen to contract with high-quality—"

"Julia?" She heard Sergio's and Dean's voices seconds before she heard the police cars.

"Julia, where are you?"

"Oh thank God," she muttered. What was she doing? She was about to get into a pissing match with a ghost. Who wasn't real. Who was a figment of her imagination and probably a sign she needed to contact her cardiologist to adjust her medications.

She walked toward them, ignoring the see-through man trailing behind her. Sergio opened his arms, and she collapsed into them. "I never want to see anything like that again in my life."

"Thank God we were at the house." Sergio brushed her hair back. "Darling, what on earth?"

Dean had a hand on her shoulder. "What happened? Was it some kind of horrible accident? I already called Lily."

"I'm pretty sure he was murdered. There was so much blood." Julia wiped her eyes. "I'm sorry. I feel so shaky now that you're here. I was trying to be really cool, but—"

"We're here." Sergio hugged her tight. "How horrible. You said it was Lily's Justin? She's going to be devastated."

Julia saw police spilling through the garden gate and wondered if Dean knew how to open the driveway gate to let them in. A uniformed officer was striding toward them.

"You're the real estate agent?" she asked Julia. "Do you know how we can get that gate open? The coroner's van will need to get in."

"Not a medical examiner?" Sergio asked. "We are talking about a murder here!"

"This is Palm Springs." The officer tried to keep her face straight. "The body'll be going to the coroner first to determine cause of death."

"I'm the agent," Julia said, "but I just took over the house, so I'm not sure about the gate."

Dean stepped forward. "I know the gate code. Let me walk over and I'll take care of it. The house was originally listed with me, and I know the owners."

"Thanks." The officer glanced over her shoulder, then followed Dean.

Before they could reach the driveway, Lily Putnam burst through the gate. "Dean! Oh my God, Dean, what happened?"

Lily was intercepted by two uniformed officers who spoke quietly to her, but the woman was hysterical. She reached for Dean, shoving the police away.

"It's not him! Tell me it's not him!"

Dean caught her, but Lily nearly collapsed in his arms. He put his arms around her and spoke quietly into her ear. Julia turned to Justin, who was looking at the ground, his face somehow shrouded in shadows.

Sergio tried to nudge Julia toward the gate. "Come on. This is going to be horrible for a while, so let's get you home and get a Valium or two in you. Dean will tell them where you live if they have questions." He frowned. "Wait, can you have Valium with your meds?"

"Probably not."

"God, the kind of hell you're living through right now." Sergio pressed her head to his shoulder and patted her hair. "How are you supposed to get through life without Valium?"

"Amazingly, it's been pretty manageable the first fifty-one years." She glanced at a shadow from the corner of her eye. Yep. Justin's ghost was following them, but his face was still unreadable.

"It's okay," Sergio said. "I'll have one for you."

As soon as they'd cleared the line of police waiting outside Casa de Lirio, Julia decided if there was one person she could talk to about the ghost that was still following her, it was Sergio.

"Hey, Serg."

He put on his sunglasses and turned. "Yes, my darling? Are you feeling sick? Please don't puke in the car. We can walk if you want."

"Not going to puke, but tiny question: Have you ever seen a ghost?"

Sergio stopped and took his sunglasses off. "Did you see Justin's..." He lowered his voice to a whisper. "...ghost?"

"Yeah." She glanced to her right, where Justin had positioned himself and didn't seem to be budging. "You could say that." She let her eyes drift to him.

"Mother of Golden Girls, he's here, isn't he?" Sergio seemed to be frozen in place.

"Ever since I found the body in the kitchen."

"We need to find Evy." Sergio yanked the car door open and nearly shoved Julia inside. Then he let out a whole-body shudder. "Fuck, did he just walk through me?"

"Don't be dramatic—he's already in the back seat."

"Can I start talking again?" Justin sulked in the sculpted leather rear seat of Sergio's Audi.

Julia ignored Justin and waited for Sergio to get in the car. "Why do we need to find Evy?"

"Because she'll know where Auntie Marie is."

Julia muttered, "Oh, of course. It all makes sense now."

"And Auntie Marie will know how to get rid of the ghost. She knows things, I'm telling you."

"Good!" Justin spat out. "I don't like this situation any more than she does."

"She will?" Julia buckled up and tried to resist the urge to fall asleep. She was hit by a sudden wave of nausea and exhaustion. "On second thought, Sergio, I think I can live with Justin for a little while. I need to go home."

The ghost piped up from the back seat. "Do I get a vote in this? I vote we find Aunt Mary. Or Maria or whatever."

"Shut up, Justin. I feel horrible."

"What's he saying?" Sergio's eyes were the size of saucers. "Are you sure you want to go back to the house?"

"I'm sure." She glanced at her phone. It was only two hours since she'd headed over to Casa de Lirio to survey her newest listing and everything had gone sideways. "Sergio, I don't understand my life."

"Darling, just go with it." Sergio backed out before he flipped the car in a quick U-turn. "You're in Vista de Lirio now. This is only the third-weirdest thing to happen to one of my neighbors this month."

Chapter Four

J ulia woke up to the afternoon sun streaming through her window and an unfamiliar shadow slumped in the corner of the room.

She sat up with a jolt and stared. "Damn it!"

Justin sat and waved from the corner. "Not a dream?"

"What are you still doing here?" She flung the light chenille blanket off her legs and jumped out of bed. "What the hell?"

"You know, I really should be the one saying that," he muttered. "I'm the dead one. You're still alive, as unfair as that is."

"What?" She put a hand on her chest. "Why is me being alive unfair?"

"You're what? Fifty or something? You had a lot more years than me."

Oh, that was the wrong thing to say. "Excuse me?" Julia crossed her arms and raised an eyebrow. "I'm not the one that pissed off someone so badly they wanted to murder me."

Justin's jaw dropped. "Are you saying being killed is my own fault?"

"I don't know. Maybe."

Someone tapped on the door. "Uh... darling Julia?"

It was Sergio.

She walked over to the door and yanked it open. "He's still here."

Without preamble, two thin figures slipped inside her room like determined cats.

"Excellent," one hissed.

"Boring," the other said. "Nothing looks out of place. This is a perfectly mundane haunting."

Julia spun around and saw two dark-haired girls inspecting the corners of her room. One accessorized her mundane plaid school uniform with neat loafers and simple gold hoop earrings, the other with black Doc Marten boots and spiderweb gloves. Other than that, they were mirrors of each other.

Julia turned to Sergio. "You told the girls I saw a ghost?"

"Of course not." Sergio sat on a corner of the bed. "I told them one was haunting you. If he's still here, I think he's haunting you."

Julia looked at Justin. "You're haunting me?"

"Whatever." He shrugged. "I tried to leave, but I couldn't go much farther than the front of the house."

Julia felt her stomach drop. "Oh, this is not okay."

"Is the ghost speaking?" One of the twins appeared in front of her. Julia hadn't even heard her move. "Auntie Julia, we need answers."

It was Aurelia, and she was also wearing black lipstick. That was new. While Aurelia demanded answers from Julia, her sister was staring into the corner of the room with narrowed eyes.

Justin looked more than a little creeped out. "Can the weird kid see me?"

"That's Juliana, and I don't think so. Juli, can you see the ghost?"

While Aurelia wore her hair in dark twin braids, Juliana's hair was cut in an angular bob that framed her heart-shaped face.

"Aurelia and I have long suspected that the estate is haunted," Juliana said calmly. "The apparitions startle Paco."

"Oh yeah," Justin said. "There's a shit ton of ghosts around here. Bunch of old people. I think I even saw Marilyn."

Julia blinked and turned to him. "Marilyn?"

Sergio perked up at the name. "Marilyn who? Is Marilyn haunting our house?" He seemed ridiculously excited at the prospect. "And girls, why is this the first I'm hearing about our home being haunted?"

Aurelia turned to her father. "Pai, you and Dad are just... too conventional to sense the otherworldly. Frankly, I'm surprised that Auntie Julia can see them."

Julia tried to smother her smile when she saw Sergio's expression.

"Did you just call me conventional?" He was horrified. "You take that back, Aurelia Augusta."

Julia was starting to feel claustrophobic with Justin's ghost, Sergio, and both her nieces in the small studio apartment. "Can we take all this outside?"

"Only if you want to talk with the police." Sergio lowered his voice. "The chief of police is here."

"The chief of police?"

"It's a small town, okay? He and Dean have mutual golf friends, so he decided to come over and take your statement about this morning." He glanced at the windows. "Dean is distracting him right now since we heard you yelling at Justin from the patio."

"Shit." She closed her eyes. "I'll tell him I was on a phone call."

"That should work. We couldn't make out much of what you were saying through the walls."

"Okay." Julia looked down and realized she was looking pretty rough. Her hair was pulled into a messy bun, her shirt was hanging open, and she wasn't wearing a bra under her tank. "Okay out. All of you, out."

The twins plopped down on the bed in unison.

"But Auntie Julia, we have important questions about being a woman that our fathers cannot answer," Juliana said, her brown eyes wide and innocent.

Aurelia mirrored her expression in practiced guile.

"Oh no. I fell for that last summer and ended up getting an education I didn't want." Julia pointed at the door. "Out. I'll answer your womanly inquiries later."

Sergio stood and walked to the door. "What kind of questions can you not ask me?" he asked the girls.

"Pai, you don't menstruate," Aurelia said.

He huffed. "We have a fully stocked closet for that."

The twins followed him out, leaving only Justin with Julia.

"You too." Julia kept her voice low. "Out."

"Where am I supposed to go?"

"You said you could make it to the front yard? Then make like a tree and leaf."

Justin curled his lip. "I think that joke is beneath you."

"Out!" she hissed, wary of the police on the patio.

Justin stood, walked to the door, and tried to open it, but his hand passed right through the doorknob. "Oh, for fuck's—"

"Just walk through. I am not opening it for you."

"It feels weird!"

"Too bad."

He sucked in a breath, then stepped through the closed door, emitting a dramatic "Ugh!" on his way out. Julia turned in a circle, finally feeling like she had some privacy.

Her room didn't look any different than when she'd left that morning. A neat queen bed with a pile of silk and velvet pillows in neutral colors, positioned on one side of the cottage. Earthen-colored walls with terra-cotta-tile floors covered in thick Persian rugs. An original Georgia O'Keeffe hanging over a gas fireplace in the cozy sitting area on the other side of the two-room guesthouse.

The bathroom door was open, and light spilled out from a lamp she'd left on. She walked into the bathroom and tried to make something out of her face, but the shock of the morning, the makeup that she'd slept in, and fifty-one years of sun weren't doing her any favors.

Ever since her heart attack, she hated looking in the mirror when she woke because all she saw was her grandmother. Her grandmother had been a beautiful woman, but Julia wasn't quite sure she was ready to look like her grandmother's sister.

She quickly washed her face and immediately felt better when she slathered on a heavy cream. The dry air of the desert had done wonders for the dark circles she usually got from allergies, but her skin was rebelling.

Why wasn't being pretty effortless like it had been when she was thirty? She used to think she spent a lot of time making herself look presentable—a necessity in the real estate world of Southern California where everyone was so damn perfect—but that was nothing to her daily preparations now.

It wasn't that she resented taking care of her skin since she knew that was good for her health, but staring at her bare face, she realized she didn't have to put on an armored face of makeup for *everyone*.

She was fifty-one years old. She was independent and successful. She'd survived a fucking heart attack. And a police officer probably didn't give two shits if she had on eye makeup or not.

Julia took a deep breath and stepped out of the bathroom. She put on a bra, tossed on a clean white T-shirt, then slipped on a pair of sandals to walk across the patio.

Here goes nothing.

CHIEF OF POLICE JOHN MARCOS WAS A HANDSOME man in his late thirties by Julia's estimation. He had tan skin and dark hair with soulful hazel eyes and an expression that apologized before he opened his mouth.

"I know you're probably still shocked from this morning, but I do appreciate your speaking with me," Chief Marcos said. "Can you tell me what time you went to 41 North Vista Drive today?"

"Forty-one...?" She frowned.

"Casa de Lirio." Dean handed her an iced tea with a chunk of pineapple in it. "Sorry, John. Julia's spent so much time here, she thinks in landmarks like me."

They were sitting in the early-evening sunshine on the back patio between the main house and Julia's guesthouse. Sergio and the girls were helping Jim prepare dinner, but Justin was nowhere to be seen. She couldn't hear him or feel him.

"You would think I'd know the address." Julia took a sip of her iced tea. "But that house is so... I mean, everyone in the neighborhood knows Casa de Lirio."

"It definitely has a personality." Chief Marcos smiled a little. "Yes, so what time did you get to the place?"

"I'm honestly not sure what time I got there, but I left here about ten thirty, and it's probably only a five-minute walk or so."

He jotted down a note. "Exactly ten thirty?"

"Pretty exactly? I remember glancing at the clock. It may have been a few minutes after when I left."

"So you walked to the house, went through the garden gate?"

"The driveway gate was locked."

"And you had a key for the garden gate?"

"I did."

He narrowed his eyes. "You're sure the garden gate was locked when you got there?"

"I put my key in, and it felt like the dead bolt turned. I didn't try the gate before I unlocked it though if that's what you're asking."

"I'm just trying to get a picture of the morning." He kept taking notes. "So you walk up to the house... Do you remember seeing anyone on the grounds?"

She closed her eyes and pictured the grounds of the estate. "I don't. And I remember looking around because it was the first time I was visiting the place and thinking about buyers. Thinking about what kind of yard it was. Thinking about the potential for entertaining, stuff like that. Just trying to see it like a buyer might."

"Makes sense."

"But I don't remember seeing anyone. I didn't go behind the house though. I was just in the front.

"Okay. And again, when you got to the house, you had a key?"

"I did." She frowned. "But the door was unlocked. I just remembered that."

Dean straightened. "Are you sure?"

"Yeah." She turned to Dean. "It didn't even register as weird at the time because something felt so off when I went inside, and that's when I called you. You were there last week with the stagers. Is there a chance you left it open?"

Chief Marcos put up a hand. "Stagers?"

"When the Putnams moved out, they took all their furniture with them," Dean said. "But houses sell better when a buyer can imagine living in a space. So we hire a company that brings in temporary furniture to style and create a home atmosphere for buyers. They're called stagers."

"I'm going to need their name and number."

"Of course," Dean said. "I'll email you."

Julia asked. "Did they have keys?"

"No." He shook his head. "I opened and closed the house for them. And I'm sure the place was locked. I always do one last pass through when they finish and make sure a listing is secure. Remember I told you about finding that squatter in a property, one who had passed away from a heart attack? I never want a repeat."

Chief Marcos looked at Dean. "But you did go to the house after Miss Brooks called you, right?"

"Only with the police." Dean frowned. "Sergio and I headed over to Casa de Lirio to make sure Julia was okay. I also wanted to see if anything was missing. If it was a robbery of some kind or just... I don't know. I knew Justin."

"We were both so upset," Sergio said. "We got to the house just a little before the police, but we didn't go inside without them."

Chief Marcos was still scribbling notes. "Dean, you and Lily identified the body, correct?"

"We did."

Marcos looked at Julia. "But you'd already recognized him. You told Dean it was Justin Worthy."

And his ghost if we're being precise.

"I *thought* it was him," Julia said, "but I was on the phone with Dean and I probably wasn't making much sense. I was pretty sure." *Especially after seeing his ghost.*

"Why did you call Dean?" Marcos asked. "You're partners in the company, right?"

"Yes. I don't know if you know, but we also used to be married a long time ago; we stayed business partners," Julia said. "I called him because..." She thought back. "I thought someone was inside. I went in and... I don't know. It just felt like someone was in the house, so I called Dean."

Chief Marcos leaned forward. "I have a feeling that you have good instincts, Miss Brooks. You've been in and out of a lot of empty houses. What made you feel like someone was in that house?"

"I don't know." She saw Justin appear in the corner of her

eye, hovering near the palmettos under the kitchen window. "I felt a presence, but I can't tell you I heard a noise or saw anyone until I got to the kitchen and saw..." She shuddered. "Until I saw Justin's body. I remember smelling copper. Or I thought it was copper. I thought they'd been cleaning the sink in the kitchen."

Chief Marcos nodded. "Do you remember smelling anything else?"

"Um... roses." She remembered it just then. "But I think there were roses on the kitchen table."

Dean said, "Pretty sure the stagers left them on Friday."

John Marcos continued to watch her. "You met Justin Worthy the night before?"

"Yes." She motioned toward the house. "In the front yard. He was with Lily Putnam at Sunday Dinner."

Chief Marcos looked at Dean. "Your regular monthly party, right?"

Dean smiled. "It's kind of a free-for-all in the neighborhood. Everyone in Vista de Lirio usually stops by."

"And that included Lily Putnam and Justin Worthy. They came together?"

Dean nodded. "Yes, but I don't remember them leaving. And I don't know where Justin went after."

"Neither do we," Chief Marcos said. "Lily went home—her driver told us she was there all night—but Justin Worthy wasn't with her, and his roommates say that he didn't come home. They assumed he stayed at Lily's house."

"You think he went to Casa de Lirio after Lily went home?" Julia glanced at Justin, who was making "I have no idea" hands behind Chief Marcos's back.

"It's where he died," Chief Marcos said. "So we know he went there. The main question is why."

Chapter Five

J ulia woke the next morning to the blessed feeling of solitude. She took a deep breath and rolled out of bed, heading toward the bathroom and hopeful that the ghost haunting her the day before—

"Hey."

She nearly screamed when she saw Justin sitting on the toilet. "Why are you on the toilet?"

"Where else am I supposed to go?" He looked around the small bathroom. "You live in a studio apartment. I don't want to be weird and hang around while you sleep, but I'm not super into the ghost party that's happening outside every night either."

She frowned and waved him out of the bathroom. "I'll ask about the ghost party later, but I need to pee. Scoot."

Was this what it was like to have a little brother? Julia only had one sister, and she enjoyed her solitude. It was one of the main reasons she and Dean had never really worked. She'd loved being married to Dean when he was a realtor who only spent about half the time in Los Angeles while they were setting up the Palm Springs branch of their business, but when it came to living together every day, he drove her crazy.

She didn't want to be alone, but she didn't want to be with someone all the time either. Julia estimated that at this point in her life, she had about three months of a happy romantic partner in her before she would need at least a month or two of space.

Men didn't get that.

No matter what they said at the beginning, they all ended up wanting her attention full time, which just didn't work for her. There weren't too many men who wanted a part-time girlfriend. There were plenty who wanted a full-time girlfriend and a part-time one on the side, but Julia wasn't into that scenario either.

She used the toilet, jumped in the shower, then quickly brushed out her hair before she wrapped herself in the thick robe she'd brought from Laguna Beach and left the bathroom, only to find Justin staring at the Georgia O'Keeffe over the fireplace.

"Okay, before you say a word." She stopped the ghost before he opened his very talkative mouth. "I am fine with your sleeping—or whatever you do—in the bathroom, and I appreciate the consideration. However, once I am awake, I'm going to need to you pop your apparitional ass out of my apartment and give me some real privacy while I get ready in the morning. I know you don't want to deal with the other ghosts—"

"No, that's fine." He was halfway to the door. "They're mostly gone by morning."

"Okay then." The apartment was empty, and she was alone. Kind of. She still had that weird prickly feeling on the back of her neck that told her Justin was close.

"How do I get rid of this?" She grabbed her phone and called Sergio, putting him on speaker while she got dressed.

"Hello?"

"Are you taking the girls to school?"

"Just on the way back. What do you need?"

She laid out her clothes and grabbed a pair of socks. Then she sat on the edge of the bed and tried to put them on. "Damn it, I should not have to be a gymnast to put my socks on in the morning. I hate being old."

Sergio's "hmm" carried a lot of judgment. "You need to join the Morning Club, darling. Tai chi is excellent for balance and flexibility."

The Morning Club was Sergio, a bunch of old ladies, and a few gay men from Vista de Lirio who all met on the front lawn in their bathrobes at six in the morning and did forty minutes of tai chi before they drank Bloody Marys and gossiped about who was getting divorced or having an affair that week.

They were probably all more flexible than Julia though, so Sergio had a point.

"Listen, Justin is still here," Julia said. "And by the end of the day, I want to *not* be seeing his ghost. Can you call your friend Evy about her aunt or whatever you were talking about the other day? Justin has to go."

"I'll call her right now, but she might be working."

"I thought she did puppet shows or something." Who would be having a puppet show at eight thirty on a Tuesday?

"She does, but she also cleans pools. It's pretty lucrative around here."

"Okay. I'm not going anywhere today. Dean is meeting with the police, trying to figure out when they're going to clear the house for cleaning, and that's going to take a specialist I'm sure." She closed her eyes. "Has anyone talked to Lily yet?"

"I called this morning, but it went to voice mail."

"That sucks." Julia didn't want Sergio distracted. "But call Evy too."

"I will, my darling. Now hang up the phone so I can do your bidding."

Sᴇʀɢɪᴏ ᴘɪᴄᴋᴇᴅ ᴜᴘ Eᴠʏ ᴀɴᴅ ʙʀᴏᴜɢʜᴛ ʜᴇʀ ᴛᴏ ᴛʜᴇ house while Julia was getting dressed. The comedian and pool cleaner was drinking a Paloma with fresh grapefruit juice by the time Julia found her on the front patio. She seemed completely nonplussed by the idea that Julia was seeing ghosts.

"So my aunt Marie is Romanian," Evy said. "And... I don't know. She just knows stuff. She knew my uncle was going to die in a car accident and tried to warn him, but he ignored her. She knew about my uncle Marty getting cancer like six months before he was diagnosed. She kept calling him up and saying, 'Marty, you have a cancer in your ass!' But we all assumed she was talking about his ex-wife because no one liked her very much."

"But he did actually have cancer in his ass?"

"Colon cancer." Evy nodded. "Stage four by the time they caught it. He almost died."

Lesson learned. Listen to Aunt Marie.

Evy continued, "She also says our great-grandmother comes to her in dreams and asks her about the family." She shrugged. "She'll probably have an idea about your ghost. Totally sucks about Justin though. How's he doing?"

"With being dead?" Julia asked.

"Yeah."

She looked at Justin, who was sitting next to her on the patio.

He just shrugged. "I guess I'm okay."

"He guesses he's okay."

"I really wish I remember who did this to me though because that sucks."

"He doesn't remember who killed him," Julia said. "He wishes he did."

"That's so weird." Evy frowned. "So why was he even at Casa de Lirio in the first place? I mean, I go every Thursday to

44

clean the pool, but I haven't seen him over there since Lily moved out."

"Wait, you clean the pool over there?"

"I clean the pools of half the neighborhood. Geoff and I don't make enough to pay the rent."

"Geoff?"

"My comedy partner."

Justin said, "Her dummy."

"Oh right." Julia nodded. "So where can we find your aunt Marie? If there's a way to get rid of Justin, I'd like to get on it." She turned to him. "No offense."

"I guess none taken?" He shrugged. "Whatever. This sucks."

ACCORDING TO EVY, THEY HAD JUST ENOUGH TIME TO catch Aunt Marie, and they'd better do it before her scheduled root canal. Julia drove to Dr. Vivian Wei's office, a neat midcentury bungalow just west of Palm Canyon Drive.

"I should probably make an appointment." Julia got out of the car with Justin following. "I haven't had my teeth cleaned in ages."

Evy got out of the car and looked around. "And I should probably not drive down to Tijuana to get my teeth cleaned, but it's a lot cheaper and you get the good drugs when you go."

"That's one hundred percent true," Justin said. "I had a friend who got an entire mouth of crowns for less than a thousand."

Julia looked at him. "That seems... dodgy."

"No, it's cool." Evy walked across the small parking lot. "There are plenty of great dentists down there, and it's way cheaper."

Julia pushed open the door to Dr. Wei's office and walked to the counter. "Hi, we're here to—"

"We'll be fast." Evy grabbed Julia's hand and opened the door to the back office without preamble. "We're just dropping something off for my aunt Marie. We know where we're going."

"Right." Julia blinked but followed Evy's lead, walking down the hallway and ignoring the sputtering secretary at the front desk.

Justin's ghost followed at a short distance.

"Marie?" Evy peeked in half-open doors until she found the right one. "Oh! There you are."

A small woman with salt-and-pepper hair, a red headscarf, and a sour expression glared at them. "What are you doing here?" She looked at Julia. "And why did you bring a channeler to my doctor's office?"

"Okay, Ms. Landa, are we ready to—?" Vivian walked into the office but stopped short when she saw Evy and Julia. "What are you doing in here?"

Julia offered Vivian a timid wave. "Hi. We were meaning to get your number the other night and we forgot. Otherwise, we definitely would have called."

"Evy, remember?" Evy put a hand on her chest. "Marie is my aunt."

"Okay...?" Vivian looked confused but not unfriendly. "I already gave your aunt the nitrous she requested, and she'll be feeling the effects of it soon. She's getting a root canal, so you need to—"

"That's why we barged in, and I'm so sorry, but she's not going to be able to talk for a while, right?"

Vivian nodded. "Yes, so you need—"

"And Julia saw a dead body yesterday—horrible, it was a whole thing, the police think it was a homicide—but now the murder victim's ghost is following her and she has to get rid of it."

"Tha's not good." Marie lifted her head. "Girl, have you

channeled bufor?" The old woman's words were starting to slur a little.

"No." Julia moved to a corner of the room, as far away from Vivian as possible, and spoke to Aunt Marie. "And it's really freaking me out. Is there a way to get rid of... it?"

"Oh, I'm an *it* now? Thanks." Justin looked annoyed by the whole scenario.

"Listen," Julia hissed at him. "Do you want eternal peace or not?"

Vivian's eyes were taking it all in, and she was clearly questioning their sanity. "Okay, I don't know if this is some kind of elaborate prank on Ms. Landa or not, but both of you need to leave and take your pretend ghosts with you."

"Gimme..." Marie tried to sit up. "I can jus say a quick pray." She blinked. "I pray for you and yer ghose to... fine peace." She reached toward the counter. "Evelyn, my bag."

"Right." Evy reached for the shoulder bag on the counter and handed it to her aunt.

"What are you doing?" Vivian asked. "Evy, your aunt has taken nitrous, and I'm about to do a root canal. She needs to—"

"Jus got my rosary." Marie held up a beaded red rosary with pride. "This belonged to my great-great... great—"

Vivian was reaching over the dental chair and trying to grab Marie's handbag. "Ms. Landa, I need you to put that away and—"

"Kay, give me your hand." Marie reached for Julia's hand, and she gave it to her. Marie immediately lifted the rosary to her forehead and began praying loudly in a language that Julia guessed was Romanian.

"Ms. Landa, you need to—"

"If you just let her finish—"

"I don't know what this is supposed to do, but—"

Julia closed her eyes and tried to block out the chaos in the small procedure room, but Marie was shouting in Romanian, Vivian and Evy were nearly coming to blows, and Justin was still whining in the corner about Julia calling him an "It."

"This is a medical office!"

"—just think you should be more flexible—"

"It? I mean really... It?"

Julia felt a roaring in her ears like heavy wind and pressure in her temples like the beginning of a migraine. Evy and Vivian were in each other's faces, and Justin was leaning against a wall in the corner.

"Listen, I am trying to be nice about this, but this is my place of *business*, and if you don't leave right now—"

"All we need is another five minutes and we'll—"

"I mean, can you understand how offensive it is to not even be considered a person? I am barely dealing with being dead here and—"

Marie's voice rose over the chaos. "Inna nameofdafader 'n son an... holy..." Her eyes closed for a minute as everyone fell silent. Julia worried that she'd fallen asleep. Or maybe died.

Then they popped back open and Vivian let out a small "eep!"

"AMEN!"

Julia felt the pressure release in her ears with a loud POP! Then Marie muttered something in Romanian, fell back on the dentist's chair, and a shining line of drool fell from the corner of her open mouth.

Vivian was frozen. "What just happened?"

Evy reached for Julia's hand. "Okay, we'll just... get out of your hair now. Again, I am so sorry that we interrupted Marie's procedure, but she can be superstitious, so we knew that praying whatever that was would put her at ease and now we're going to go and it was really nice seeing you again we should definitely go out for drinks when you get a chance and bye."

Julia was pulled out of the procedure room with a familiar feeling of nausea in her belly. Her ears were clear and her head felt lighter, as if she'd just drained water from her ears.

But most importantly, Justin was nowhere to be found.

Chapter Six

Evy drove Julia's Mercedes back to Dean and Sergio's. Neither of them said anything for a long time.

Finally Evy let out a soft, "Hmm."

"What?" Julia turned to her. She had her sunglasses on because the light was beginning to make her head pound.

"So that was weird."

Julia looked at her from the corner of her eye. "Tell me something in the past two days that hasn't been weird."

"I mean, Justin getting killed was weird, but..." She scrunched up her face. "I guess not that surprising? He fooled around with a lot of married women."

Despite herself, Julia couldn't stop her curiosity. "Was he cheating on Lily?"

"I don't think so. Yet. But I'm pretty sure his last relationship broke up because he was still seeing his ex-girlfriend. You know, the one his own age?"

"Got it." Julia kept glancing over her shoulder as if Justin was still listening in. Weird. He'd only been her ghost for a couple of days, but she already felt his absence. "But you think he and Lily were serious?"

'Hey, Lily might have been old enough to be his mother, but she was still a stunning woman. She didn't require much of Justin. Cook for her, keep her company, and go to parties and events. Hang out in the evenings and watch *Antiques Roadshow*. The rest of the time was his own. It was a pretty good gig if you ask me."

'Lily was an *Antiques Roadshow* fan?" Julia didn't know why that surprised her, but it did. Lily Putman didn't strike her as PBS's target viewer.

'She likes to think she's a collector," Evy said. 'She's always talking about some piece of furniture or art or jewelry she picked up at an estate sale that she got such an incredible price on. It drove Richard nuts."

Julia was partly curious, but she was more interested in letting Evy fill the air. She didn't really care about Justin's murder. After all, he wasn't hanging over her shoulder anymore, reminding her of her ticking mortality.

And so what if fate had thrown the mystery in her lap? She wasn't a detective! Sure, there were some odd things about the case, but that was for the police to figure out. The last thing she needed on her plate was an unsolved murder.

"—probably never going to know who killed him."

Evy's last statement got Julia's attention.

'Why do you say that?"

Evy threw a glance her direction. 'I mean, over a third of all homicides are never solved nationally. It was probably a vagrant or someone like that whom he interrupted, so that's pretty random. Plus this is Palm Springs; our police department has more experience finding Rolex thieves working in swanky hotels than it has with murder."

'I hadn't thought about that." Julia wasn't going to dwell on it. It wasn't her business, and she didn't want to know. After all, Justin was gone now. Whatever magic Aunt Marie's prayers worked seemed to be holding.

Julia looked at Evy. "So the whole ghost thing didn't seem to surprise you all that much."

Evy shrugged. "I mean, if you hang out in Vista de Lirio for any length of time, you start to feel like there's something kind of... otherworldly about the place, don't you think? If there's a place in Palm Springs that's haunted, it's your neighborhood."

"I guess I didn't think about anyplace being haunted." Which wasn't exactly true. Julia had been in enough old houses to know that most of them carried... Well, she'd always called it energy. Old places had a vibe. She could walk into a house recently vacated by an older couple or a big family and almost immediately know if the home had been a happy one. Happy homes had a lightness to them. Unhappy homes had weight.

"Oh look," Evy said. "Dean is home." She glanced at the clock. "Sergio is probably picking up the girls. How are you feeling?"

"A little bit like someone is jabbing my temple with an ice pick."

"Fun!" She brought the car to a halt just inside the gate. "I'm going to see if Dean can give me a ride home then. Geoff and I have a gig tonight."

"Geoff and... Oh right." Geoff was Evy's dummy. "Evy?"

"Yeah?"

"Is there a proper term for a ventriloquist's dummy that doesn't sound offensive?"

"Well, the very proper name for Geoff is a ventriloquial figure." Evy was obviously trying to keep a straight face. "But he really doesn't mind if you call him a dummy." She smiled and hopped out of the car, leaving Julia hiding in the shade of the passenger's seat.

Her car was quiet and cool under a clump of Mexican fan palms. She was very tempted to lean her seat back and sleep right there.

Luckily, she didn't do that. She did walk to the pool area,

find the shadiest lounge chair, and collapse face-first, her shoes dangling from her toes.

She wanted to forget that morning and the chaos in the dentist's chair. She wanted to forget the past three days. And she definitely wanted to forget seeing Justin Worthy's ghost.

Moments after she closed her eyes, Julia was asleep.

"...STILL THINK SHE'S ASLEEP."

"But is it real? The young man said—"

"We've seen ones like him come and go, Mrs. G."

Julia heard the voices around her before she opened her eyes. They were soft and whispering, but they felt close, like an adult speaking over a sleeping child.

"...seems cold, don't you think?"

"It is winter. Of course she's cold."

"It's winter in Palm Springs, honey. No one wants to be cold."

Julia's eyes fluttered open, and she was surprised to see the pool lights glowing cool blue in the darkness. She was still passed out, facedown on the lounge chair, but someone had come and draped a thick blanket over her, so the only part that felt cold was one foot that had slipped off the chaise.

"Oh look, she's waking up." The voice was gentle and lilting. "Do you think we—?"

"I can hear you." Julia rolled over, pushed herself up to sitting, and rubbed her eyes. "I don't know why you're all..." She blinked. Rubbed her eyes. Blinked again.

In front of her, three shadowy figures hovered. There was the elegant woman in the emerald-green dress Julia had seen at Sunday Dinner, a man in a fedora with one shoulder slouching as he leaned against a patio umbrella, and then... there was Marilyn.

"Oh my God." Julia couldn't stop staring. "It's... I mean, is it?"

The night of the party, Julia had thought it was an impersonator.

She'd been wrong. So wrong.

Julia's eyes swept the patio in a panic; then she sat up and pinched her arm. Hard.

"What are you doing that for, honey?" Marilyn smiled, and just as in life, it was incandescent. Her iconic beauty mark was visible even in the dimness of the outdoor lights. "You feeling all right?"

"No." She felt the sick feeling in her stomach again and pressure in her temples. "What are you doing here?" She pointed at all three of them. "You should... you should not be here."

The familiar woman in white draped herself on the lounge chair next to Julia and smiled, her eyes crinkling in the corners. "But where else would we be, silly?"

It was a fair question. As Julia took in the soft gold lights that illuminated the palm trees, the crystal-blue pool, and the flickering firepit, it seemed like a ridiculous question. Given the option of where you might spend eternity, a luxurious estate in Palm Springs that hosted regular social events was probably one of the better options.

The imperious, formal woman in the green gown hadn't budged. "The young man says that you can both see and hear us," she said. "I admit, I was skeptical, but it seems he was correct."

"The young man?" Julia felt a knot form in her stomach. She looked into the shadows past the woman in green. "What young man?"

Justin stepped out from behind a screen. "Hey, Julia."

"Are you kidding me?" She sat up straight and pointed at him. "You were gone!"

"But I wasn't really." His expression twisted into something that probably meant he was thinking. "It was weird. It was like I could see you, but I felt a little frozen. I was there, but I wasn't. And then, sometime when you were sleeping, I just felt like myself again." He shrugged. "And these guys were way clearer."

Julia was speechless. All that drama at Vivian's office, and it had done nothing. Absolutely nothing. She'd gone into the dentist's office with one ghost and now she had four!

"Now, Miss... I do apologize," the woman in green said. "How would you like to be addressed?"

Julia waved a defeated hand. "Julia. Just... Julia."

Marilyn leaned forward. "I think that's a beautiful name. You can call me Mae."

Julia blinked. "Mae?"

The face known around the world was just as perfect in the afterlife. She winked at Julia with a coy smile. "Just Mae. I like my privacy."

Justin piped up. "That really is her, isn't it?"

"Young man," intoned the woman in the green dress. "Compose yourself. You may have come to an undignified end, but that doesn't need to predict your afterlife."

Julia watched the interplay between the two ghosts, both of which were as clear as if she'd been seeing them in the flesh. "I don't understand what's going on."

"It's quite clear to us." The woman in green stepped forward, clearly the leader of this odd little group. "I'm Mrs. Griffin, my dear, and you are a medium."

The man in the fedora muttered, "Some might call you a channeler, but you get the idea."

Mrs. Griffin's long-sleeved green gown was decorated with intricate embroidery, her hair in a sleek chignon. Julia was guessing by her dress and makeup that she died sometime in the 1940s.

"I can't be a medium." Julia said the words, but she didn't believe them. "I'm fifty-one."

"And I'm sixty-seven, dear. I don't know what that has to do with anything."

"Thirty-six," Mae said. "What a fix." She winked at Justin.

"Holy shit." Justin looked like he was about to pass out. "It's really you."

Julia shifted to the end of the lounge chair. "People don't just flip on a ghost-seeing switch, do they? I've lived my whole life without any ghosts, and now I have..." Julia turned to the fourth ghost at the party, the muttering one. "Four? This is not real. It's... a dream or a hallucination or something."

The man in the fedora was younger than Mrs. Griffin, but not by much. His face had a worn and tired expression that told Julia he wasn't the least bit impressed with her and he was even less impressed by Justin.

"That's your rationale?" the man in the fedora asked. "The name's Elton Woods, PI. And lady, if you don't want to believe us—"

"I *don't* believe you."

Mae put a ghostly hand on Julia's knee. "Well, of course you do."

"I don't know how you can continue to deny the truth with so much evidence all around you," Mrs. Griffin said. "It would be very illogical."

"What's illogical is my seeing ghosts!" Julia stood and started to pace.

"See." Elton tossed off a wave. "I told ya girls."

"I'm having some kind of mental breakdown." Julia stared at the ground while she paced. "That's what this is. It's not super-natural. It's not some freakish mystery. This is me finally reaching the end of my rope and just... crashing."

It was the only thing that made sense. At least she was in the right place. Dean and Sergio probably knew of any number of mental hospitals that could help. Half of Sergio's family were in show business, the rest were in psychology, probably to keep the first half from going off the deep end.

Mae leaned forward. 'I know it's a lot, honey. Have you had any shocks lately? Any near misses?"

'Near misses?" Julia was genuinely confused. 'You mean has anyone tried to kill me?"

Mae let out a tinkling laugh. 'Oh, don't be silly! I'm talking about life. Maybe... a car accident or a little bump on the head? Something like that."

Julia froze.

'She knows," Elton said. 'I could see it a mile away. She knows exactly what's going on here."

Piece after piece falling into place.

Julia's paranoia after the heart attack. The feeling that she was being watched. Never feeling alone. Fear of the dark. The strange noises she'd begun to hear in empty houses.

Had all those curiosities been leading to... this?

She'd pushed it all to the back of her mind, convinced she was just stressed out. Nearly dying could do that to you, right? She'd taken the invitation Dean and Sergio offered like a lifeline. She'd known she needed a fresh start, and Palm Springs seemed like the perfect place for it.

Now four ghosts were staring at her in the flickering light of Sergio's gas fireplace and nothing made sense, but everything was starting to.

'You're not the first around here," Mae said, stretching out on the lounger. 'But you look like you could be the most fun. What do you say, Jules?" She sat up. 'Can I call you Jules?"

As if on cue, Juliana, oldest of the twins by ten minutes, opened a door and walked out. She sat on the lounge chair where Mae was sitting and looked around.

"This is about the ghosts, isn't it?" the girl asked without preamble. 'You're talking to them."

Despite being part of their lives from birth, Julia still found her nieces slightly terrifying. "No."

Juliana swept her eyes around the patio ominously, her hands crossed demurely over her pleated plaid skirt. "I'm Juliana Augusta. My fathers named me after a Roman empress who poisoned her husband."

Julia pursed her lips. "I think they named you after me."

"And you." Juliana didn't stop her severe glare. "Whichever spirit is tormenting Paco, our beloved rescue alpaca, I will ask you only once to stop. If it happens again, my sister and I will call the exorcist."

Mrs. Griffin smiled. "I have always approved of this one."

"Why does that not surprise me?" Julia muttered. "Juliana, I don't think any of these people are messing with Paco."

"Eh." Elton shrugged. "I have been, but I guess I'll stop. We've got a lot more to entertain us now." The corner of his mouth turned up in a smile as he looked at Julia. "We got a medium." Then he looked at Justin. "And a murder."

Chapter Seven

J ulia was lying awake at eleven o'clock that night, helped by her four-hour nap that afternoon and her new ghostly acquisitions. She'd fled the patio, and the ghosts had the sensitivity to leave her alone. Justin seemed to be more at ease with the three resident ghosts since he'd returned.

She glanced at her phone and saw four texts from an unfamiliar number. Probably junk calls; they got worse every year. She was just stretching her legs and working out the regular kinks in her back when someone pounded on her door.

"Julia!"

It was a woman, but Julia didn't recognize the voice. She was confused more than worried; no one could have gotten on the estate unless Sergio or Dean let them in.

"Julia Brooks!" the woman yelled again. "What the hell did you do to me?"

Now Julia recognized the voice. She got out of bed and opened the door to a furious Evy Landa. "Why are you yelling at me in the middle of the night?"

"What did you do to me?" Evy looked wild. She was wearing

a slim black suit and white shirt with a loose bow tie hanging around her neck.

"You look great in a suit." Julia was sleepy, and she wasn't very clear on why Evy was at her house. "I could never pull one off. I think my boobs are too big."

"Will you listen to me? I need to know what you did to me so you can make it stop."

Julia closed her eyes, then opened them. "I should... Your aunt, the thing with the ghost? It didn't work."

"What are you saying? Are you trying to blame my aunt Marie?"

"I had one ghost; now I have four. You do the math."

"What are you talking about?" Evy took a step back. "Are you saying Justin came back after Marie did the thing?"

"Yeah. And he came with three more friends. They're more of them now and they're clearer. And one of them is..." Julia stopped. Mae had mentioned valuing her privacy. Maybe she wouldn't want Julia to tell people who was there. "Several of them are quite old ghosts. I think they've been around a while."

"Okay." Evy nodded. "Okay, but how does that explain the voices?"

Julia froze. "What voices?"

"The voices." Evy put her hands next to her ears and gestured wildly. "I am hearing people's thoughts, Julia!"

She blinked. "Oh, that's not good."

"Ya think?"

"Like everyone? Are you hearing *my* thoughts right now?"

"No. It's not that regular. I first noticed it when I was at Restful Palms for the show tonight, and I heard Mr. Everett—"

"Restful Palms? Is that a club?"

Evy paused and blinked a couple of times. "It's not exactly... It's kind of a club."

"Restful..." Julia started to smile. "Were you at a retirement home? Is that where your show was?"

'Okay fine. Yes, Restful Palms is a retirement home, not a club. But you know what? Those places pay better than the clubs, so I don't want to hear any shit from you or Sergio. Those old people fucking love Geoff. You think the cowboys at the casino are begging for some snazzy ventriloquist action? The elderly appreciate the *art*, okay?"

'I'm not..." Julia shook her head. 'I'm not saying a word. Tell me about the voices."

'It started with Mr. Everett, and then I started..." She took a deep breath. 'I need a drink."

'Why the hell not?" Julia reached for her robe, shrugged it on, and followed Evy out to the back patio between the main house and the guesthouse. The moon was hanging over the silhouetted line of palm trees in the distance, and the mountains were dark slashes against a riot of stars in the desert sky.

Dean and Sergio's house was dark save for a light in the kitchen and a dim gold glow from a second-floor window. She pulled out a chair from the patio table and lowered herself into it as Evy walked to the bar.

Julia asked, 'Who's Mr. Everett?"

Evy pulled a bottle of champagne from the outdoor kitchen fridge. 'Glasses?"

"Try the cupboard to the left of the sink."

Evy opened it and grabbed two plastic champagne flutes for poolside sipping. Then she walked to the patio table and popped open the bottle of champagne. 'Sergio owes me."

'I wasn't going to say a word."

'Mr. Everett was thinking about my boobs. The man is older than my father, and I've hugged him so many times in his wheelchair. The whole time? He's thinking about copping a feel. How messed up is that?"

"That's pretty messed up."

'Men are gross." She opened the bottle and immediately poured two glasses in expert style, proving that cleaning pools wasn't the only side job Evy Landa had taken over the years. "I mean, even when they're ninety, they're thinking about boobs."

Julia took the offered plastic champagne flute. "To be fair, boobs are pretty great."

"Says the woman with lots of them." Evy rolled her eyes.

Julia glanced down at her breasts. They'd held up well, and she gave most of the credit to the lack of children attached to them. "Okay yes," she said. "But yours must be pretty nice if you caught Mr. Everett's eye."

Evy almost spit out her champagne. "You have a point." She groaned and slid back in her chair. "This isn't okay! At first, I thought he'd said something. Then I realized that I could also hear what his wife was thinking next to him. Kind of. It was all flashes and a mix of voices and pictures. Not easy to understand at all."

Julia was feeling punchy with lack of sleep and a glass of champagne. "So what was Mrs. Everett thinking about if it wasn't your boobs?"

Evy raised an eyebrow. "Someone who wasn't Mr. Everett."

"Seriously?"

She sat up in her chair. "And then I realized that this other muttering I was hearing wasn't coming from someone hanging out near the exit, it was coming from Nora Perkins, who was thinking about running away with Mr. Stafford."

Julia's eyes went wide. "Another torrid affair?"

"Mr. Stafford is her dachshund. I got the feeling she wanted to make a break for it and hit the casino."

Julia frowned. "From what you said, it seems like retirement homes are hotbeds of sex and gambling. That makes me feel better somehow." After all, she wasn't getting any younger. "But you're not hearing me now?"

"No, it was only while I was onstage."

"So what was different between now and when you were onstage?"

Evy shook her head. "Nothing. I packed up Geoff and came straight here after. I had to sweet-talk Dean to let me through the gate, but he finally gave up because I'm a lovable pain in the ass, and then I drove up here, parked my car" —Evy motioned to a vintage Cadillac that looked like it had been new in the 1980s — "and I knocked on your door."

A man leaning against the Cadillac was smoking a thin cigarette and wearing an outfit very much like Evy's. Black suit, high collar, bow tie.

"Evy?" Julia turned to her. "I don't suppose you picked up a friend on the way here?"

"No, why?"

Julia had a sinking suspicion she knew what was different between Evy onstage and Evy now. "So you were doing the show with Geoff, right?"

"Of course." Evy refilled her champagne.

"And what would you say Geoff's... personality is? What's his character, you know? Most ventriloquist's acts that I've seen, the dummy has its own character so the comedian and the dummy—"

"Oh right. Yeah, I know what you mean." She took another long drink of champagne. "I always imagined Geoff as kind of s stuffy Professor Higgins–type character, right? Like a very proper Englishman who's all fancy and shit. And I prank him all the time and torment him for laughs. Geoff is definitely the straight man. Comedically, I mean."

"Mm-hmm." Julia nodded. "And how did you come up with that?"

Evy frowned. "I can't really say. It just felt right, you know? How some things just seem to take on a life of their own? The name, his personality? It all just kind of came to me. From the minute I picked Geoff up at the shop—"

"So he's a vintage dummy?" Julia saw the pieces falling into place once again.

"Yeah, I found him at a specialty shop in New York years ago. He was originally made for someone in London in the 1920s. Maybe that's why I assume he's British, you know?"

How was she going to break it to Evy?

Julia looked at her. "I think I know why you were hearing the voices onstage but not now."

Evy's eyes lit up. "How? Have you been reading or something? We have got to find out where Aunt Marie went. I got home the other day after leaving here, and there was a very messy note with something about her taking off for a couple of weeks, but I couldn't make out where she said she was going. Which isn't unusual for her—she's in her eighties, but she's still really spry. In fact—"

"Evy, I'm pretty sure your dummy is haunted." She stared at the elegant man leaning on the Cadillac. "And I'm pretty sure I know why you named him Geoff."

The ghost turned and caught Julia's stare. He looked behind himself, then back to her, putting one hand on his chest in disbelief.

Me? his expression seemed to ask.

Evy was not amused. "What are you talking about?"

Julia raised her hand and gave a small wave. "I'm pretty sure I just met Geoff."

JULIA SAT NEXT TO EVY, WHO WAS STARING AT A TWO-foot tall puppet with a black bow tie and a monocle.

Not unlike the ghost that was sitting next to the puppet. Both had arrow-straight postures, a severe mouth, and slicked-back hair.

Evy was shaking her head slowly and staring at the doll. "It's like I don't even know you."

"That seems rather harsh." Ghost Geoff's mouth turned down at the corners.

Julia kept looking between the man and the dummy. "So you just had him made to look exactly like you?"

"Yes," Ghost Geoff said. "That was part of the act. He was the outrageous one, and I was the gentleman."

Sergio, who had been drawn outside by Evy's earlier screaming, lounged on a chaise, his head propped up with his fist as he examined the two women and the dummy. "I don't get it. Geoff is possessed?"

Ghost Geoff didn't like that much. "I say—"

"I think it's more like..." Julia struggled to explain. "And please understand, I am going completely on my very new instincts here, but I think that it's more like when Geoff the person passed away, he kept hanging around with Geoff the dummy because...?" Julia looked at Ghost Geoff.

The man crossed his legs elegantly and brushed an invisible piece of lint from his pants. "It seemed appropriate at the time."

"He was really happy around Geoff the dummy," Julia said. "It's like the other ghosts around here. I'm pretty sure they're all hanging around because this place has good energy and happy memories."

Sergio waved a hand. "I mean, it's not a surprise that the place is haunted. I guess I'm a little disappointed that no famous ghosts picked our house to haunt; according to my mother, the previous owners had some legendary parties."

Julia had made the executive decision that "Mae" and her true identity definitely needed to remain a mystery from Sergio. The ghost had asked for privacy, and Sergio would immediately spread that news to everyone from his favorite vendor at the farmers' market to his chiropractor.

"So a society matron named Mrs. Griffin, a socialite named Mae, and a detective named Elton?" Sergio rubbed his hands together. "I have to know who all of them are."

'Don't forget Justin," Julia said. 'He's still hanging around."

Not at the moment though. Julia looked around and didn't see a hint of any of them. Did ghosts sleep? That seemed unnecessary. Maybe they just got supernaturally tired and had to build up energy after talking with live people.

'I bet Mrs. Griffin is Adelaide Griffin," Sergio said. 'She and her husband built the house in the 1920s. She lived here until she passed in the early fifties. Then the house went to some studio executive—"

Evy burst out, 'Can we focus on the fact that Geoff has seen me naked please?"

Julia wasn't quite sure what to say about that one, so she looked at Ghost Geoff, who was definitely uncomfortable.

He shifted in his seat. 'I say..."

'What *do* you say?" Julia asked him point-blank. 'She's shared a dressing room probably more times than she can count. Did you turn around?"

'Of course I did! In a manner of speaking. I can fade when I need to. And certain... shall we say, *private* times—"

'Oh God, that valet at the Palmer a few months ago." Evy slapped a hand over her eyes. 'Geoff was still sitting outside his box when we got home because I'd been washing his clothes." She seemed to curl into herself. 'Oh Goooooood..."

Julia put her hand on Evy's shoulder. 'Ghost Geoff says he turned around. That he kind of fades away when you need private time. He seems pretty buttoned-up to me, so I'd buy it."

'I would really prefer to be called by my given name, Geoffrey," the ghost muttered. 'No one has ever called me *Geoff*."

'Hush, Geoffrey," Julia snapped. 'Evy's just had a shock; you get to be quiet now."

Evy stared at the puppet with hollow eyes. 'I don't know how I can ever trust you again."

'I never lied to you," Geoffrey said. 'I told you immediately who I was. You just didn't realize it was me speaking and not the puppet."

Julia shook her head. "I don't even know how to translate this conversation." She sighed. "Evy, Geoffrey the Ghost feels very bad about haunting Geoff the puppet, but I think you can be fairly confident that your relationship with Geoff the puppet is fine. Just try to ignore Geoffrey the ghost. Knowing he exists doesn't have to change who you and Geoff are."

Sergio smiled softly; his blinks growing longer and longer. "You're like a beautiful, beautiful ghost therapist, Julia."

"Thanks." She turned to face Evy. "Now, I think you need to hold Geoff."

Evy looked confused. "As part of the ghost therapy?"

"No. I am not a ghost therapist. You need to hold him so you can see if you can read thoughts when you do."

"Oh right." Evy didn't look happy about it. "Last time it wasn't all at once. What if now that I know what's happening, it's stronger?"

"I think you'll still need to concentrate on people to make it happen," Julia said. "After all, you didn't hear everyone in the room when you were onstage, just the people you were looking at."

"Okay." Evy reached for Geoff and settled him onto her lap. Then she looked at the empty chair where the ghost was. "This feels awkward now."

"Same Geoff, remember?" Julia focused on Evy, mentally speaking to her. *Can you hear me?*

Evy blinked. "Holy shit, I can."

Sergio sat up. "Do me next!" He closed his eyes in concentration.

"Why are you singing 'The Piña Colada Song' at me?" Evy asked.

Sergio opened his eyes and clapped. "Oh, this is so cool!"

"I don't think it's cool," Evy said. "What if I start hearing shitty things people think about me? I don't want to be that self-aware!" She pointed at Julia. "She already thinks I'm overreacting to the Ghost Geoff thing, and she's a little judgy about the valet at the Palmer."

Julia's eyes went wide. "I am not!"

"You are a little," Evy said. "It's okay; I judged myself after that one too." She set Geoff down. "That's going to take some practice. I may not be taking many gigs for a little while."

"I think we can all agree on one thing," Julia said. "Me suddenly seeing ghosts. You suddenly hearing people's thoughts. Aunt Marie trying to lift some curse on us while she was under the influence of whatever drugs Vivian gave her..." She looked at Evy.

Evy's eyes went wide. "We need to find Vivian. She was the only other person in the room. Only God knows what Aunt Marie did to *her*."

Chapter Eight

Julia stepped onto the patio midmorning with her hair in another messy bun and a thrumming headache behind her eyes. Champagne and paranormal revelations after midnight were probably a lot easier to handle when you weren't fifty-one.

"Hello, my darling!" Sergio sang from the patio, clearly unbothered by a ghostly visitation and three a.m. alcohol. "Come join me and Mick, Jules. I was just telling him about your new little ghost thing."

New little ghost thing.

Yeah, Sergio would describe it that way. And he'd likely share the news with literally everyone he met, which meant that any fresh start she was hoping for in Palm Springs would be colored by the rumor that she was a medium.

Fantastic.

"Great." She squinted. "Sure thing, just give me..."

It took her a second to recognize the man sitting on the patio as the film director from Sunday Dinner, Michael O'Connor, the one who'd been talking to Lily and Justin. He was just as frustratingly handsome as he'd been two nights ago, while Julia was looking like a disgruntled Persian cat in need of a visit to the groomer.

She tried to make excuses. "Maybe I'll just see if Jim can get me—"

"Breakfast." Sergio's voice was firm. "Now. Jim made eggs Florentine, and I know you love his hollandaise."

Dammit, she couldn't resist Jim's hollandaise sauce. "Fine. But..." She wrapped her robe more tightly around herself and reached for a pair of sunglasses on the small table by her front door. "This is as fancy as it gets this morning."

As she approached the patio table, Michael stood and held out his hand. "Sorry for intruding on your morning. Sergio and I have a standing breakfast every couple of weeks when I'm in town, and he's been entertaining me with your..."

Julia shook his hand and sat. "Being at a loss for words would be appropriate in this situation. I don't know what to call it either."

Michael smiled, and his eyes crinkled in the corners in a way that told Julia he liked to laugh. She appreciated that. She also appreciated that his face looked like a grown man's and not a middle-aged executive who was desperately trying to stave off the passage of time.

Not that she'd seen too many of those in LA.

"So I'm not going to pretend to be coy or cool," Julia said. "I've seen your movies, and I like most of them."

"Thanks. I like most of them too." He squinted. "The ones from a few years ago weren't my favorite, but the money was really good."

"I've sold some houses that I think are absolute eyesores, but it's a job." She reached for the coffee cup Sergio poured for her. "Thanks, handsome."

"You got it." Sergio sat back. "You know, Evy is still sleeping, but I'm glad you woke up, because I wanted you two to meet."

Oh dear. Not Sergio playing matchmaker again. Not that

Michael O'Connor was a bad specimen of a man, it was just that she never had much luck with anything more than a fling.

Sergio continued, "Jules, I'm going to be an oversharer—"

"When are you not?"

"And tell Mick here that you had a pretty bad scare with your heart a few months ago."

"Sergio!" She thought he'd be oversharing about himself, not her. "What the hell?"

"I'm only sharing that because this didn't get a lot of press, but Mick—"

"Died about two years ago." Michael looked at her. "For three minutes and twenty-two seconds, that is. It changed my life pretty dramatically, so I'm sure that's why Sergio is being completely intrusive and violating your privacy."

Julia blinked. "Oh. I'm so sorry to hear that."

"Don't be. I was on a set and it was a freak accident. I don't remember much, but..." He frowned. "Well, I haven't done a movie since. Guess I'm trying to figure out if I still want to make them."

"Wow." Julia shook her head. "I'm lucky, I guess."

"I think I was pretty lucky too. There were great doctors on the production, but it was a close call."

"Yes, my doctor was really great too, but I guess..." What had she been trying to say? "I definitely think I'm reevaluating things since the health scare, but I never wondered whether I was in the right line of work."

Michael nodded. "I see what you mean."

"I genuinely love real estate. I mean, I don't love all my clients, but there's something really satisfying about matching the right home with the right buyer."

"I can see that."

"And it's not always the high-dollar places, you know? Sometimes it's finding a little place for someone in a niche neighborhood where they've always wanted to live. Or it's helping someone move back to a city they left." She shrugged and sipped her coffee. "It's not art or anything, but I do love helping people find home."

Michael turned to Sergio. "She's gonna end up convincing me to buy a house, and Dean is going to be pissed."

Sergio laughed, and Julia looked between the two men. "What?"

"It's been a joke for years," Michael said. "I've always traveled so much for work that I never bought a house."

"Oh my God, where...?" Julia blinked. "I honestly can't wrap my brain around that. You've got to have possessions of some kind, right? Where do you put them?"

"He has a plane hangar!" Sergio said. "Can you imagine? And there's this little tiny apartment in it. Right here in Palm Springs. It drives Dean up the wall. The man has more money than God, and he lives in a shitty hangar apartment."

"I beg to differ." Michael held up a hand. "It's a very nice hangar apartment." He looked at her. "It is small though. I had to rent another hangar last year to store my plane."

Julia couldn't stop the smile. "So you have two hangars? One for storage and one for your plane? But no house."

"I love flying. I've thought about doing that instead of making movies, but then it would be a job instead of pure fun. A lot of people were shocked I didn't die that way, but it's something I've enjoyed since I was a kid. My grandfather was a pilot."

"And you live in a hangar and are trying to decide if you still want to make movies."

"Right now I'm actually house-sitting for some friends and taking care of their dog and just..." He pursed his lips. "Living in the moment."

Sergio handed Julia a plate with Jim's perfect eggs Florentine on them. "Okay, enough talk. Eat something. Mick is a very cautious pilot; he's the only one I'd trust to fly the girls in a small plane. He's as careful as he is rich. But he is, essentially, homeless."

Michael laughed and shook his head. "I prefer to say I'm a nomad." He turned to Julia. "When I'm not working, I usually stay with friends." He shrugged. "Like Lily and Richard when they were together. Or Dean and Sergio."

She looked over her shoulder. "So did I take your bed?"

"You did, but I surrender it with pleasure."

The way the man said *pleasure* should be illegal.

Julia cleared her throat. "So you know Lily and Richard, huh? Did you hear about Justin?"

Michael winced. "I did. I don't know what to think. Sergio said the police ruled it a homicide?"

Sergio nodded. "Officially yesterday. Blunt-force trauma to the back of the head." He shuddered. "Horrible."

"The kid was..." Michael shrugged. "Annoying, if you ask me. I don't really know why Lily was with him. There were rumors..."

Julia perked her ears. "Rumors?"

"That Richard was seeing a much younger woman. I don't know if it's true. I tried to stay out of that kind of stuff because I was friends with them both. But I can't think of any other reason that Lily would be with someone like Justin."

"I don't know," Julia said. "Most people don't have a problem with older men and younger women. What's the big deal?"

Michael lifted a hand. "And if the guy was a doctor or in business or even if he was a starving artist or something, I wouldn't question her taste. But Lily—despite the stereotypes about blond, socialite actresses—is a brilliant woman. It's one of the reasons that she and Richard were married so long. She's witty and has an incredible sense of humor. This Justin kid..." He shook his head. "He just wasn't on her level."

Julia, having only known Justin after he'd already been dealt the indignity of death, felt the urge to defend him. "He was a personal chef. That's an important job. Especially if you have, like, special diet needs or something."

Sergio snorted. "Justin was a chef because he couldn't make it as a trainer. And he was a trainer because he couldn't make it as an actor, but he'd invested too many years on his muscles to let them go to waste. He didn't create menus, darling, he *was* the menu."

"Still," Michael said, "it's absolutely horrible that he was killed. I'm guessing it might have been something personal. Maybe an ex-girlfriend or something. Lily complained about one of his exes stalking him, but I don't know if that was just a rumor."

Julia didn't know if it was a rumor either, but she knew a few people, living and dead, that she wanted to ask.

EVY WAS WEARING SUNGLASSES AND LOOKED distinctly more hungover than Julia was by the time they made it over to Vivian's house that afternoon. They'd tried to reach her at the office but were told she'd gone home for the day.

Suspiciously absent on a Wednesday afternoon? Yeah, it piqued their interest.

A quick call to Sergio netted them her home address in Rancho Mirage, a short drive from Palm Springs.

"You know..." Julia was thinking about breakfast with Sergio and Michael. "I'm thinking that if you want anything kept quiet in Palm Springs, the number one rule is to not tell Sergio Oliveira."

"You're just now figuring that out?"

"I admit I've been a little slow since my health scare last summer."

Evy turned to look at her. "What health scare? You seem right as rain."

"I had a mild cardiac event." Julia turned off Palm Canyon Drive and toward the guard house for Vivian's development. "The houses out here bother me, but I know I need to get over it. Dean says we have three or four listings coming up in this area. Even though the homes are custom, they feel so... suburban. So much money, not enough taste."

"A mild cardiac event? You mean a heart attack?" Evy stared out the window. "Yeah, I wouldn't have pegged Vivian for golf course living, but I guess I only met her once."

"Same, and I had a *mild cardiac event*." Julia maneuvered between two golf carts and three old women walking toy dogs. "I had laparoscopic surgery and a couple of stents. My doctor says I'm perfectly healthy now."

"Holy shit." Evy took off her sunglasses. "My mom was a nurse. You don't get stents for an irregular heartbeat, Julia. Are you sure you're okay?"

It was a question that Julia was thinking more and more about the longer she kept seeing dead people. Was their presence a portent of things to come? Everyone died, but not everyone saw ghosts, right? Maybe the universe was trying to ease her into the idea of joining the afterlife a little early.

"I'm fine." She wasn't sure if she was reassuring Evy or herself. "I'm on some medications now, and I know to be careful. I'm exercising more. Paying attention to stress. Stuff like that."

"Is that why you moved out to the desert?"

"Kind of." She scanned the high walls of the houses along the golf course and spotted Vivian's house number among the sea of slightly customized midcentury and Italianate homes surrounding a verdant golf course. "It's part of the less-stress plan."

"And you've already found a dead body and have started seeing ghosts. How's that working for you?"

"Right?" She pulled into the driveway and put her car in park.

The glowering ghost in the back seat of her Mercedes wasn't exactly a zen master.

Julia wasn't sure what the universe had planned, but so far it wasn't working. Justin had shown up around noon, but he'd remained silent and sullen. She could feel angry energy from him. It wasn't unlike when her mother's geriatric shih tzu glared at her when she was visiting.

"Okay, how do we want to do this?" Evy asked. "You think we should play it casual? Ask how she's feeling?"

"Do you remember yesterday? She already thinks we're lunatics. We might as well just go with it." Julia exited the car and walked up to Vivian's gate, ringing the doorbell without stopping to think. It sang with an electronic chime that told Julia she was being recorded. She and Evy hung back; she could feel Justin behind them.

A few moments later, she heard noises coming from the house. Someone was coming to the front gate quickly.

Dr. Vivian Wei yanked the metal gate open and stared at Julia and Evy.

"What did you do to me?" She held up her hand, showing an open palm. "Whatever this is, you need to make it stop. Call your aunt, call your priest. I don't know how you Catholic people do things—"

"We're actually Romanian Orthodox, so it's pretty different from Catholic."

Julia frowned. "She had a rosary."

"Eh." Evy shrugged. "It's a little bit of a cheat because Orthodox prayer beads have a hundred prayers, which takes a long time, but the rosary only has fifty-nine, so I think she maybe used it as a shortcut, but the actual rosary was a gift from a dear friend of hers who passed and—"

"I don't care!" Vivian did not look like the calm and collected professional they'd met a few days before. She looked frazzled and a little scared. "I don't care what kind of prayer beads or rosary or weird Christian things you have to do, but I need you to make this stop."

Evy and Julia exchanged a look.

"So...," Evy started. "How've you been?"

"You said something about ghosts yesterday?" Vivian looked at Julia. "Well, I'm feeling things. Like, when I touch people, I am *feeling* them. And I'm not talking about physically feeling their bodies—very little grosses me out, I'm a dentist—I'm talking about their feelings. I am feeling their *feelings!*"

Julia whispered, "That doesn't seem good."

"No, it doesn't!"

"Yeah." Evy cleared her throat. "I'm going to say that probably... is bad."

"I have to have my hands in people's mouths!" Vivian was practically yelling. "I already know way too much about them. I do not need their feelings too!"

"So the medical gloves you use—?"

"Not thick enough!" She looked over Evy's shoulder and lowered her voice. "Apparently they are not thick enough." She widened the door. "Come inside. I don't need my neighbors thinking I'm a crazy person. I may have inherited a very nice house, but I'm not rich enough to get away with that."

Evy looked at the line of luxury homes stretching on either side of Vivian's. "Are you sure?"

"Come on."

They entered Vivian's shade-covered courtyard, which was precisely landscaped with tropical plants, and entered the two-story ranch-style house that looked like it had been built in the 1970s.

Vivian walked to the right where Julia saw an updated kitchen. "I need some tea. I'll make some for you guys too. You both look hungover."

Julia noticed the distinct smell of incense as soon as she entered the house, along with a calming energy that immediately set her at ease. She looked over her shoulder, but Justin was nowhere to be found.

"She reads people well," Evy muttered. "I could definitely use some tea."

"And my ghost doesn't like her house." Julia was delighted by a sense of relief.

Driving through the development, she'd expected Vivian's home to be a generic, tasteful-but-bland, mirror of the outside. Instead, she was delighted to find a warm, light, bohemian sanctuary with eclectic art, scattered rugs, and a ton of personality. A small altar was tucked into a corner near a plate glass window overlooking the courtyard—that's where the smell of incense was coming from—and deep greens with pops of orange and purple filled the room, which was also home to a veritable jungle of thriving houseplants.

Julia couldn't stop smiling. "Vivian, you're living in the wrong house."

The woman poked her head out of the kitchen. "What are you talking about?"

Evy was turning in place, taking it all in. "Your plants are amazing. I can kill a cactus."

"Oh thanks." Vivian returned to the living room with a clear glass pot of green tea and a couple of mugs. "I don't know if you guys want tea, but you need it."

"Why did you buy this house?" Julia asked. "You need something with more age. More personality. You have to be the youngest person in your neighborhood, right? There are some midcentury bungalows set to go on the market that I think would—"

"Wow." Vivian held up her hands. "And I thought I got enthusiastic about flossing. Can we focus on the ghosts and the empathy and...?" She looked at Evy. "I'm almost afraid to ask."

Evy plopped down on Vivian's emerald-green sofa. "Oh, I just discovered that when I'm holding my ventriloquist dummy, I can hear people's thoughts. And that's apparently because my dummy is haunted by a stuck-up British ghost named Geoffrey."

Vivian looked at Julia, who nodded.

"I don't even know how to classify that," Vivian said.

"Join the club!" Evy said. "And ever since Aunt Marie's little blessing, Julia is seeing even more spirits than she was before. The ghosts who are hanging around Dean and Sergio's house, the one haunting my dummy, *and* the one from the murdered guy who was killed on Monday."

Vivian was staring at them, her eyes the size of the golf balls that were whizzing through the air behind her house. "What murdered guy?"

Chapter Nine

As they explained, Vivian kept shaking her head. "Oh, this is so bad."

"You're telling me," Evy said. "I don't know how I'm going to ever look at Geoff again, much less go onstage with him. I mean, even if you set aside the fact that I seem to be able to hear voices when I'm holding him—and who needs that in the middle of a show?—I am having a hard time getting past the fact that a ghost has seen me naked. I mean, he says he looked away, but how can I ever trust him?"

Vivian frowned at Evy. "I was talking about the murder."

"Oh!" Evy sat up straight. "Yes, that is definitely horrible too."

"I think the key is the murdered man." Vivian held her tea with both hands. "Don't you? You said that you hadn't seen any ghosts before you found Justin's body. Maybe that means you need to make sure he's at rest and then he'll leave you alone. And if *he* leaves you alone..."

Evy jumped in. "Then maybe all the ghosts will go away. Or at least we won't know about them anymore. Because they'll be at *peace*."

Julia wasn't keen on turning into a detective. "How am I supposed to help a spirit find peace? I'm not a priest. I don't know anything about his murder. I don't know anything about his life except rumors."

"Maybe..." Vivian arched her immaculately groomed eyebrows. "I mean, maybe he just needs an advocate. A voice among the living. Does he have any family living in the area? A squeaky wheel gets the oil, right? If there's no one pestering the police about his case—"

"I would think Lily would do that," Evy said. "His girlfriend."

Vivian nodded slowly. "You would hope so. But I don't know. Your friend Michael mentioned that he didn't think Lily was serious about this man. He may be easily forgotten."

"Maybe we should go talk to Lily," Evy said. "I know where she's living now. We could ask her how she's doing, see if she knows anything about the investigation. We should be able to tell if she's going to be on the police about finding Justin's murderer."

Julia said, "Also, Michael mentioned that Lily told him an ex-girlfriend of Justin's had been stalking him. Maybe there's something there. Maybe she still cares about him. Maybe she'll bug the police."

"But it could also mean she might have murdered him," Evy said. "For being with Lily."

"Oh right." Julia shook her head. "I'm not a detective. I don't think like that."

Vivian took a deep breath. "Listen, I know we're not the police, but we're all three bright, mature, intelligent women. I'm a dentist, and my mother is a doctor; I know a ridiculous amount about the human body. Plus I listen to a ton of murder podcasts."

"Oh, I love those!" Evy smiled. "Did you listen to the new

one about the guy who they thought killed his boss but they were actually partners and she was killed by...?"

Julia was glaring at her.

"What?" Evy shrugged. "It's a really good podcast."

Vivian nodded. "It is, but they made the real murderer a little too obvious about halfway through."

"Can we get back on track?" Julia asked. "Obviously we are not trained detectives, and this is none of our business."

Vivian raised an eyebrow. "Except it is. Especially for you."

Evy scooted forward in her seat. "Okay, I know murder podcasts are not the same as police training, but I think Vivian has a point. I know a lot of people in this town, and old people love talking to me. Between me and Sergio, there isn't a rumor we can't dig up. If Justin was fooling around on Lily, I can find out."

"And what about me?" Julia said. "I'm a fifty-one-year-old real estate agent who doesn't know very many people here. I have zero interest in murder podcasts. I don't even like detective shows."

"But you have an in that neither of us have," Vivian said. "You can talk to ghosts."

"That would be helpful, except Justin says he can't remember how he died," Julia said. "He doesn't even remember why he went to Casa de Lirio in the first place."

"Okay..." Vivian narrowed her eyes in an expression that Julia was quickly coming to realize meant she was thinking about something. "How many ghosts did you say were around Sergio and Dean's house?"

"At least three, but there might be more." She was sure there had been more shadows on the estate during Sunday Dinner.

Vivian leaned forward. "So how many ghosts do you think there are in the whole of that weird, kooky neighborhood where you live?"

Evy smiled. "For that matter, how many ghosts are there at Casa de Lirio?"

Vivian nodded. "And what did *they* see?"

THE GATE AT CASA DE LIRIO WAS HANGING OPEN when they arrived. The sun was starting to go down, and a dim blue filter seemed to settle over the estate.

"Is the gate supposed to be locked?" Vivian asked.

"There have been workers in since the police cleared it," Julia said. "Dean texted me this morning. They probably left it open."

Evy said, "I know I still have a key for cleaning the pool. No one asked for it back or anything."

"Still, maybe we shouldn't go in the house," Evy said. "Just in case."

"If there are ghosts around" —Vivian boldly walked through the gate and onto the flagstone path— "they'd probably be hanging around outside, right Julia?"

"You're asking me?" She had a heavy feeling in her chest, and while she looked over her shoulder for Justin's presence, he was nowhere to be found.

"Yes, because you're the one who's seeing ghosts," Vivian said. "Give me someone to touch and I'll tell you their feelings, but I can't talk to the undead."

Evy cocked her head. "Are they technically undead? I think that's just vampires and zombies."

"Wait, are vampires and zombies real too?" Vivian froze. "Because I don't know if that's a level of weird I can handle at this point in my life."

"Pretty sure it's just psychic stuff," Julia said. "At least so far."

Vivian's jaw clenched. "Move to Southern California, they

said. The sunshine will be so good for your depression, they said."

"No one mentioned the ghosts and psychic phenomena?" Evy walked toward the house, scanning the grounds. "Julia, are you seeing anything?"

"Not so far." She felt the same oppressive feeling around her, but nothing appeared. "Maybe the ghosts are hiding."

"Maybe they don't know you can see them," Evy said.

"If they didn't realize she could see them," Vivian said, "wouldn't they *not* hide?"

"Oh right." Evy shook her head. "I knew I should have brought Geoff."

"Justin?" Julia could feel the little bastard, but he wasn't showing himself. "Hey, can you come out and tell the spirits around here to talk to me?"

Nothing. If anything, the oppressive feeling just got worse.

Julia, Evy, and Vivian followed a brick path around the side of the house, which was shaded by a palm grove and lemon trees. The bricks wound through a gravel courtyard with a glistening pool in the distance. Beyond the pool stretched a view that was unparalleled in Palm Springs—the reason people fell in love with Casa de Lirio. The side of the mountain swept up from the hills, outlining rocky outcroppings against a blanket of stars in a blue velvet sky.

The pool of Casa de Lirio was surrounded by terraced planters holding palms, bougainvilleas, and hibiscus bushes. The three women circled the grounds, passing the massive pool, luxurious cabanas, and lush gardens, but no ghosts appeared. Julia could feel them around, but something was holding them back.

Evy was kneeling on the pool deck. "I swear, did the police actually kick trash in here? I think I see police tape at the bottom of the pool. How am I supposed to get that out?"

"I feel like there's something around here," Julia said, "but I can't see it. It's almost like I can hear a party in another room, but I can't really hear what anyone is saying."

After their second circuit around the house, Evy put a hand up. "This isn't getting us anywhere."

"Ideas?" Vivian asked. "Julia's spoken to the ghosts at Sergio's house, maybe they could offer a kind of introduction? Is that possible?"

Julia shrugged. "Maybe?"

"I have a better idea." Evy was still staring at the pool.

Julia and Vivian both turned to look at her.

Evy put her hands on her hips. "Margaritas."

"ADMITTEDLY, I DIDN'T THINK I COULD DRINK ANY more after this morning." Evy sipped her salt-rimmed glass. "But I somehow found the motivation. Maybe it was all the trash in the pool that I'm going to have to fish out tomorrow."

"It's a gorgeous house." Vivian turned to Julia. "Have there been many offers?"

"A couple of lookers and one party who was set to make a serious offer, according to Dean, but that was before all this happened. Who knows if it'll be a draw or a problem?" She sipped the frosty concoction of tequila, Cointreau, and sweet lime. "Notoriety can work with you or against you in real estate. There's no predicting it."

"It's like those strange women who fall in love with murderers," Vivian said. "Some people are attracted to the macabre."

Julia looked around the bustling Mexican restaurant near the airport. It wasn't fancy and the servers weren't the model/actor types, but the place smelled amazing. "Evy, is this your regular Mexican place?"

"Yep. Avoid Palm Canyon Drive unless you want to pay

through the nose. Some of the restaurants there are really good, but they're crazy expensive."

"This is what I've been needing." Vivian raised her glass. "Local friends. Margarita friends."

Julia smiled. "Hard to make margarita friends when you're living in a retirement village."

"Are you kidding?" Vivian smiled. "My neighbors drink like fishes."

Evy nodded. "Lots of functional alcoholics at the retirement homes around here."

"That's depressing," Julia said.

"I said they were *functional*." Evy looked at Vivian. "Did you really move out here to cure depression?"

Vivian's eyebrows went up. "You're very direct."

"If by that you mean nosy, I know. I'm the queen of etiquette compared to my family though. You met my aunt Marie."

"The one who cursed me with psychic empathy? Yes, I remember her."

"I'm trying to track her down, but with Aunt Marie, it could be weeks. There's no telling."

"Okay sure." Vivian took another sip of her margarita. "I moved here to help with the depression, but I mean... I've been living with it my whole life, so that's not really anything new." She stirred her drink. "I guess I was looking at another cold, snowy Chicago winter, still processing my grandmother's death —my mom was having a really hard time—and then thinking about coming out here for a vacation, you know? Then I thought about coming back from vacation and thought... why? Why am I staying here when I could be there? I have a house in both cities now, and I've never loved snow."

"So do you go back in the summer?" Julia asked. "It's pretty miserable here with the heat."

"No, I love the heat." Vivian shook her head. "And Chicago is hot in the summer too, but humid. I'd rather be here."

"So has it helped?" Evy asked. "The sun thing."

"Yeah." Vivian nodded. "I mean, I'm not throwing out my meds or anything, but it's better. I love the sunshine." She turned to Julia. "Your turn."

"Why did I move out here?" She shrugged. "I kind of told you the other day. I'm semiretiring, but I don't want to be bored."

"I heard rumors of a heart attack," Vivian said. "From Sergio, in case you're wondering."

"I'm not surprised." Julia sat back and lifted her margarita. "Yeah, my doctor wouldn't approve of this, which is why I'll be sticking to one drink and playing designated driver later."

"I'm a lightweight too," Vivian said.

"I... am not." Evy smiled. "Showbiz, you know?" She set down her empty glass. "Let's talk about Julia more."

Julia smiled. "Dean and Sergio are probably my best friends. Their daughters call me Auntie. My own family is friendly but kind of distant. It felt pretty natural to come stay with Dean's family for a while after the... heart thing."

"No kids?" Evy asked.

"Never wanted any," Julia said. "I love being an aunt though. You?"

"Can you imagine me with offspring?" Evy shook her head. "My brothers are keeping my parents happy and making sure there's a plentiful crop of Landas for the future. I'm off the hook."

Vivian had a small smile on her face that told Julia there was a story there.

"Okay, spill Dr. Wei."

Vivian smiled. "Well, I can't believe I'm sharing this with virtual strangers, but I'm starting fertility treatments next week."

She raised her glass. "So I will also be keeping to one and please don't tell my doctor."

"Oh wow!" Evy said. "That's awesome. So you're just doing it on your own? Or do you have a partner we haven't met?"

"I got tired of waiting for the right partner, and I'll be forty-one next month, so..." Vivian shrugged, and it looked awkward on her. "I thought it was time for the next logical step."

Julia had a feeling that the organized Dr. Wei had very little experience with the unplanned or spontaneous.

Evy seemed to be the definition of spontaneous.

And Julia? Just like everything in the past few months, she kind of felt like she was along for the ride. Faced with the idea that she'd been minutes from dying alone in her house in Laguna Beach minutes after closing a ten-million-dollar deal, her fast-track, high-paced life had gone off the tracks and never found its way back.

Now she was sharing margaritas with two strangers who were unexpectedly tied to her by psychic phenomena that none of them could explain, a murder they needed to solve, and a town with way more secrets than it revealed on the glossy surface.

"Speaking of next logical steps," Julia said. "What do you say to paying a visit to Lily Putnam tomorrow?"

Chapter Ten

L ily Rose Putnam was nothing if not picturesque in grief. She sat across from Julia, Vivian, and Evy on a chaise, giving the impression that she might swoon at any moment, necessitating the intervention of one or both of the uniformed maids and butler who hovered at either end of the bouquet-filled room.

The three would-be detectives shared a tufted sofa. Julia was trying not to feel awkward in her stocking feet, but Lily's residence was apparently "no shoes allowed."

The house was not what Julia had expected after seeing Casa de Lirio so many times, but she supposed Lily was between homes. This estate was a midcentury masterpiece with a minimal design aesthetic while Lily Putnam screamed *excess!* down to her three diamond-studded toe rings on perfectly manicured bare feet.

"I just can't believe he's gone." She dabbed her eyes. "I keep expecting him to walk through the door with some silly story he heard about a celebrity."

Julia was trying hard to be sympathetic, but Justin's ghost was hovering behind her, she was self-conscious because she just realized she had on one cream-colored sock and one white, and she was having a hard time focusing on Justin's grieving girlfriend.

'Silly story? She begged for gossip," Justin muttered. 'She lived for it. Half the shit I made up just to keep her entertained. Is she wearing waterproof mascara?"

'How are you sleeping?" Vivian asked. 'Nights can be the worst when you've just lost someone, and sleep is so important."

Lily turned damp eyes toward Vivian. 'Do I know you?"

'I'm..." Vivian looked at Julia in a slight panic. 'I'm Sergio's dentist?"

'Oh, of course." Lily nodded as if that explained everything. 'So you're a medical professional. I know this could drastically affect my health because I'm not sleeping well at all. Justin's side of the bed is just... so empty."

Had she paired a white sock with an off-white? Was it a loose-sock situation? Julia was feeling scatterbrained and couldn't remember. And where were all her socks? Did the dryer eat them in some sort of desert pique, offended that someone in the house was wearing shoes and not sandals?

'Lily sleeps with a CPAP," Justin muttered. 'Half the time she sent me to a different room if I stayed the night."

Julia leaned forward. 'Excuse me, Lily? I am so sorry, but I drank so much coffee this morning. Can you tell me where your bathroom is?"

'Oh dear, don't even think of it." She lifted a hand and pointed down the hall of the light-filled mansion. 'That way, second door."

"Thanks." Julia rose and walked calmly toward the bathroom. In her socks. When she was behind the closed door of the rose-scented powder room, she whispered, 'Justin!"

He passed through the door with a curled lip. 'I'm not watching you pee. That's weird."

"You need to shut it," she said. "I am already feeling thrown off without my shoes."

"Yeah, she's weird about that. She doesn't even have white carpet, she just thinks shoes are dirty, and I guess she has a point when you think about—"

"Shut. Up! If you want to leave here and vent to me in the car about all of Lily's faults, then you can do that, but right now? When I'm trying to have a conversation with her, I need to not look like a delusional person who's talking to herself."

Justin sulked against the wall. "Fine."

"Am I going to have to talk to you about this again?"

"Quiet during convos with the living. Fine."

Julia looked around the powder room. "Now I have to hang out in here for a few minutes or it'll look like I didn't wash my hands. Anything you want to tell me about her before I go back in there? Does her grief seem genuine?"

He shrugged. "Yeah. I mean, why *wouldn't* she be sad? Lily was lucky to be with me. She wouldn't have killed me."

His disdain made her skin itch. "Are you sure? Maybe you pissed her off." *God knows you're pissing me off plenty.*

"Okay, even if she wanted me dead, she's not that strong. I know, I trained with her. Whoever hit me..." A light flickered in his eyes, and he rubbed the back of his head. "Oh! I remember that part. They came at me from behind. I never saw them."

She nodded. "That fits with what I remember from the crime scene. It looked like you were bleeding from your head."

"But I was..." Justin frowned. "I was bent down. Why was I bending over? I was looking for something, but I don't know what. Maybe I forgot something at the house."

"So whoever hit you was strong but not necessarily tall. It could have been Lily."

"No, I told you, her arm strength was ridiculous. She focused on cardio too much; I kept trying to get her to train with weights more, but she didn't want to get bulky." He rolled his eyes. "Like that would happen."

Julia realized she'd been in the bathroom for several minutes. "Dammit."

Justin looked at her. "What?"

"Now I've been in here too long."

He still looked confused as Julia flushed the toilet.

"What if she thinks I'm pooping? That's just rude."

"I hate to quote a children's book, but everybody poops."

Julia turned on the faucet to wash her hands. "Not in a grieving woman's powder room when she stops by for coffee."

"I mean, if you're drinking coffee—"

"Just be quiet," Julia whispered. "No more interrupting Lily."

Julia walked out of the bathroom with her mobile phone in her hand. "Sorry," she said when all the women turned. "I got a phone call I had to take care of."

Lily eyebrows furrowed together. "In the bathroom?"

"I didn't want to bother you all." She gingerly took her place in a scooped armchair. "Lily, on a professional basis, I did want to ask you if you had any idea why Justin was over at the house. Is there something he maybe lost or misplaced? Something I need to keep an eye out for?"

Lily shook her head. "I told the police too. I have no idea why he would have gone over there. Bernardo drove us home after Sunday Dinner, and then Justin said he was meeting some friends for drinks." She shrugged. "I know my friends aren't always his favorite, so I didn't think anything of it. They usually go for drinks at that little bar on Gene Autry Trail. The one in the strip mall?"

Evy nodded. "I know that place. They have great cocktails."

"I went to sleep and didn't worry when he wasn't home the next morning. I figured he'd decided to stay at his own place." Her eyes started tearing up again. "And then I got...

Dean called and…" She pressed her lips together and dabbed her eyes again. "I have to get control of myself. His parents are coming into town tomorrow. I told them they could stay at the house, but they wanted to stay at some hotel." Lily looked confused. "I don't know why. Wouldn't they rather stay in a nice home?"

"They probably just don't want to be an imposition," Vivian said. "They must be in so much shock."

"Justin was from Ohio," Lily said. "I've never been to Ohio —have you? It's in the middle of the country, isn't it? Is it close to Chicago? I've been there."

Julia sensed that the productive part of the conversation was quickly coming to a close unless she got it back on track. "What have the police said? Do they have any idea who could have done this?"

"I told them it was probably that Serena girl who was stalking him."

Vivian leaned forward. "Someone was stalking Justin?"

Lily rolled her eyes. "His ex, of course. She couldn't face that Justin was in love with me. I know she thought he was only with me for my money, but that's not the way we were."

Vivian nodded. "It's horrible that people are so judgmental. Did the police say that they were questioning this ex-girlfriend?"

Lily grabbed a throw pillow and hugged it. "I think so. I mean, I don't know much about law enforcement, though I did do a pilot in the nineties for a police procedural that would have absolutely been a slam dunk if *Cop Rock* hadn't bombed the season before. Can you believe that? We were cursed by that show. All the networks were wary of police series for three years. So unfair."

"Right." Vivian nodded. "I remember that a little bit. But are the police giving you updates? Are they in contact with you or his parents? Do you know—?"

"Nothing." Lily leaned forward. "And honestly? I don't

think I want to know. It was probably a homeless person or something, don't you think?"

Julia had to bite her tongue. "It's... possible."

Lily's manicured hand waved away a fresh box of tissues one of the maids held out. "I think it's really better if I don't know. I don't want to interfere with their work. Too many chefs spoil the broth and all that." Her eyes started to tear up. "Chefs... Celia, come back." She beckoned the maid with the tissues and grabbed three. "I just remembered that Justin was a chef."

"Oh, Lily." Evy was by far the best at showing concern. "I'm just so sad for you. You two seemed so happy."

"We were!" Lily sniffed. "Justin promised... he promised he would always be there for me. He understood the age difference was unconventional, but after all, age is just a number, isn't it?"

"It is." Not that Julia had any interest in a man in his twenties. Middle-aged men were immature enough. "Is there anything we can do to help? Meals? Help with arrangements?"

"No, no. I have staff for that." Lily sniffed. "Can you believe Richard called? That woman probably told him to call me to make himself look good."

"What woman?" Evy said. "I hadn't heard he was with anyone."

"His secretary. The young one? I know they're together." Lily's lip curled. "She practically flaunts it."

Evy exchanged a look with Julia that told her this was news to her. "Isn't that good though?" Evy asked. "If Richard called, he must be ready to move on. You both can."

Lily snapped, "I will never move on from what that man did to me! What he's still doing to me. What he forced me to accept in the divorce that I never—" She pressed her lips together and closed her eyes. "My therapist said I need to work on that." She nodded. "The outbursts, I mean. It's just so hard when my feelings are raw."

"Of course it's hard," Vivian said. "Focus on healing right now. That's way more important than anything about Richard."

Julia nodded, but all she could think about was if Lily held that much venom for Richard, what would have happened if she'd found out Justin had been cheating on her too?

"THOUGHTS ON LILY?" EVY GOT RIGHT TO THE POINT. "I think she's dumb, and if she killed Justin, she'd probably already have confessed by now."

"I have my doubts about her too," Vivian said. "But not because she's dumb. I think the dumb-blonde thing is a complete facade, but she does seem pretty fragile. Justin might not have taken that relationship seriously, but she clearly did."

"I never said I didn't take it seriously." Justin sat on a nearby lounger. "I had big plans for Lily and me."

Vivian, Evy, and Julia were back at Sergio and Dean's house, this time with a full complement of ghosts. Elton the detective was sitting at the table, as was Mrs. Griffin. Mae was hovering near Dean's shoulder as he grilled some steaks. Justin was in the lounger and even Geoff was present, but he was hanging out near Evy's old car.

"So Lily is likely out," Julia said. "And according to the police, her driver alibied her, but is that really an alibi? All he can confirm is that he didn't drive her anywhere. She could have driven herself."

Elton muttered, "It's always about a dame, kid."

Julia wasn't quite sure why Elton was calling her kid when he appeared younger than she was. Then again, he'd been dead for a long time. Maybe anyone in the living world seemed like a kid to him.

"Most people in real life don't have alibis," Vivian said. "If you don't know a crime is going to happen, you don't need one.

Think about the crazy questions police ask. Where were you on October seventh at eight p.m.?" She spread her hands. "Does *anyone* know that off the top of their head?"

Julia looked at Elton. "Where were you on October seventh?"

Elton smiled. "Right where I always am, kid. Hangin' around here. But your pretty friend has a point. Sometimes an alibi doesn't mean much."

Evy pointed at Vivian. "That sounds like an excuse a guilty person would make though. 'I don't have an alibi because I didn't know anything was going to happen.' Remember *Seven Kills for Seven Brothers*?"

Julia frowned. "Seven brothers killed..." She shook her head. "This isn't a murder podcast."

"That was a documentary, but Evy's point is valid," Vivian said. "Those brothers alibied each other, and it ended up being because they were all conspiring."

Julia raised her hand. "Do ghosts count as alibis? Because they won't leave me alone."

"I say," muttered Mrs. Griffin a moment before she faded away.

"Don't worry about her," Elton said. "She has no sense of humor."

Dean walked over with a plate of steaks in one hand and a vodka tonic in the other. "Ghosts don't count as alibis because they can't testify in court. And dinner is served."

"This looks amazing," Julia said. "Thanks, Dean."

"Staff!" Evy clapped her hands. "Lily Putnam has household staff. Couldn't they confirm what the driver told the police?"

Vivian muttered, "Is it really an alibi if you pay the people who witness it?"

"Not live-in staff." Dean took a steak and passed the plate. "Lily and Richard never had live-in help. It was a thing with them. The closest they ever got was a housekeeper who lived in the guest cottage at Casa de Lirio for a while until her mother got ill. But never anyone in the house."

"Interesting," Julia said. "So Lily's only alibi is her driver. But again, does she need one?"

"I say no. I didn't really touch her enough to read her today, but she seems innocent to me. She was really broken up about Justin."

Dean said, "I can't imagine Lily hurting anyone. She's a very kind person beneath all the celebrity stuff."

"Agreed," Evy said. "It would be nice if we could rule her out completely, but I just don't see how she even has a motive."

"No one had a motive!" Justin said. "Everyone loved me." He shook his head. "If I have to depend on you three to solve my murder, I'm going to be hanging around forever."

Julia stared at the ghostly image of Justin's carefully coiffed and highlighted hair. Then his immaculate white polo shirt and his pouting face.

Justin the chef-trainer-pool guy hanging out with her for the rest of her life?

She was going to solve his murder even if it killed her.

Chapter Eleven

The next day, Evy and Julia met for coffee on Palm Canyon Drive, a block from the luxury spa where Justin Worthy had once worked. They'd called Vivian, but she was booked with patients for the day and "not a fan of overpriced spas that pretended to be medical clinics."

Julia could see her point.

According to Lily, Justin's ex-girlfriend Serena still worked there. So since Vivian couldn't come, Julia and Evy had booked a couple's facial and asked for Serena by name, saying they got a recommendation from a friend.

"You realize they probably think we're a couple." Evy sipped her coffee. "It's pretty much the norm down here."

Julia looked Evy up and down. "Eh. I've done worse."

Evy laughed. "Seriously, I have often thought that life would be much easier if I were attracted to women."

"You know, I hear that too, but my friends who are with other women still complain about all the same shit." Julia smiled. "Personally, I think all long-term relationships are doomed to failure. I never met a man I wanted to keep around for more than a few years."

"All relationships except Dean and Sergio," Evy said. "If they ever broke up—"

"My faith in humanity would be destroyed. I completely agree with that." Julia finished her cappuccino. "Ready, babe?"

"You know it." Evy gathered up their trash and tossed it in the garbage as they headed out the door. "So how are we going to play this? Go the direct route? Should we say we know Justin? Or maybe Lily? And is Justin here? I kind of wish Vivian was with us. She asked really good questions the other day."

"I know what you mean. She must take the murder podcast thing seriously. And no Justin. I told him we'd be getting undressed and asking people about him. He decided to fade. I don't exactly know how that works, but I think he can kind of hear what's going on but he's not actively *here*, if you know what I mean."

"I have no idea what you mean, so I'll just nod and smile."

"If they ask us, we'll just say we knew Justin," Julia said. "We met him through Sergio, who knows everyone."

Evy patted her backpack. "The trick will be how I'm going to get Geoff in the treatment room with us."

Julia froze, nearly tripping the retired couple walking behind her with their Westie. The terrier barked and the man muttered, but they swerved around her and Evy.

"You brought Geoff?"

"Well, yeah?" She patted her backpack. "Trust me, it was not easy fitting him in here, but how else was I going to read Serena's thoughts?"

"I honestly haven't thought about it." This changed everything. With Geoffrey, Evy was a human lie detector. She would always know if someone was telling the truth. They started walking again. "Okay, I say you just go with the eccentric pitch. Tell them you *need* the dummy in the room with you. It's probably not the weirdest thing they've ever heard."

The spa entrance was in sight.

"I probably should have thought about this before the actual appointment," Evy muttered. "Oh! I have an idea. Bless you, Palmer valet."

"What?"

"I'll explain later." Evy pulled the frosted glass door open, and they entered a small hallway filled with dim lights, breathy flute music, and a smiling receptionist.

"Hello," Julia said. "We're here for a joint treatment. It's under Julia Brooks."

"Oh right." The girl behind the counter brightened. "I have you listed for a couple's facial; is that correct?"

"With Serena?"

"Yes, it'll be Serena and Martisse."

"Perfect."

The receptionist walked around the counter. "Just come with me then. Is this your first time here?"

"It is." Julia had to admit that as long as Serena wasn't a murderer, she would probably be back. The hallway where they walked was filled with bright indoor gardens and trickling fountains on either side. Two wooden doors swung open and revealed a completely different world than the bustling traffic and tourists on Palm Canyon Drive.

Heck, even if Serena *was* a murderer, that was hardly the spa's fault, right?

"How long have you been here?" Evy said. "I didn't even know this place existed."

"I think the spa itself is about five years old, but the owner has been in the business for much longer. She used to run Restoration Spa in La Quinta."

"Nice." Julia looked around. The hallway with gardens had led behind the main building on Palm Canyon Drive and into an open garden area where more fountains bubbled and two women lounged on reclined chaises. To one side of the courtyard was a room that read MEDITATION, and opposite that, there was a "Welcome Room" where they walked with their hostess.

"Please find a robe and slippers in comfortable sizes." She handed them two keys. "These are for your lockers. You can change and meet Serena and Martisse in the courtyard." The hostess motioned to a station near the door. "There's tea and cucumber water available, and we encourage drinking a lot of it when you're here so you can cleanse." She smiled again and said, "Welcome to Infinity Room. I'm Ashley if you need anything. I'll be in front." Then the smiling girl left them alone in front of a wall of neatly folded robes and stacked slippers in plastic wrap.

"No cucumber water for me," Evy muttered, "or I'll be peeing every fifteen minutes."

"We can't even bring our purses in the rooms," Julia said. "How are you supposed to get Geoff in there?"

"Don't worry about it." Evy grabbed a robe and slippers. "I have the perfect idea."

FIFTEEN MINUTES LATER, THEY WERE LYING ON reclined treatment tables in a candlelit room with more flute music. Julia was on one side of the room with Serena gently cleansing her face while Evy was on the other, Geoff tucked into her side like a baby.

"That's so interesting," Martisse was saying. "I had no idea method acting could include props."

"It's not a prop," Evy clarified. "The dummy is an integral part of the new act. My coach said I need to think of him like an extension of myself, which is why he needs to be with me all the time."

Serena kept an eye on Julia to gauge her reaction, but Julia caught her eye and shrugged. "If her acting coach tells her to do it, I don't even try to object."

"I feel like he is... another me," Evy said.

"Luckily, her other me doesn't also need a facial," Julia said.

The corner of Serena's mouth turned up, and Julia felt a spike of triumph. So far the woman had proved to be far from the chatty type.

"So how did you hear about Infinity Room?" Serena asked. "Thanks for asking for me."

Julia glanced at Evy from the corner of her eye. "You were a recommendation from a friend of ours. Justin Worthy?"

Serena froze for a second, then resumed the gentle cleansing on Julia's skin. "You heard about what happened, right?"

"That he died?" Evy asked. "Oh my God, I'm so glad you already know."

Julia watched Serena's face closely for her reaction. It was hard to read her; she kept her face very blank. If she had to guess, Julia would say that Serena looked a little sad and numb.

Evy was still chattering. "Julia was worried you were going to ask us how we heard about this place and then we'd have to mention Justin and we didn't know if anyone here—"

"The police actually came by to tell us," Martisse said quietly. "He used to work here about a year and a half ago."

"He mentioned that."

"They weren't telling us," Serena said. "They were *questioning* us."

Martisse let out a small laugh. "Yeah. I think they must figure it couldn't be one of Justin's new rich friends who killed him, so it must have been someone from his past. No offense, of course. But none of us have really seen Justin for a while, so it was kind of weird that they asked so many questions."

"Yeah, that's so awkward." Julia kept her eyes wide. "That must have been intimidating."

Serena shrugged and turned on the steam machine to let it heat up before she covered Julia's face with a warm cloth to wipe off the cleanser. "Justin and I used to date, so I'm sure someone told them that I was like, a jealous ex or something."

Evy piped up. "Were you?"

Julia tried not to wince, and was relieved when Martisse laughed.

"Are you kidding? No offense to Justin, but she broke up with him, not the other way round."

"I'm in a really great relationship right now," Serena said softly. "For a million bucks, I would not mess that up. Justin and I didn't exactly have a clean breakup—he was cheating on me—but I let it go a long time ago."

Cheating? That was definitely a motive for murder, but who kills an ex a year and a half later when they're in a solid relationship? That wasn't ringing true to Julia. She'd have to wait and hear what Evy heard from Serena's thoughts.

For a few long moments, everything was quiet as the steam machines and the flutes took over the room. Martisse and Serena exited the room, leaving Evy and Julia alone for a few minutes.

"Hey Julia?"

"We should probably wait until we're done—"

"I know, I know. I just need to know if Geoffrey is here."

"Oh." Julia peeked out from the steam machine to see Geoffrey in the corner, his face turned to the wall. "Yeah, I don't see him. You're good."

"Okay, thank God." She paused. "Is Justin here?"

"No, but I'm going to ask him about the cheating later."

"It was with Lily."

Julia nearly jumped out of her skin when she heard Justin's voice. "Don't do that!"

"You asked."

"I told you I'd ask later, not—"

The door opened, and Serena and Martisse walked in.

"Okay, ladies." Martisse's voice was soft. "How are you feeling?"

Like I just saw a ghost. "So relaxed." Julia struggled to keep her voice calm. "Just really... really relaxed."

"Mmm." Evy let out a deep sigh. "So peaceful."

"Great. Then it's time for extractions."

"Okay." Julia looked at her fresh face in a mirror outside a shop as they were walking back to the car. "Even if Serena was a murderer, I'd probably still be going back. Homicide and skin care have nothing to do with each other. I can compartmentalize."

"No need." Evy tried on a pair of sunglasses, then put them back. "It was kind of hard to read all the thoughts in there because there was you and Martisse and Serena, plus there's the whole combination of words and images thing, but once you asked about Justin, I just felt this huge, overwhelming sense of sadness. No guilt. No happiness. No sense of satisfaction." Evy turned to Julia and yelled, "Justin, if you're here, you never should have broken up with Serena. She really loved you, and she's heartbroken you're dead."

Justin was walking at Julia's side, staring straight ahead. "I'm dead, not hearing impaired."

"So that settles Lily's theory." Julia stood at a crosswalk, waiting for the light before crossing the street to reach her car. "Evy, leave the glasses. Teal is not your color."

"I guess you're right." She put the glasses back on the rack, then walked over and stood by Julia. "Who else could have done it? I wonder if the police questioned Richard."

"Richard, Lily's ex?"

"I mean, it makes sense to be jealous of the new boyfriend, right?"

"Please," Justin said. "That old man loved me. He and I were both praying that Lily would marry me."

"Justin says Richard wouldn't have wanted to kill him because Richard wanted Lily to marry Justin." Julia frowned. "Alimony, right?"

"Oh yeah," Evy said. "Richard was paying a boatload of alimony."

"Which would have stopped if Lily married Justin." The light changed and Julia and Evy started to cross, only to jump back as a black BMW darted into traffic from a parking spot and nearly ran them over.

"Holy shit!" Evy pulled Julia back. "What the hell?" She shook her fist at the rapidly moving car. "You could have killed us, asshole!"

Julia felt her heart skip a beat and paused with a familiar sense of dread.

Was this it? Would this be the moment it revolted?

She took three deep breaths.

Five things she could see. Four things she could touch. Three things...

"Julia?" Evy touched her shoulder. "You okay?"

"Yeah." She nodded. "Just a shock."

Julia had seen the car heading straight toward them and had a flashback of falling in her kitchen, reaching for anything to break her fall.

Nothing. There had been nothing to catch her.

"I was shocked too," Evy said. "People are usually way more observant about pedestrians here. Even the tourists."

"I'm fine." Julia's heart was pounding, but it didn't feel dangerous. She laughed a little. "Reached my target heart rate for the day though. My cardiologist will be thrilled."

Evy looked suspicious. "You better tell me if you feel faint or dizzy or something."

"You were telling me about Richard paying Lily alimony." Julia tried to change the subject.

"I only know through the grapevine, but rumors say he's

paying a lot. Not that Lily didn't have plenty of money of her own," Evy said. "That's probably what Justin was after. That and whatever she ended up making from Casa de Lirio. Richard and Lily were splitting the profits from that."

They made it safely to the other side of Palm Canyon Drive and turned right to the parking lot where they'd parked the car.

"How long did they live there?"

"Probably thirty years at least."

"So they probably own it outright." Julia quickly did the math. "It's sitting on three acres of prime real estate in a historic neighborhood. If it goes close to the asking price—which it was supposed to before a murder happened there—they'd be looking at fourteen or fifteen million dollars split two ways." She glanced at Justin. "Not a bad inheritance for a young husband."

"Hey, I never claimed it was purely a love match," Justin said. "But I wasn't cheating on her."

"Supposed to?" Evy asked. "Do you think the murder will keep it from selling?"

"Dean said he was talking with another agent who had an interested party just a day or so before the murder. They were pushing numbers under the asking price but still in the neighborhood. They're not returning calls now. We already told Lily's and Richard's attorneys about it, but it looks like nothing will come of it now."

"Bummer."

"No kidding." Julia had her keys out, unlocking their vehicle when she saw a familiar face near the back entrance of a different spa. "Hey, Evy?"

Where had she seen him? He was a handsome man with pewter-grey hair and a trim beard, tan the way that athletes and sailors tan. He was standing next to a green Mercedes SUV with black California plates.

"What?"

Where had she seen him? It was driving her crazy. "See the guy in the green Mercedes?"

Evy craned her neck. "Well, speak of the devil and he does appear. That's Richard."

"I think I've seen him in pictures at Dean and Sergio's house."

"He and Dean golf together, so that doesn't surprise me."

Justin whipped his head around. "Where? Dammit, why can't I see farther? I hate that asshole."

"Lily's Richard? I thought you said he loved you."

"He loved *me*; I thought he was a snob."

"Richard loved me?" Evy sounded confused.

"No, Justin said that Richard loved him because he was hoping Justin would marry Lily so he wouldn't have to pay alimony. But Justin thought Richard was a snob."

Evy said, "Oh right. Yeah well, that's him. Lily's ex."

And friend of cute Director Michael.

Why had she thought about Michael? That was annoying. "What's he doing...? Ohhhh."

Richard stood up straight when a very young, very blond woman walked out of the spa door. He opened the door for her, she got in, and then he walked around to the driver's side.

"Huh." Evy cocked her head. "I'd heard rumors, but I'm a little surprised to be honest. I never pegged him for the trophy-wife type."

"All men are the trophy-wife type," Justin said.

"You're just being cynical because you were a trophy boyfriend." Julia slid into her car. "Let's get back to Sergio and Dean's. I want to pick their brain for a couple of ideas."

Chapter Twelve

J im and Sergio were cooking while Dean served drinks to Evy and Julia.

"Did you invite Vivian over?" Dean asked. "I adore that name. It's so classic."

Sergio put down his paring knife. "We should have another baby."

Dean's eyebrows shot up. "We are not having another baby just so you can name it Vivian."

"But the girls are growing up!"

"And we're getting old." Dean shook his head. "I'm not becoming the father of a newborn at fifty-two."

Sergio sighed. "We're rich. We can hire all the people."

Julia snorted. "Says the father who wouldn't leave his twins with his own mother for three years because he couldn't stand the separation."

Evy got the conversation back on track. "I wonder why Lily and Richard never had kids."

Sergio frowned. "That's actually quite sad. Lily was pregnant three times and lost every pregnancy. I think they stopped trying after that. They never adopted; I don't think Richard wanted that."

"As far as I know," Dean said, "It never caused any friction. They both wanted kids, and I know they were both broken up about it. It just wasn't in the cards for them."

"So what did cause the divorce?" Julia asked.

"Cheating," Sergio said. "What else? They both did it."

"According to Richard," Dean said. "I've never asked Lily. Two sides to every story, remember?"

Sergio started paring vegetables again. "Well, Richard initiated the divorce. I think he got to the point where he didn't feel like pretending anymore. They'd been living separate lives for a long time."

"And they're still not done with each other," Dean said. "Until the house sells, the financial settlement is up in the air."

"But Richard is still paying alimony?"

"Spousal support can start at separation if a judge approves it," Dean said. "Lily is doing very well at the moment."

Evy and Julia exchanged a look. "So if the house sale dragged on, would it benefit her?"

"Hardly. She'll likely get far more in the divorce settlement. They were married a long time. She's angry about Casa de Lirio, but she can't do anything about it. Richard wouldn't budge."

Evy looked confused. "What do you mean?"

"Neither of them can make an offer on the house for ten years," Julia told her. "That's part of their financial settlement."

Dean nodded. "Lily's only in her sixties; she might still have plans for that place."

"I don't understand the fascination with that house," Evy said. "I mean, have you seen the place Lily is renting? It's amazing."

"I understand it," Julia said. "It's not the house at all really. It's the acreage. The trees and the gardens are impossible to reproduce in Palm Springs now. They just don't make estates that big anymore. And the view of the mountains..." Julia shook her head. "Richard might not be the only one who would kill for it."

"Wait," Dean said. "You think Richard—?"

"I know he's your friend, but surely the police have looked at him," Julia said. "His wife's new boyfriend was killed by a blow to the head in his old house where he still has keys."

Justin appeared in the arched doorway to the kitchen. "It can't be Richard. I told you, he loved me."

"I just can't see it," Sergio said. "Murder is so... unlike him."

"You don't know Richard." Dean glanced over at Julia. "He doesn't have a temper like that."

Justin laughed. "Richard the robot. That's what Lily called him."

"He would probably say murder was too gauche for a Putnam!" Sergio snorted. "You just have to know his personality. He's the opposite of hot-blooded."

"But maybe there was another reason he killed Justin," Julia said. "One based on logic, not temper."

Sergio and Dean exchanged a look.

"Okay," Dean said. "I might actually be able to believe that. He can be ruthless in the business world. But a crime of passion? No way."

"According to Lily, anything of passion was pretty much out of the question." Justin stuck his index finger in the air, then slowly let it tilt down. "Poor Richard."

Evy rapped on the table. "I say that after dinner, we go back to the house. Give Julia another crack at interviewing some ghosts."

"I'll text Vivian." Julia pulled out her phone. "I'm so glad that all my friends seem to be adapting to my life as a psychic medium so well. Be aware, I will be charging you full rate for palm readings."

"Don't disrespect the ghosts, Jules." Sergio narrowed his eyes. "They might take revenge."

She put down her phone and turned to Dean. "You and Chief Marcos are friendly, right?"

Dean shrugged. "We golf."

"Have you heard anything about the case? It's been days; do they have any leads?"

"Last I talked to him, they're still looking at locally known burglars. They interviewed all the usual suspects and no one jumped out, so they're figuring it was random."

"The house was unlocked, right?" Evy asked. "I'm assuming Justin had keys."

Julia looked at Justin, who nodded. "He had keys," she said. "So he could have let himself in."

"Justin would have left the door open when he was inside probably." Evy shrugged. "Maybe a thief didn't know that Justin was there and he surprised him."

"That's possible."

Dean waved a hand. "It wasn't a thief. There wasn't anything taken."

"What if there were secret compartments in the house?" Sergio wiggled his eyebrows. "Secret safes. Maybe that's where the Putnam Diamond went. Maybe that's what the thief was after!"

Evy raised a hand. "Uh, I haven't heard about this. Explain please?"

"It's a huge point of contention in the divorce, and they're still arguing about it," Dean said. "The Putnam Diamond is a twenty-carat diamond choker that has been in Richard's family for generations. His version is that he loaned it to Lily for events but that he never gave it to her, and so as an heirloom, it remains his property. She says he gave it to her as a gift, so she should keep it."

Sergio walked from the sink to the bar to grab a drink as the smell of fajitas filled the air. "Richard says he doesn't have it and claims that Lily is hiding it. She basically says the same thing about him. Neither one will admit to having it."

Julia raised her eyebrows. "Is anyone buying that either of them just lost a twenty-carat diamond necklace?"

"Well, that is one theory though," Evy said. "That a thief was looking for the missing diamond and killed Justin in the process."

Julia looked to see if Justin was still around, but he had faded almost as soon as mention of the Putnam Diamond came up. "How much was it worth?"

"I don't know anything about antiques," Dean said. "And I know very little about jewelry. But according to Richard, the Putnam Diamond was more valuable than Casa de Lirio. It was worth somewhere around seventeen million dollars."

Julia nearly choked on her drink. "So that is... definitely a motive."

VIVIAN JOINED THEM AFTER DINNER, ARRIVING JUST IN time to meet Aurelia, who was standing in front of the garage, Paco held on a long lead. Julia waved at Vivian, who approached the house but gave the alpaca a wide berth.

"Why do they have that thing again?" Vivian asked.

Sergio sighed. "It's a rescue. Aurelia, we are not taking the alpaca to a crime scene."

Aurelia stared at him with wide eyes.

"I don't care what you say, it is not a good idea. Paco can stay here."

Juliana joined her sister and continued staring at their father.

He huffed. "It's not a good idea."

"If anyone dangerous is hanging around," Vivian said, "Paco would probably scare them off. He seems very protective."

Sergio pointed at Vivian. "Not helpful."

"Don't care," Vivian countered. "I'm more interested in being protected by the guard alpaca."

"Fine, he can come." Sergio muttered, "This is all because they made me feel guilty for getting a purebred dog." He stomped down the driveway.

Vivian turned to the twins and offered them a slight nod. "Ladies." She looked at the alpaca. "Paco."

Julia sidled up to her nieces. "But seriously, now that you're done tormenting your pai, you should stay in the yard at Casa de Lirio, and if you see anything weird, tell me."

Juliana narrowed her eyes at Vivian. "I like the dentist."

"Thank you?" Vivian seemed unsure of whether it was a compliment or not.

Aurelia asked, "Do you ever have any extra teeth at your practice? Can I have them if you do? I'm working on a necklace."

"Definitely no."

"Okay, let's walk." Julia grabbed Vivian's arm and marched ahead.

They followed Sergio down the wide sidewalk and turned right at the corner.

Vivian turned to Julia when they were out of earshot of the girls. "I don't like being judgmental, but what is wrong with those girls?"

"They've been raised to question everything and disdain dominant popular culture. Plus they aren't affected by peer pressure because they only care about each other's opinions."

"Yep, that sounds about right." Vivian looked around. "Are there any ghosts around us right now?"

"Yes." In fact, the entire residency of Sergio and Dean's home—both corporeal and incorporeal—seemed to be joining them.

Mrs. Griffin and Mae were leading the way, floating up the

street before Sergio and Evy. Mrs. Griffin was in her typical dinner gown, and Mae was wearing a floaty robe over her bathing suit and a pair of chunky heels that showed off her legendary legs.

Elton hung close to Julia, peppering her with questions she was trying to ignore.

"Who've you talked to so far? The police have any leads? When did the kid die exactly? I heard he was bashed on the head. Any idea what the murder weapon was?"

Justin trailed behind them all, a mere shadow of his normal ghostly self. He seemed to have nothing to say to either Mrs. Griffin or Elton and would only occasionally speak to Mae.

"So do you think having the other ghosts with you will help?" Vivian asked. "Maybe the other ones won't be shy."

"I hope so." She glanced at Elton.

"Tonight?" Elton seemed to glow a little. "Tonight you're gonna see some things, kid."

"What does that mean?"

Mae turned and giggled. "It's a special night, honey."

Julia turned back to Elton. "Because?"

"It's better to see it for yourself."

Julia turned to Vivian. "Elton says I'll definitely see some ghosts there tonight, but he's being mysterious. Mae says tonight is special. I don't know what any of that means."

"Oookay."

Julia turned to Elton again. "You guys aren't the only ones who hang in the neighborhood, right?"

"Not by a long shot." Elton passed under a streetlamp, rendering himself nearly invisible for a few seconds. "I hang out here because it's the place where I was killed, but most spirits? If they don't move on, they linger in places where they were happy." He looked around the narrow street filled with walled estates, lush gardens, and towering palms. "I mean, it's a pretty nice place to haunt, all things considered."

"Except for the being-killed part?"

"Who was killed?" Vivian asked. "Was someone else killed?"

"Around here?" Elton said. "More than a few someones. You think you see Vista de Lirio, doll, but you only see the surface. As for my own death?" Elton shrugged. "I choose not to focus my eternity on that part. Tell me more about the ex."

"Justin's ex-girlfriend or Lily's ex-husband?" She glanced at Vivian. "Elton is asking about the case."

"Okay, if you're going to talk to ghosts," Vivian said, "I think I might go walk with the living."

"Fair enough."

Vivian dropped back, and Julia asked Elton, "Okay, which ex were you wondering about?"

"Both."

"So according to Evy, the ex-girlfriend wasn't involved. We went to meet her, and nothing in her thoughts even hinted at her being guilty, and the police already questioned her too. Doesn't seem to be a good lead."

"And the ex-husband? He'd be the first one I'd look at."

"More possible, but we can't figure out a motive."

"The schmuck's sleeping with his wife; you need more of a motive?"

"But Richard wanted the divorce. We just saw him with a new woman. According to Justin, Richard liked that Lily had a new man. He was hoping to avoid some alimony if they got married."

"Twisted," Elton said. "And let me guess, the kid doesn't remember squat."

"Nothing from the day of his murder."

"Yeah, that's pretty typical. I don't remember mine either. It's like our minds—whatever is left of them—just wipe that part clean."

Julia glanced up, noticing the street they were passing. One more block to Casa de Lirio. "Well, despite what Justin said, I think Richard the ex-husband is worth looking at. Dean has his doubts. Says he's not the crime-of-passion type."

Elton nodded sagely, then muttered, "There's gotta be a dame involved."

Julia blinked. "Well yeah, the ex-wife. Lily."

The ghost shook his head. "I say there's another dame involved."

Julia wasn't too sure Elton was an unbiased consultant in all this. He seemed to have a very definite point of view about "dames being involved" even without knowing much.

Just because he's a private detective doesn't mean he was a good one.

Elton said, "What about the new woman?"

"Whose? Richard's?"

"Yeah, the new woman of the ex-husband."

"Why would Richard's new girlfriend be angry with Justin?"

"I don't know." Elton frowned. "Maybe Justin was trying to drag out the divorce for some reason and the new girlfriend got angry because she wanted to marry Richard."

"It's possible." Maybe Julia shouldn't be so quick to dismiss Elton. He had been around for more than a few years.

Elton pointed toward the dark trees at the end of the street. "Guess we'll find out if anyone at the house has anything to say."

"You think they'll talk to me this time?"

"Sure they will," Elton said. "Now whether they tell you what you want to hear? No way of knowing that."

They walked the last half a block to Casa de Lirio in silence save for the skipping steps of Aurelia and Juliana tapping along with Paco's soft hoofbeats.

When they arrived, the garden gate was hanging wide open.

Chapter Thirteen

"Again?" Julia shook her head. "We have to talk to the workmen about this. It's not safe; especially with that pool."

Dean was the first one to poke his head inside. "Hello?"

Julia was dying to follow Dean, but she felt her phone buzzing. She took it out and answered it, not reading the screen. "Hello?"

"Hi, is this Julia?" A deep male voice said her name. "Did Sergio give me the right number? If he didn't, I apologize."

Why did she recognize the voice? Something was familiar about it. "Who is this?"

"I'm sorry. I was looking for Julia Brooks, and a mutual friend—"

"Michael?" The name hit her suddenly. "Is this Michael?"

"Julia?"

"Yes." The smile came without warning. "Hi, you caught me at a funny time. Can I call you back?"

"You could," he said. "Or you could meet me for drinks tomorrow at Tequila and we could just talk in person."

Tequila was, predictably, a tequila tasting bar and modern Mexican restaurant a few minutes from Vista de Lirio.

Before she could talk herself out of it, she said, "Sure, that sounds great."

"Good. I'll make a reservation. Does six o'clock work?"

"Sure?"

"Is that a question?"

Julia smiled. "That's a yes. Tomorrow at Tequila around six o'clock. See you then."

"Looking forward to it."

As she hung up her phone, she glanced at Vivian, whose eyebrows were nearly at her hairline. "We're ghost-hunting and you just made a date?"

"He already knows about the ghost thing, and he asked me out anyway. You think I should turn that kind of interest down?" Julia tucked her phone away. "It's Michael O'Connor."

"The director who was at the party?"

"Yep."

They started walking again.

"I love his early stuff," Vivian said.

"Same."

Dean and Evy had already disappeared inside the gate. Vivian and Julia followed. When she walked through the bougainvillea-covered arch, she was immediately hit with the same feeling of *presence* she'd felt before, but this time there was something pleasant about it, like a weighted blanket on a cold night.

"What is going on here?" There was something unearthly about the house that night. "Elton?"

In the distance, Mae let out a laugh of pure glee before she ran to the back.

"And there she goes," Elton muttered. "Typical."

"What's up with Mae?"

"Jules!"

She turned and saw Dean and Evy walking toward the sprawling Spanish house.

"We're going inside," Dean said. "I want to take a look around, make sure the house is locked up and everything is clean."

"Sounds good."

Sergio stood beside her, scanning the grounds. "I'm not sure the girls should be here, even with Paco. Something feels strange to me."

"I feel something, but I wouldn't call it bad energy." In fact, it was getting lighter and lighter every step she took toward the house. "I think if you stay here with them, nothing will happen." She felt herself drawn to follow Mae, just like Mrs. Griffin and Elton seemed to be doing. They were walking, not running, but both spirits were heading toward where Mae had disappeared.

Vivian stayed at her side. "What is happening?" She touched Julia's arm. "You're both tense *and* excited. And very curious. What are you seeing?"

"It's more what I'm hearing."

There was a low, resonant hum in the air that seemed to emanate from the backyard and the same low chatter she'd heard the first time she came, like a party in a distant room. "I want to check out the back."

"I'm with you."

Julia turned to Sergio. "I think you and the girls will be fine here. Just hang in the garden and let Paco explore."

"If something bad happens, yell," he said. "Other than that, I'm sticking with Paco."

As they walked around the house, a breeze rustled the trees, adding a shushing background to joyful voices that whispered in the distance.

When the pool came into view, Julia froze. "Oh my ghosts."

Vivian let out a deep breath. "It's so dramatic at night. They must have had some awesome parties when Richard and Lily lived here."

"Had parties? Try have." Compared to the eerie pressure of a few nights before, Julia couldn't believe what she was seeing.

Vivian frowned. "What do you mean?"

There weren't a few ghosts. There was a mob of them.

Apparitions of every age and era filled the area behind Casa de Lirio. They waded in the pool, sat on the grass, and lounged in the cabanas.

But Julia's eyes were fixed on something far more unearthly than human spirits.

Past the pool, hidden among the greenery, was a gold-outlined archway. Sitting around it were dozens of spirits, but no one walked through the glowing portal.

"Julia?" Vivian snapped her fingers. "Are there ghosts?"

She whispered, "So many ghosts."

Surprisingly, it didn't feel creepy or scary at all. In a way, it was the shadow version of Sunday Dinner at Sergio and Dean's. There were even more spirits than she'd seen originally—lounging in the bushes, leaning against the umbrellas, dipping ghostly feet in the crystal-blue water.

Julia couldn't take her eyes off the gold doorway. "What *is* it?"

"What's what?" Vivian frowned. "The pool?"

Elton appeared beside her. "It's a gateway, kid. There aren't very many of them, but there's one in Vista de Lirio. Maybe because there's a natural oasis here. No idea, but it was here long before any of us. Spirits are drawn to it even if we don't realize what it is."

Julia looked around, and the backyard was teeming with them. "There are so many."

"So many what?" Vivian slapped a hand on her forearm just as a ghost nearly walked through her. "These mosquitos are killing me."

"There's some kind of doorway here," Julia said. "And there are... so many ghosts."

Vivian looked wary. "Nice ghosts?"

A burly man stood a few feet away from Vivian, glaring at the small Asian woman.

Under her breath, Julia asked, "Elton, can ghosts hurt people?"

"Not physically."

"Yeah," she said to Vivian. "They're perfectly nice. They're not really paying attention to us, you know?" The glaring spirit was still staring at Vivian, so Julia put herself between the ghost and her new friend. "Are you feeling anything?"

"I think the empathy I was feeling only works on live people, but I can say whatever weird psychic power Aunt Marie cursed me with feels really strong." Vivian reached for Julia's hand and gripped it. "You're a little scared and a lot lying to me about the friendly-ghost thing. Do I want to know why?"

Julia glanced at the angry man. "Probably not."

"I'm going to trust you on that one. You're also completely digging this even though you kind of don't want to. And I feel like you're hiding something from me, but that's normal because we don't know each other all that well. I'll try to respect your boundaries." She released Julia's hand and walked slowly around the brick deck of the pool area.

Julia blinked. "That was kind of freaky."

"And your seeing ghosts isn't?" Vivian spun in place. "I can't describe what I'm feeling! It's electric. Did Evy bring Geoff? She needs to feel this."

"I don't think so." Julia turned to Elton. "What does the gateway do?"

"Every now and then," he said, "It opens. Then anyone who's tired of killing time in this world can move on to the next."

"Does anything ever come out of it?"

He shook his head. "Death is a one-way street, kid. You go in; you do not come out."

"So if you miss your first chance—"

"The doorway is your only ticket out," Elton said. "It's that or eternity here."

"So all these people want to move on?" Julia scanned the crowd. While some were sitting very close to the portal, most were lounging or laughing with friends in the crowd.

"Not all spirits want to move on." Mrs. Griffin had moved close to listen to their conversation. "But the gate creates an aura that transports us, Miss Brooks. For those who had a troubled life, it makes them forget their past mistakes."

Elton continued. "Every embarrassing moment, every sin, and every failure?" He shook his head. "None of that matters here."

"No wonder ghosts love it." Julia turned to Vivian. "The doorway I was talking about, it's like a contact high. This gate opens to the afterlife, so if you go in, you're in. But if you just hang around you get a whiff of heaven without giving up your life here."

"I can see that being an attraction." Vivian looked around. "I think I can feel some version of it. I don't feel any urge to leave. *At all.* I just want to hang out."

"Same." A thought popped into Julia's head. "Hey, Elton, are there any permanent residents here?"

"What do you mean?"

"I mean, most of these ghosts are here for the glowing gate, right? Is there anyone who came here or lingers here because they lived here? I thought I felt someone the other night, but they didn't show themselves to me."

"There is." Elton frowned. "But I don't know if she'll talk to you. She's not friendly like me and the girls."

He guided them away from the pool and toward the back of the house where a series of shaded cabanas provided a bridge between house and garden and small round patios were tucked against the house, each one leading to a set of french doors and a guest suite of the house. Julia could see Evy and Dean moving around the kitchen, but she couldn't hear what they were saying.

The resonant hum that filled the air around the gate was softer here, and the whispers of ghostly voices echoed against flagstones, brick, and smooth white plaster.

Lying on a chaise tucked away in one patio, her face turned up to the sky, Julia saw a ghost and knew immediately that she was the spirit Elton had spoken about. It wasn't an air of negativity or danger, but something about the spirit was fleeting, as if she might fade away in a heartbeat.

She was dressed in a white string bikini and a gauzy robe. While her wardrobe was similar to Mae's, Julia got the impression that this spirit was much newer. Her long blond hair fell nearly to her waist, and her blue eyes were distant.

"Hey, doll." Elton leaned against the house. "You got a visitor."

The spirit's eyes flicked to Julia, then away again, trained on the sky.

"Now don't be a drag." Elton walked toward her. "When was the last time a live one could see you?"

Still no answer.

Vivian walked over and scanned the seemingly empty patio. "This is pretty, but what are we staring at?"

"Ghost," Julia said. "More recent." She spoke softly. "Miss, a young man was killed here a few nights ago. Can you tell me anything? I'm trying to help."

The ghost turned her eyes to Julia for a moment, then melted into the night.

Elton sidled up to her. "Bad luck, huh? She's a quiet one. Most of the spirits around here, they come and go, drift from our place over to the gate here. They wander in and out of all the houses. Party with the rock stars down the street. We're mostly a happy bunch."

"Rock stars?" Julia hadn't heard of any rock stars in the neighborhood. "Are you talking about ghosts?"

Elton ignored the question. "But her? She never leaves. Rarely talks to anyone. She's always here." He shrugged. "That's all I know."

"Julia?" She heard Evy's voice. "Viv?"

"I hate the name Viv," Vivian said. "We're going to put a stop to that right now." She marched toward the sound of Evy's voice. "Come on. Is there anything else you need to ask the dead?"

Julia followed. "Do you have to make it sound so ominous? Most of them seem pretty harmless." Except for the angry man who was *still* glaring at Vivian. He sent a chill down Julia's spine.

"I don't mess around with the ancestors," Vivian said. "There are rules about that kind of stuff. And I definitely don't fool around with them when I don't have an offering."

An offering? Hmmm. That was a thought.

She turned to Elton. "That woman? Is she always like that?"

"The attitude? Sure."

"So we can assume she's not here because she was happy and peaceful here."

The ghost frowned. "I see what you're getting at."

"If she isn't here because she's the happy, peaceful type, then the only other reason she'd be hanging around here and not some other place is because she died here."

Vivian spun around. "What? Someone else died here?"

"Maybe." Julia caught up with her and continued walking toward Evy's voice. "It seems like Casa de Lirio has more secrets we haven't discovered yet."

"There." Evy was pointing to a cabinet under the kitchen island. "That's where I found it."

Julia had underestimated how disturbing it would be to return to the place where she'd found Justin's body.

She stared at the Saltillo tile. "They already replaced the floor."

"Richard had tile people in here the day the police cleared it," Dean said. "About half the floor needed to go."

"Huh." She pointed to the spot where Justin had lain, the image bursting into her mind so clearly that she nearly gagged. "He was here. Dean, do you remember? He was sprawled out here. So whoever hit him..." She tried to imagine it.

Dean stood next to her and shifted her to the left. "Imagine you're Justin. To end up in that position, someone had to come at you from behind. Someone really tall."

"Not necessarily, because he was bent over," Julia said. "He can't remember why."

"I remember you saying something about that." Evy flipped open a lower cupboard. "Which is why I decided to look down, not up."

"It paid off." Dean crouched down to look inside the cabinet. "At first we just assumed that the space below the cabinet here was cosmetic. No cupboards lay right on the floor, right? There's going to be some trim that lifts it up a little." He reached in and scrunched up his face. "But then we realized..."

There was a click and a pop. A small door flipped up, revealing a hollow space under the cupboard. That false bottom was lined with green velvet, and the surface was dust free.

Evy held up a hand. "Okay, who had suspicious kitchen cupboard on their bingo card? Just me? Say it was just me."

"What was in it?" Julia looked at Dean. "Was it empty?"

"It was when we found it," he said. "But when Justin came through? Your guess is as good as mine. It could be that he found the cupboard but nothing was inside. Then again, maybe he found something—"

"And whoever killed him took what he found," Vivian said. "The question is, why was he snooping in the first place?"

"Justin was Lily's personal chef," Julia said. "It's possible he discovered that hiding spot ages ago along with whatever might have been in it. Maybe he was just waiting for a chance to take it when he could be alone."

"The point is," Evy said, "we don't know what Justin found, but we're pretty sure this is what he was doing when he was killed."

"If the hiding spot was empty," Julia said, "there would be no reason to kill Justin."

"So we can assume he found something," Vivian added. "And whatever it was, it was worth killing for."

Chapter Fourteen

Tequila Bar and Restaurant was renowned for two things: the widest selection of tequila in the valley and really great tacos. It was never a bad bet for dinner or a drink, so when Julia pulled into the tiny parking lot across the street, she was feeling optimistic.

The date? That could go either way. But good or bad, she'd be drinking and eating well, and that was always a plus.

There was a break in traffic, so she walked across the road, keeping an eye out for Michael.

Julia was almost at the opposite sidewalk when she heard the screeching tires. A black sedan darted around the corner in a sharp right turn and nearly clipped her. She gasped as her purse thunked against the right fender before the car sped away.

"Holy shit." Julia's heart was in her throat.

Again.

"What is it with drivers in this town?" She shook her head and reminded herself to just use the crosswalk next time.

Tequila was half a block away, and Julia spotted Michael leaning against a pillar near the hostess station and looking at the wall of succulents that decorated the outside of the building. She stopped for a moment and smiled, noting that unlike every other person waiting, he was not looking at an electronic device.

How quaint.

Michael turned and saw her, a huge smile spreading across his face. "Hey."

"Hi." She walked toward him and pointed at the lush green wall. "Are you a gardener?"

"I'm not." He nodded at the waitress who immediately grabbed menus and place settings so she could lead them to their table. "No house, remember?"

"That's right; you're kind of... Homeless doesn't seem like the right word."

He smiled. "I identify as a nomad."

"That's right! I'd forgotten you said that. Nomad sounds intentional. Good call."

They followed the hostess, who wound through the small tables lit with flickering lamps. Every now and then, Michael touched his hand lightly to the small of Julia's back. She felt a tingle that had nothing to do with ghosts sizzle up her spine.

"I like gardening," Michael continued. "Or I should say I like gardens. More now than when I was younger. I lived in a Buddhist monastery for about six months and found myself in the garden for a lot of my time there."

"A monastery?"

Michael waited for Julia to be seated before he answered her. "It was right after the accident." He sat across from her and took the menu from the waitress. "I was healed physically, but I was still having a hard time sleeping. Believe it or not, my doctor recommended the place. It was in Hawaii, and it was very simple. I worked during the day, slept at night. There was electricity in the kitchen but nowhere else, so when the sun went down, that was pretty much it. The bed might have been hard, but it's the healthiest I'd felt in a long time." He took out a pair of horn-rimmed reading glasses from his pocket and perused the menu.

"I invited you for drinks, but I haven't eaten since lunch. Do you mind if we get some food too?"

"I'd be irritated if we didn't. I love the tacos here." Julia found herself curious about the monastery. She wondered if women could stay there. Probably not. "So did you sleep?"

Michael looked up with a frown. The glasses were giving him a little bit of a sexy-professor vibe, and Julia couldn't fault it. She'd always been an overachiever.

"Did I sleep?" Michael's eyes cleared. "Oh, at the monastery? I did. It got me straightened out. I've slept really well ever since. I also got interested in gardening, but I've never had a home of my own, so no garden."

"Not the easiest thing to transport." She smiled. "Pets?"

"I had the best dog in the entire universe for thirteen years." A shadow fell over Michael's eyes. "He was a shepherd mix named Bruno, and he went everywhere with me. He passed last year, and I haven't been able to face getting another one." He nodded at her. "You?"

"I really love cats, but I'm allergic to them. And I like dogs, but I worry that I work too much for one." Julia shrugged. "I don't know. I like the idea of pets more than the reality maybe. It's kind of like having a boyfriend."

Michael threw his head back and laughed. "You know what? I know what you mean. I've never been married, which the tabloids speculated about for years."

"Not gay?"

"Not even a little." He smiled. "And I don't have anything against the institution of marriage or anything, I just haven't met anyone who wants to live like I do."

"I was only ever married to Dean, and you know how that turned out." She set her menu down. "Tacos al pastor and that tequila cocktail with pineapple."

"Good choice." He frowned at the menu. "I think I'm going spicy."

"You're not one of those men who eats hot peppers because you think women will be impressed by that, are you?"

"Do I look like I'm twenty-five?" He glanced up. "Maybe don't answer that. I do love spicy food, but only if it doesn't kill me or give me heartburn. I've had their green chili tacos here, and they're great."

She set her menu down. "I like being with a decisive man."

"Oh yeah? Well, I was looking at the al pastor tacos, so I might end up stealing a bite. I'm not *that* decisive."

Julia's smiled grew wider. "I like a decisive man who shares food even more. Life's too short to only eat one thing off the menu."

"Hear, hear." He lifted his water glass and they toasted. "So tell me, Julia Brooks who was married to Dean, why haven't we met before now?"

She shook her head. "I don't know. I feel like we should have."

Michael lifted a finger. "Ah, but then it might not have been the right timing. I used to be a complete bastard."

"I have a hard time believing that."

"Don't be too sure. A lot of drugs were floating around in the eighties and nineties. A *lot*."

Julia smiled and waited while Michael gave their order to the waitress. "So it sounds like you haven't worked much since your accident."

His eyebrows went up. "It sounds like you've faced some big life changes since your... What did you call it?"

"Cardiac event."

"An *event*." He smiled. "You're right; that sounds much friendlier than attack or scare."

"I know." She sipped her water. "I think that's why I'm seeing ghosts."

Michael looked around furtively. "Are we talking about that?" he asked in a quiet voice.

"I don't think anything really surprises people in this town." She flagged down a server who was walking by. "Hey. If I told you I'd just recently started seeing ghosts around Palm Springs, would that surprise you?"

The server's eyebrows went up. "I mean..." He shrugged. "Anyone famous?"

"A few." Julia sat back in her seat, and the server returned to the bar. "See what I mean?"

Michael nodded. "Fair enough. So I can be open about the whole 'dead for several minutes' thing."

"I'm pretty sure it just makes you slightly more interesting at cocktail parties."

Their server returned with their drinks, and Julia took her first sip of the pineapple tequila drink she'd ordered. "Oh, this is dangerous."

"I just got a basic margarita on the rocks, but it's so good." Michael set his drink down. "So Sergio tells me that Casa de Lirio is still on the market."

Julia's professional antenna perked up. "Are you interested?"

"It would be a little weird to buy Richard and Lily's old place." He smiled. "I might decide to start looking, but that's too much of an estate for me. Stunning though, right?"

"Hmm." Julia nodded slowly. "Lots of ghosts."

He leaned forward. "Are there?" He smiled. "Yeah, that doesn't surprise me. That house has a big personality."

"Speaking of Casa de Lirio..." Julia pursed her lips. "Do you know of anyone who died there? A former owner or anything like that?"

"Oh man, not that I know of." He rubbed his fingers along his jaw in a thoughtful gesture. "But I wasn't here every year or anything. I guess it's possible."

"But no one was murdered?"

Michael's eyebrows went up. "When Lily and Richard lived there? No way. Nothing until Justin."

"Interesting." She sipped her pineapple cocktail. "This is excellent; you should try it."

"Thanks." He held his margarita to her. "Try?"

She shook her head. "No, thanks."

Michael sipped the pineapple tequila and nodded. "You're right—it's dangerous."

"Both of them wanted it," Julia said. "The house, I mean."

"That doesn't surprise me. They poured thousands and thousands into the restoration." Michael frowned. "As long as I've known them, they considered Casa de Lirio their home even though they had houses in other cities."

"You've been friends with them for a long time it sounds like."

"I've known Richard and Lily for... Has to be twenty years. Damn, I'm old. I met them right after I moved out to LA."

"From?"

"Minneapolis. I'm a midwestern boy. Whole family is still there." He waited as the server set down their tacos. "Food's better out here; don't tell my mom."

"I won't." Julia paused to take a bite of her first taco. "These are delicious."

"So much better than hotdish." He wiped his mouth with a golden-yellow napkin. "So I moved out here, and I met Lily first. She was still in soaps, and I'd just gotten my first commercial directing gig. She was already married to Richard, but he was that stuffy guy from the East Coast, you know?" Michael sipped his margarita. "I bet if you'd asked people then how long those two would last, they would have given them five years max. But they stuck together. They were really devoted to each other for a long time."

"What changed?"

Michael frowned. "I don't know. They both worked a lot. Richard got more and more into producing, which he was really successful at, and then Lily started to work less. Pretty soon he was the one everyone wanted to talk to at cocktail parties, and I'm sure that bugged the shit out of her."

"Infidelity?"

"You know... what's rumor and what's reality?" He spread his hands. "It's so hard to know, and I didn't ask. If there was cheating, it was nothing obvious from either of them; they were respectful that way. Which was why I think Richard finally pulled the plug when Lily started with her trainer. That one was obvious."

"I was her fucking personal chef."

Julia glared at Justin, who'd decided to appear sitting at the table next to them, lounging like he hadn't a care in eternity. "Take off," she said sternly. "You decide to show up just now after being gone all day?"

Michael turned to look at the empty chair. "Is someone... there?"

"Yeah, the trainer."

"Wait, the ghost you're seeing is...?" Michael's eyes went wide. "You're seeing the guy who was murdered?"

"Ever since I found him at the house." She nodded. "He appears to be stuck to me. That's why Vivian, Evy, and I are trying to figure out who killed him. We're hoping he moves on once he has inner peace or something, because if *he* moves on then maybe the others..." She shrugged. "It would be nice to have some privacy."

"Your privacy means shit if you're listening to lies," Justin said. "I was her personal chef. And we didn't even start fucking until Richard called it quits with Lily. I mean... okay, there were probably a couple of days of overlap, but he was out of town so it didn't count."

"Justin, that is... so messed up. That's not how infidelity works."

Michael was looking ever more confused, and Julia was

starting to feel like a lunatic. 'Okay, he's going to take off, and we're going to ignore him."

'Whatever." Justin faded from view, but Julia could still sense him.

This was going to be fun.

'How do you plan to find the murderer?" Michael asked. 'Don't the police think a vagrant or a thief—?"

'As far as we can tell, there have been no violent break-ins reported anywhere in the city lately," Julia said. 'And it just seems too strange that Justin was killed at Casa de Lirio if it wasn't personal."

Michael frowned. 'Does he know who did it? You know, the... ghost."

'No. He was hit from behind. And a lot of his memory of that day is fuzzy. He doesn't even remember why he was at the house." Julia decided that she didn't need to share everything with Michael. The secret compartment felt confidential. 'So we're trying to figure it out. Doing the best we can anyway."

'Well, obviously you have a leg up on the police," Michael said. 'I don't think they've made any progress. I know they questioned Richard, but he obviously had nothing to do with it."

Julia lifted her drink and sipped carefully. 'Why obviously?"

'I mean..." Michael smiled. 'He's not the jealous type—not that he loved that Lily cheated on him—but the affair made him the sympathetic husband, which I think he liked. And he was probably hoping Lily's new boyfriend would want to get married."

'Which would save him a bundle on alimony, right?"

Michael nodded. 'Lily hasn't worked in years." He lifted a hand. 'But like I told Richard, she's the main reason anyone gave him the time of day in Hollywood, so alimony was definitely due. He might be supporting her these days, but she was the only reason he has the career he does. Outside of finance, that is."

Julia made a face. "And who cares about finance in Vista de Lirio, right?"

"Very boring." Michael smiled, and his eyes crinkled in the corners. "I like you, Julia Brooks."

She liked him too. Liked him enough to try another date, and she knew he was interested. Plus—and this was purely a bonus—it was useful to know someone who knew Lily and Richard by more than just gossip.

"So" —Julia leaned across the table, showing just a hint of cleavage— "Sergio invited me to a gallery opening this Friday. You interested in being my date?"

Michael put his elbows on the table and mirrored her position, letting his eyes drift down to the offered cleavage for a moment before he smiled. "I just happen to have been invited to the same gallery opening. How about that?"

She leaned forward even more, motioning him closer before she kissed him lightly on the lips, enjoying the sting of chilies as she pulled away. "Sounds like a date."

Chapter Fifteen

J ulia called Evy and Vivian the next morning, asking for a meetup, and Evy suggested her house "for a good reason" that Julia was hoping had something to do with the mysterious Aunt Marie coming back into town.

She drove to the Sunrise Park neighborhood east of downtown and turned right on McManus to find a street of orderly midcentury modern homes with towering palms swaying behind whitewashed block walls. She parked on the street behind Vivian's sleek electric sports car and got out, enjoying the warmth already emanating from the sidewalk.

It was spring in Palm Springs, and while summer teased the afternoons, the mornings were still perfect.

Julia knocked on the turquoise-blue door and waited.

Evy opened it and immediately began talking. "Hey. Good, you're finally here and we can start. I've got everything set up in the study. It's kind of the den, and Aunt Marie uses it for her sewing room most of the time, but since she's still nowhere to be found, I moved all that stuff to the guest room and set up the murder board in the den because honestly, when do we have guests anyway?"

Julia was trying to process all that when she smelled the coffee. "Coffee."

"Yeah, in the kitchen." Evy waved at her to follow. "Sorry, the house hasn't changed in fifty years."

"No, it's very cool." Julia assessed the potential sale value of the home, which she did with pretty much every house she entered. "Is your aunt the original owner?"

"She's not. She bought it in the eighties, but she didn't change much. She loves wood paneling."

"Smart lady." The original features of the house already set it apart from the average middle-class family home of the era. The pale wood paneling was still intact, as were all the built-ins. "It's worth a bundle right now."

Evy turned to her. "Seriously?"

"Seriously." Julia entered a kitchen that overlooked a friendly dining room and a wall full of windows looking into the crystal-blue pool that dominated the backyard. "This place is great."

"It's funny, you hear about places in the neighborhood going for a million dollars and up these days, but they were all just little family homes when they were built." Evy poured a cup of coffee into a bright purple mug and handed it to Julia. "Milk in the fridge. Sugar in the cupboard."

"Just milk for me." She walked to the fridge. "What's this about a murder board?"

"I told you I love murder podcasts, remember?"

Julia nodded and followed Evy from the family room, down the hall, and into another wood-paneled room where Vivian was standing in front of what looked like a freestanding blackboard.

"What is...? Oh my God, you weren't joking about the murder board."

Evy had somehow gotten her hands on pictures of all the major players they were looking at. There was a small picture of Justin in the middle of the board and an array of pictures shooting out from the center with pictures and notes next to them.

A voice came from over her shoulder. "Okay, that is really weird."

Julia recognized Justin's aura before he spoke. "Are you done pouting now?"

"I'd like to point out that you're the one who told me to get lost."

She explained when Evy and Vivian turned to look at her. "Justin just showed up."

"Does it have any pattern?" Vivian asked. "The way it appears to you."

"I am not an it." Justin was still seething with attitude.

"He comes and goes. It seems like if we talk too much or I'm away from Vista de Lirio, it's harder for him to show up. I do think there's a geographic limit for him."

"Stop talking about me like I'm not here." Justin pouted.

Julia finally turned to face him. "Then stop showing up when you know it's not appropriate. You knew you weren't welcome during my date with Michael last night."

"That guy is a tool."

"So mature." Julia rolled her eyes. "Justin doesn't like Michael. Big surprise."

Vivian perked up. "That's right! How was the date?"

"You know, it was really nice." Julia smiled. "He seems like a very thoughtful person, and he's led an interesting life."

"And he's a certified silver fox," Evy said. "I'm pretty sure it was in *People* magazine."

"Definitely two-date material then," Vivian said.

"Yeah, we're going to that gallery opening this Friday that Sergio's promoting."

"I'm going to that too," Vivian said. "I've never been to a gallery opening before, so I have no idea what to expect."

"Free food and wine," Evy said. "I always go. Even if Sergio doesn't invite me."

Julia tried not to laugh. "You gate crash gallery openings?"

"I guess." She shrugged. "I mean, it's all the same people at them unless it's festival season, so if you show up to enough of them, they just assume you're always on the list because you know the artist or the organizer. Free food and all the champagne I want, baby. I love free food."

"Good to know." Julia turned to the board. "Okay, so we've got Serena up here, but I thought you said she was eliminated as a suspect because you read her thoughts."

"I'm not exactly a professional at this whole telepathy thing," Evy said. "I don't want to completely rule her out. That said, I don't think she's likely." Evy pointed to the board. "The other suspects are Richard Putnam, Lily Putnam, the mystery blond lady who was with Richard, an unknown thief, or Michael O'Connor." Evy winced. "Sorry, Julia."

She frowned. "Wait, why is Michael up there?"

"There are rumors that he's always had a thing for Lily," Vivian said. "Sergio told me the rumors were pretty intense a few years ago, right after his accident. It was before Justin was in the picture."

Justin muttered, "Yeah, that guy could have done it."

Julia turned to him. "You're just saying that because you think he's a tool. And you only think he's a tool because he told me that you weren't on Lily's level."

Justin's eyes went wide. "What the fuck?"

"Really?" Vivian said. "Because that would kind of fit with him having a thing for Lily if he thought Justin was beneath her. I don't even get what that means though. That he didn't have money? That's kind of shitty."

"My impression was that it wasn't age or bank account. Michael said that Lily was smart and talented; he clearly didn't think the same about Justin."

"Again, none of that rules him out," Evy said. "Okay, for now let's focus on how we can get me in contact with some of these people so I can try to read their thoughts."

"The gallery opening." Vivian smiled. "Just bring Geoff as your date."

"That's not funny." Evy pursed her lips. "I could bring him in a backpack or something, but it would be very noticeable."

"Why don't we ask Sergio if you can perform there?"

"Sure, and we'll see how well Geoff's upstate New York summer-camp humor plays with the under-seventy Palm Springs crowd. That sounds like a complete winner."

Julia looked at Vivian. "Do you know what that means?"

"No idea."

"Dad jokes, ladies! So many dad jokes." Evy tucked her black hair behind her ear. "That stuff is for retirement homes for a reason, Julia."

"Maybe Sergio could bring Geoff to the gallery early," Vivian offered. "And tuck him away in an office or something until the opening. You don't have to be touching the person for the telepathy to work, right?"

"I don't think so? I'm pretty new at this, but when I was doing that first show where I freaked out, I was onstage. I wasn't touching anyone."

Vivian asked, "Have you been practicing the telepathy thing?"

"No! Other than that first night and taking Geoff to the spa when we questioned Serena, absolutely not."

"Poor Geoff," Julia murmured.

"I think it might be a good idea to practice," Vivian said. "It seems like the kind of thing that would get better over time."

Evy looked tortured. "But I don't want to hear people's thoughts. Do you know how often women think about how fat their stomachs are? Even when they're old? It's a lot."

Julia frowned. "That's very depressing."

Vivian was clearly a fan of the practice-until-perfect school. "Still, I think you need to experiment with this. For instance, the first time you read minds, you were onstage. You may need a level of attention trained on you rather than just being able to eavesdrop." Vivian stood up and stared at the murder board. "And I'm going to have to learn how to be way more handsy in a nongross way if I'm going to question any of these people and use my empathy."

"You can do it," Julia said. "I'll stick with you and try to steer the conversation. Everyone knows I discovered Justin's body, so it would make sense for me to be curious. I'll make sure you at least shake hands with everyone."

Vivian cringed. "So many germs."

Evy said, "The one thing we have going for us here is that people love to gossip. This town runs on solar, wind, and unconfirmed rumors." She pointed to the board. "Richard will probably be there. I don't know about the blonde." She pointed to Lily's picture. "Lily's grief and confusion when we saw her last week seemed genuine to me, but if we're not ruling Serena out, we shouldn't rule her out either."

Vivian nodded. "I only touched her for a moment when we arrived at her house, but it didn't seem like she was hiding anything." Vivian stared at the board. "If anything, she felt like an oversharer. I kind of remember this massive wave of emotions that hit me all at once. I have a hard time imagining that woman keeping a secret like murder."

"Without a doubt." Julia pointed at Richard. "Richard Putnam had the most motive. He hated Justin, didn't want Lily to be happy, and he claimed that she stole an incredibly valuable heirloom from his family. I'm sure he thought Justin was a gold digger. He might have even thought Justin stole the Putnam Diamond."

"Oh!" Evy's eyes lit up. "What if that's what was in the secret compartment?"

"I was thinking about that," Vivian said. "Maybe Justin did steal it, and he was keeping it there so no one knew."

"It wouldn't be the dumbest reason someone was killed." Julia turned, but Justin was nowhere to be seen. "Hey, Justin?"

He drifted into the room through the wall that faced the hallway. "Oh, I'm sorry, do you need me now?"

No, because you're a prick!

Don't say it aloud.

"The Putnam Diamond," Julia said. "What do you know about it?"

"You've gotta be kidding me." Justin crossed his arms over his ghostly chest. "I told Lily how dumb it looked the last time he gave it to her to wear. It was old as shit. Looked like it belonged in a museum or something."

"So it wasn't Lily's?"

"No." Justin shrugged. "But she was claiming it. She was hoping Richard might give her the house if she gave him the necklace. But then it went missing and completely screwed up that plan."

"When was the last time you saw it?"

Justin looked like he was thinking hard, but it was so easily confused for his "don't really remember" face that she had no idea where the conversation was going.

"She wore it to a dinner they hosted... maybe six months before they split and we got together?"

"Where was it kept?"

"In Richard's safe," Justin said firmly. "He was the only one who had the combination. So he has to be hiding it if you ask me."

"Lily wore the Putnam Diamond about six months before she and Richard split, but it was in the house and stored in Richard's personal safe," Julia said. "I think that may be a dead end."

"Richard had a safe that Lily couldn't access?" Vivian asked. "Don't you think that's weird?"

Evy shrugged. "Yes and no. I can see wanting some privacy for my stuff."

"She had one too," Justin said. "Lily had her own safe. She wouldn't even let me see it."

"And they were fighting about it in the divorce?" Julia asked. "This diamond that neither of them claimed to have?"

"Yeah. It was probably the main thing holding up the financial settlement actually. Richard was sure Lily had it, and Lily was sure he was hiding it."

Julia translated for the living in the room.

Evy sat on the dark brown couch and stared at the murder board. "Rich people are weird. They're even weirder when they're suspects in a murder though."

"So we definitely talk to Richard at the opening," Julia said. "Who else? Lily? The blonde?"

"I doubt the blonde is going to show up," Vivian said. "I suspect she's going to remain hidden until that divorce is final."

"Maybe *she* has the Putnam Diamond," Evy said.

All of them laughed, but Julia was feeling exhausted.

"So on Friday we focus on talking to Richard and Lily," Julia said. "I'm going with Michael, and he's friends with Richard, so I'm sure I can get an introduction. Vivian, maybe plan on sticking with me?"

Vivian nodded. "Sounds good."

"I'll tell Michael you're new in town and want to meet everyone. Hopefully that gets us a conversation with Lily too."

"Then I think we have a plan," Evy said. "Now to convince Sergio to sneak Geoff into the gallery opening."

Julia pictured the dummy and the British ghost that followed it around. "Well, at least both Geoffs are in tuxedos."

Chapter Sixteen

J
ulia arrived a half hour after the gallery opening was set to start, a fashionably late entrance that would still afford her plenty of time to mix with Sergio's friends, mingle with murder suspects, and flirt with Michael.

She wore a camel-colored blouse with silk pants in a slightly darker shade. A pair of crocodile loafers and a small clutch completed the "casual but with money" look she was going for. Twisting her hair up in a french knot was both an elegant and practical look. The afternoon had reached nearly eighty, and she'd been running errands for the office all day.

"Yes!" Sergio pounced on her as soon as she entered the gallery. "This is who I've been wanting to introduce you to." He leaned in and whispered, "Play along."

Two people with matching black outfits and round silver glasses stood in front of her. They looked like extras from a sci-fi movie, but whatever.

"This" —Sergio put his arm around her— "is my friend Julia. She's psychic, and her aura is amazing."

The sci-fi twins nodded as if that made abundant sense.

They began speaking to each other quietly in another language. German? Swedish? Julia couldn't place it.

"Thanks," Sergio whispered. "They're wildly rich and addicted to novelty."

Julia smiled through gritted teeth. "You have to stop introducing me to people as your psychic friend. I'm starting to get weird texts."

"Julia!" Michael waved at her from a corner where three people were gathered around a bronze sculpture.

"Oops!" She wiggled away from Sergio. "That's my date."

He tapped his fingers together like an evil mastermind. "I like you two for each other."

She shrugged. "You know me. I manage to mess anything up."

"No, I don't see it. Not with Mick."

She rolled her eyes. "Now who's the psychic?"

Julia turned and walked across the room, flashing a huge smile at Michael, who was standing near another couple dressed in black.

Michael held out his arm. "Come meet Pam and Yves."

She looked for Vivian, but her new friend was nowhere to be found. "Hey!" She smiled brilliantly as Michael made introductions to the couple from London. She scanned the room discreetly, noticing that Richard was already in conversation with a dark-haired woman near a crimson painting and Lily was near the bar, whispering to a woman in a purple caftan.

Julia couldn't help but notice that there were three ghosts in the gallery, leaning against a far wall. They appeared to be in a small huddle, but when they noticed her looking, they immediately faded away.

"You're Sergio's friend."

Julia blinked and turned to the right. "I am."

It was a small woman Julia recognized from Sunday Dinner.

She wore a black tunic with black leggings, and red sunglasses that covered half her face. She had thick salt-and-pepper hair trimmed into a pixie cut, and a small ruby winked from a stud in her nose.

"You don't remember me," she began, "but I'm your neighbor Genevieve De Winter, and I have a standard poodle with three legs and two savannah cats. The cats are quite large; I do not advise entering my gate without calling ahead."

"Right." Julia blinked. "I won't. How do they get along with Paco?"

"They can't stand the beast, which is an excellent and most amusing dynamic; hello, Mick, darling, how are you? Are you finished directing the drivel yet?"

Julia turned back to Michael and noted that the couple from London was gone and Michael was leaning down to kiss the older woman on the cheek.

"Genevieve, I haven't directed anything in two years. I took your advice, remember?"

"Good, then maybe you'll finally direct something worth watching."

Michael smiled. "I haven't switched to French experimental film, but I do have an independent feature I'm considering."

"Hmmm." She pursed her lips. "I'll consider it if there's anyone good in it." She turned and left without another word.

Michael said, "Did she warn you about her cats?"

Julia nodded. "I'm not sure I know what a savannah cat is. Is it illegal?"

"Knowing Genevieve? Probably." He put his hand at the small of her back and guided her toward the bar. "There's a woman over here who's been trying to get your attention for a few minutes."

Vivian was waving near the doorway. "Hey."

"Oh hi!" Julia tried to act surprised. "You did come after all." She hooked her arm through Vivian's, forgetting about her new friend's empathy until she felt the slight flinch. She quickly unhooked her arm, never breaking her smile. "Michael, I hope you don't mind, but when Vivian told me Sergio had invited her tonight, I told her she had to stick with us. She's new in Palm Springs."

Vivian stuck out her hand and held Michael's firmly. "I promise I'll be a very unobtrusive third wheel."

"Oh, no problem." Michael, to his credit, seemed genuinely delighted to meet Vivian. "I've been in and out of this town for twenty years. I'll be happy to introduce you to anyone I know. Are you an artist?"

"Only with teeth."

"Teeth?"

Vivian smiled. "I'm a dentist."

"Oh, no kidding." Michael looked a little lost. "I don't know that I've ever met a dentist before. I mean other than my own."

"Well, we're..." Vivian stopped, her mouth hanging open a little. "Sorry, I was trying to think of a funny dentist joke, but there aren't a lot."

"Let's get you a glass of champagne," Michael said. "Maybe you'll remember them with a few drinks." He steered them both toward the bar, but not before they brushed past Lily Putnam and the woman in purple.

"Mick?"

They stopped, and Michael turned. "Lily, I'm so sorry. Did you change your hair? I didn't even recognize you."

"Oh, just a little." Lily touched the shorter ends near her neck. "I needed a change."

"It looks fantastic. You've met Julia Brooks, right?"

"Sergio's psychic friend, of course." Lily offered her hand. "And your friend who's new in town." Lily's smile was wan. "You were so kind to stop by the other day."

Did everyone in Palm Springs think she was psychic? More importantly, could she use this to sell more houses?

"We were happy to come by," Julia said. "I... sensed you might need a visit." Why not? *Just go with it, Julia.*

"It's so good to see you." Vivian reached her hand out and enclosed Lily's in a comforting grip. "How have you been sleeping?"

"Everything is so strange," Lily said. "The memorial is next week, but his parents are taking him back to Ohio."

Justin appeared behind her back, but Julia could feel him. "Are you kidding me?" He hissed. "I left that state as soon as I was legally able! This fucking sucks."

"I'm sure his parents want him close." Vivian kept her hand around Lily's palm. "But that makes it so hard for his friends and loved ones, doesn't it?"

"Very." Lily stared into the distance with damp eyes. "I keep going out to things to amuse myself, but nothing seems to take my mind off Justin."

"She wasn't looking that distraught when you first got here," Justin muttered. "Is that her third glass of champagne?"

"Why don't I take you out to a movie next week," Michael said. "We'll catch a matinee and lunch. Just like old times."

"Better than old times." Lily smiled. "No Richard acting like a wet blanket."

Michael laughed, then subtly steered them away from Lily, making polite noises and blowing a kiss her direction.

Julia leaned over to Vivian. "Have you seen Evy?"

"No."

Julia scanned the room, looking for Sergio or Evy, but both were nowhere in sight.

The three artists exhibiting that night were standing in the front, their three signature pieces displayed behind them. Two painters and a sculptor, from the looks of it. Off to the right, Julia spotted Richard Putnam speaking with another man in a business suit, both of them holding cocktail glasses with what looked like whiskey.

Their conversation could only be described as intense.

"Do you see him?" Julia muttered.

"Yes." Vivian leaned closer. "No sign of Evy."

"May I have everyone's attention?" A glass clinked near the bar, and everyone turned to look. Sergio had reappeared. "Thank you all for coming tonight to celebrate Lex, Cami, and Joseph. I know you're all dying to buy every single painting and sculpture, but please put your wallets away—only for a little while!—and enjoy these new and exciting voices in the desert art scene." He started clapping. "To Lex, Cami, and Joseph!"

As the crowd clapped, Julia tried to maneuver closer to Richard, wandering over to a canvas with an impressionistic desert scene on the back wall.

"Michael, did you see this?" She waved her date over. "I love the colors in this piece."

"Mick, is that you?" In a sea of Southern California cadence, Richard's New England tone was distinctive.

All three of them turned.

"Richard!" Michael stepped forward and gave the man a one-armed hug that included the customary manly slap on the back. They exchanged a few quiet words before Michael turned to Julia and Vivian. "Rich, this is Julia, the very kind woman who foolishly agreed to go on a date with me the other night. Now I've roped her into this nonsense too."

"Don't be silly." Julia offered her hand. "If you hadn't, Sergio would have kidnapped me and stuffed me into one of the metal sculptures." She smiled. "Julia Brooks of Steward Brooks Realty."

"Of course." Richard took her hand. "You're Dean's partner, aren't you? I don't know why, but I always assumed the Brooks in the name was a man."

"I get that a lot."

Michael continued. "And Richard, this is Vivian." He smiled. "I'm sorry, I didn't catch your last name."

"Wei." Vivian held out her hand. "Vivian Wei. Wei and Sutter Dentistry? I'm working with Dr. Sutter to take over his practice."

"No kidding." Richard's eyes locked with Vivian's, and he couldn't seem to move them. "I heard that Joel was packing up —it's nice to meet the doctor who bought him out."

"It's much friendlier than that. Joel is ready to retire, so we're trying to make it a smooth transition for his patients. I'm very happy with his whole practice so far. The office staff is amazing."

"He's a good man."

"I think so too." Vivian swallowed hard, and Julia was dying to know everything she was getting from Richard.

He finally released her hand and turned a bit awkwardly to the man on his right. "Michael, I don't know if you've met Cy before. He's my... Well..." Richard looked at Julia and Vivian. "He's my divorce attorney. An unpleasant business we're trying to make less dull by meeting out of the office."

"Cy Stevens." The man held out his hand and briefly shook everyone's. "Rich, I'm heading out. Call me first thing on Monday."

"I will." Richard lifted his drink in a vague wave. "Try to get an answer about... Well, we'll talk Monday."

Julia watched the interplay between the two men with keen interest. There was something very unhappy about Richard's expression, though he was trying hard to hide it.

Michael quickly changed the subject. "Richard, you missed a great Sunday Dinner last week."

Richard glanced at Vivian. "I haven't been to one of those in months. Lily claimed it."

"Not possible." Michael snagged two more glasses of champagne from a passing waiter and resupplied Vivian and Julia. "Sunday Dinner is for everyone."

Vivian caught Julia's eye and nodded to the side. Julia

glanced over and saw Evy poking her head out from behind a large room divider, trying to get their attention.

"Michael, would you excuse us for a moment?" Julia touched his arm. "We're going to go find the ladies' room."

"Of course."

Richard nodded at them, but his eyes lingered on Vivian. "Ladies, it was a pleasure to meet you."

Vivian and Julia walked away, heading toward where Evy had disappeared.

"Do you think she's been able to read anyone?" Vivian asked.

"Impossible to know. There are so many people here." Julia saw Evy heading toward a back hallway and followed her. To the right was another hallway that led toward marked restrooms, and to the left appeared to be an office. "I wonder if it's just too much at once."

Evy went to the left and then quickly twisted the doorknob to enter the darkened office. Julia and Vivian ducked inside; then Evy slammed the door and flipped on the light.

"This is impossible!" Evy was panicked. "I have been hiding back here for an hour now, trying to pick up single threads of thoughts with Geoff here." She pointed at the desk chair where Geoff was sitting like he had a meeting in five. Ghost Geoff was on a sofa, lounging and reading the covers of the magazines on the coffee table.

Vivian nodded. "Take a breath. It sounds like it's not going well."

"I feel like I'm going insane." Evy tucked her hair behind her ear and breathed deeply. "It's like walking into a party but everyone is shouting at the top of their lungs, and what they're shouting doesn't even make sense. It's just disjointed words and phrases. Sometimes I'm just getting flashes of images, and it all jumbles together." She took a shaky breath. "I can't do this."

Vivian took Evy's hands. "Yes, you can. This is why you need to practice. Everyone in this room shouting at you would be impossible to read. There has to be a way to muffle some thoughts and focus. Do people's thoughts sound like their voices?"

Evy nodded. "I think so. Yes. Mostly."

"Okay, so you need to focus on following a single voice." Vivian nodded. "Can you do that? Just focus on a single voice and forget everyone else?"

"I mean, I could try, but I don't know how—"

"What about him?" Julia pointed at Geoffrey. "Maybe he can help."

Geoffrey came to attention. "You believe I can be of service?"

"I'm wondering..." Julia turned to Evy. "What if Geoffrey followed *us*?" She turned to the ghost. "You can go a distance from the dummy, right?"

"I prefer that you call him a puppet or doll, but yes."

"Okay, so you can go a little ways from the *puppet*." She turned back to Evy. "Why doesn't Geoffrey the ghost follow us? Maybe he could act like an antenna or something. Focus the energy. He's like... an extension of the doll, I think. Maybe if Geoffrey is focusing in on one person, you could too."

Vivian nodded. "That's a good idea. We can try it."

Evy screwed up her face. "Is that logical though? I mean, I know the doll and the ghost are connected, but—"

"Is any of this logical?" Julia said. "I'm seeing spirits everywhere I go, Vivian is getting handsy with perfect strangers—"

"Do you really need to put it like that?"

"—and I'm on a date with a rich, famous film director," Julia finished. "None of this is logical, Evy. Not a single damn thing."

"Okay." Evy picked up Geoff and took a deep breath. "Let's try it."

Chapter Seventeen

Julia and Vivian left Evy in the back office with Geoff and a promise to return with champagne and at least three shrimp cocktails. Geoffrey the ghost followed them into the packed room.

"Quick, before we get back," Julia said. "What were you getting off Richard?"

"I definitely think he's hiding something. Also, he's attracted to me, which is weird."

Julia looked at her. "Why is that weird? You're a very beautiful woman."

"It's more the fact that we suspect he killed someone," Vivian said. "Normally he's *so* my type. I love breaking uptight bankers out of their shells as long as they don't have a weird Asian-girl fetish."

"Weird Asian... Oh." Julia wrinkled her nose. "Yeah, I know that guy."

"It's always a risk." She plastered on a smile as they approached Michael and Richard, who were still chatting. "Gentlemen, so nice to see you again."

Michael had a look on his face that Julia couldn't read but

she definitely wanted to ask about. That was until he turned to her. Then his face read all the things she found attractive.

Delight.

Humor.

Warmth.

Warning sirens were sounding. She could fall for him, and then she'd be stuck. She'd have to try a *relationship* again and not just casual dating to satisfy Sergio's relentless meddling.

Geoffrey was no help at all. "That man likes you very much, Miss Brooks."

"Quiet, Geoffrey," she muttered. "Michael! You're still looking at the bronzes."

His smile got wider. "We were waiting for you and Vivian. Your champagne got warm, so I tossed it and grabbed you another one."

"Thanks." Dammit, he was thoughtful too. "That's probably not ecologically responsible, but I can't bring myself to care."

"Life is too short to drink room-temperature champagne."

She took the glass of bubbling wine. "That sounds like a line from a movie."

Michael narrowed his eyes. "I think it might be. Probably a bad sign when I start quoting my own films, right?"

"I think it depends on the film."

"Good point."

He was everything Julia usually avoided, especially since her cardiac event. He had "serious relationship" written all over his handsome face. Plus he was her age, which only made him more dangerous. Men her age—who weren't in the midst of a midlife crisis—were focused and relentless when they saw something they wanted. Julia had dropped one relationship entirely when the man asked her on the fourth date if she was ready to get serious.

She didn't need that kind of pressure in her life.

Julia nodded at Richard and Vivian, who were engaged in an animated conversation in front of one of the bronze sculptures. Geoffrey, true to his assignment, was hovering nearby.

Julia leaned closer to Michael. "I think Vivian and Richard hit it off."

"He's attracted to smart women, so I'm not surprised." That inscrutable look she'd seen earlier crossed his face again. "Maybe warn her... I don't know where *she* is in life, but he has some unsettled business before he's free."

A dozen questions burned the tip of her tongue, but she tried to keep her expression relaxed. "The divorce, right?" She grimaced. "Those can take forever. I'll be sure to fill her in."

"Good." Michael looked both regretful and relieved. "I'm not saying he's not a solid guy—I wouldn't be friends with him if he wasn't—"

"No, I get what you're saying." She played along. "Life is complicated enough, right?"

Michael sipped his cocktail and played with the collar of her jacket. "Some people come into your life at the exact right time, don't they? And others...?" He raised his eyebrows. "It can kill or make a thing, can't it? Timing."

"Very true." Why wasn't now a good time for Richard if his ex had already moved on? "Have Richard and Lily ever talked about reconciling?"

"God no." Michael shook his head. "That's not the reason. I just think... I mean, I think some things could still get ugly with the two of them—they're both public figures—and I hate the idea of your friend being caught up in all that unless she knows ahead of time, you know?"

"I'd hate that too." *Especially if Richard is a murderer.* Julia looked around the room. "You can definitely tell the visitors versus the locals. Everyone who lives here is tan."

Michael smiled. "Yes. They are. Tanning goes in and out of

fashion in LA, but not here. Here, it's always part of the outfit, you know?"

"Sunlight is the best disinfectant." Julia nodded at a tiny white-haired maven wearing a chic black dress. She was half bent over, walking with a cane, and holding a large brandy snifter. "Maybe that's her secret."

"You'd think nobody would have any secrets with all that sunshine," Michael said. "But you'd be surprised. Desert sunshine makes for dark shadows."

Julia turned to Michael, whose eyes had turned back to his friend. "Now you're definitely quoting one of your movies."

"Am I?" Michael laughed and the worry left this eyes. "The question is, do you remember which one?"

Julia smiled, but inside, she was seeing flashes of the murder board at Evy's house.

Lily and Richard.

Lily and Justin.

Richard and the blond woman.

Richard and Michael.

She sipped her champagne and laughed along with her date, keeping an eye on Vivian as she flirted with Richard and touched his hand numerous times. There were a few moments where Vivian flinched, but it was barely noticeable.

What are you hiding, Richard?

And what did Michael know?

TWO HOURS LATER, VIVIAN AND JULIA SAT IN EVY'S living room as Evy devoured a plate of mini quiches, bacon-wrapped asparagus, and tiny finger sandwiches along with a half bottle of leftover champagne.

"You know" —Evy sipped the cold sparkling wine— "being

friends with Sergio can be a pain in the ass sometimes, but he definitely knows how to feed a girl."

"I'm dying to know what you got off Richard." Julia tore her eyes from the finger sandwiches. She'd barely eaten, she'd been so nervous juggling a date and a murder investigation.

"I feel like I have whiplash," Vivian said. "Mostly he was really interesting. Warm, and I felt this really low buzz of amusement from him. Like, I get the feeling he has a very dry, very low-key sense of humor."

Evy blinked. "Excuse me, suspect profile, not dating profile?"

"I'm just saying if we clear him, I'm definitely asking him out." Vivian tucked her long hair behind her ear. "So most of it was pretty standard, nothing surprising, but then he'd get these random punches of serious anger." Her eyes went wide. "Like, white-hot rage kind of anger."

"Just randomly?"

"I was trying to figure out what triggered it, but maybe it was something he was just remembering. You know how sometimes you'll forget about something and then it pops into your head and it makes you mad even though it happened in the past?"

"Oh!" Julia sat up straight. "The conversation with his lawyer. They were talking right before we met them."

Vivian nodded. "That would make sense. But what would his divorce lawyer have told him that would make him that angry?"

"Something about the Putnam Diamond, maybe?" Evy nibbled on an asparagus spear. "Or the house?"

"Either of those would probably piss him off," Julia said. "The question is, do you think Richard is capable of killing Justin?"

Justin appeared, sitting next to Evy on the couch. "Nah.

That dude's old. It was probably the diamond. Richard was obsessed with it because of his family or something."

"Richard seemed perfectly fit to me." Julia narrowed her eyes. "And the police never found the murder weapon. All it took was one blow to your head."

"From something heavy," Justin countered. "You think that guy could lift a rock?"

Evy asked, "Speaking of the murder weapon—"

"Wait." Julia caught on something Justin had said. "You said he couldn't have lifted a rock. Is that what it was? Were you killed with a rock?"

"It would make sense," Vivian said. "There was a lot of decorative rock in the landscaping. Most of it was river rock, so it was smooth and probably wouldn't have left a trace on the body like granite or sandstone."

"True." Evy picked up the bottle and refilled her champagne. "And once you kill the victim, you wash it off and toss it back in the yard with the other thousand rocks. Who's going to look for it?"

"Um, hello!" Justin raised his hand. "I'm here. Do they know I'm here?"

"And you never answered me," Julia said. "Do you think it was a rock that hit you?"

"How am I supposed to know? I died, remember? My memory's still a little fuzzy."

"Then why did you say *rock* just now?"

"I don't know. It was something Lily used to say, I guess. 'I couldn't lift a rock, darling.' Something like that." He frowned. "Actually, that's kind of a weird saying, isn't it?"

Julia narrowed her eyes, but it didn't seem like Justin was lying.

Could the dead lie? That was a good question. She needed to ask Elton or Mrs. G. "I think the point that's important here is whether or not Richard seems capable of murder. What did his thoughts say, Evy? Did having Geoffrey there help?"

The dummy was carefully tucked away, and Ghost Geoffrey had faded once they arrived home. Evy took a deep breath. "It was very jumbled. I don't think I ever realized before how fragmented people's thoughts are. And half of them aren't even verbal. They're images and sounds and scents, and I can't really sense those, it's more of an impression. Richard was thinking about that blond girl quite a bit, but not in any kind of sexy way." She closed her eyes. "He thought about Vivian naked about three times, but it was pretty brief and he wasn't picturing her doing anything gross. Just flashes."

"Weird." Vivian frowned. "Do men usually picture women naked that soon?"

"Yeah," Justin said. "That sounds about right. I've already imagined all three of you naked, and you're like my mom's age."

"You're twenty-eight!"

"So?"

Vivian held up a hand. "What are you saying to the ghost?"

"I have a name!"

Julia ignored his petulant complaint. "Justin was saying that Richard picturing you naked during your first conversation really isn't all that uncommon."

Evy grimaced. "Why are men?"

"Why are men what?"

"Just... why?" She shrugged. "I don't have the rest of that thought, I'm too tired. Do I think Richard is capable of killing someone who wounded his pride and stole his wife? Yes. I listened to his thoughts, and I think he's a cold one. It wouldn't be a crime of passion, but he's capable."

Vivian pointed at Evy. "Okay, I agree with that last part. It *wouldn't* be a crime of passion, because I don't get that from him. If he did it, it would be calculated. Part of that is just intuition; I'm usually attracted to very organized, analytical men."

"I agree with both of you." Julia sat back in her chair. "So where does that leave us? Richard is capable of murdering Justin and maybe hit him on the back of the head with a rock, but we have no way of proving that."

"And for the record" —Justin raised his hand again— "I don't think it was Richard. He's a pussy."

"Maybe we need to talk to the police again," Vivian said. "Or at least try to. They have to know what the murder weapon is by now, right?"

"Dean golfs with the chief of police," Evy said. "Guy named John Marcos. I know because he did a department fundraiser there and they called me for entertainment, but I was already booked that night. I guess Dean recommended me."

Julia thought about it. "Maybe Dean could tell me when the chief of police is golfing and I could happen to run into him."

"Incidentally," Evy said. "Dean's club is also Richard's and Lily's club. As far as I know, they still have joint membership."

Vivian wrinkled her nose. "How do you settle that in a divorce? Is it a shared custody arrangement of some kind? I get the snotty country-club friends on Easter if you want them at Christmas?"

"All I know is that according to Sergio, it's definitely made their social life more complicated. I think Lily considers all of Palm Springs her friends and she doesn't feel like sharing."

"The blond woman." Julia was still thinking it over. "Maybe that's what he's hiding? Maybe that's what Michael found out about?"

Vivian blinked. "Sorry, you lost me. What about the blond woman?"

Julia pointed to Evy. "She said that Richard kept thinking about the blond woman randomly. And you said that he would get flashes of anger. And when I was with Michael, I kept getting the feeling that there was something he knew or had just found out and he was hiding it. Maybe this is all about that girl." She looked at Vivian. "He wanted me to warn you, by the way. About Richard."

"What about?"

Julia frowned. "It was interesting. He said that things could still get ugly between Richard and Lily. I think... maybe he does know about Richard's little affair now. He warned me that Richard had some things to work out before he was free. What exactly did he say?" She searched her memory. "Unsettled business." Julia looked at Vivian. "That's what he warned me to tell you. That Richard had some unsettled business before he was free. Implied something about tabloids getting involved."

Vivian narrowed her eyes and looked at Richard's picture on the board. "Interesting. And interesting that he'd mention it to you. Richard is his friend."

"Is it weird that it makes me like him more for looking out for my friend that he's just met?"

Vivian looked over her shoulder. "No, I think it's nice."

"Cool."

"Could Richard have told Michael something about Lily?" Evy asked. "Or something about the blonde?"

"Well, that's a five-thousand-dollar question." Vivian pulled a business card from her purse. "Good thing I'm going to have a cancellation on Monday."

"Because?"

Vivian pressed her lips together. "It's possible that someone we met tonight mentioned that he might have a loose crown. But I cannot tell you who it is because that would violate HIPAA."

Julia smiled. "Clever Vivian."

She wrinkled her nose. "Is it bad that I'm really hoping it isn't him because I want to ask him out?"

"Hey." Evy pointed to the murder board. "Julia is already dating one suspect in this case. No reason for you not to date the other."

"That just leaves Lily, the blond lady, and the unknown burglar for you, Evy."

"I'm going to have to go with Lily," Evy said. "She wouldn't be the first woman I've kissed, but if she's a murderer, she could be the last."

"Not to put a damper on Evy's dating," Julia said, "but while Vivian is fixing... this mystery person's crown and I'm pestering Dean about meeting the chief of police, maybe Evy can go to the library."

Evy blinked. "Why?"

"Research." Julia was still thinking about another blond woman, one they knew even less about than the girl they'd seen with Richard. "The ghost at Casa de Lirio," she said. "According to Elton, she's not happy there, meaning it's possible she's stuck there because that's where she died. According to Dean, no one matching her description ever *lived* at the house. And according to Michael, Richard and Lily had a lot of wild parties but he'd never heard of anyone dying at one."

"Wild parties?" Vivian asked. "You think the ghost you saw died at one?"

"If she did, it would probably be in the paper, right?" Julia looked at Evy. "Let's try to find out if anyone else died or was killed at Casa de Lirio."

Chapter Eighteen

Monte Verde Country Club was an institution in Palm Springs. Only a few short blocks from the Vista de Lirio neighborhood, it was hidden behind high hedges, decorative walls, and a general air of exclusivity.

Dean and Sergio were members because Sergio's mother had been an avid tennis player and they'd fallen into the membership. They kept it up because Dean enjoyed his rounds of golf, it was good for business, and the girls enjoyed the screams of surprise when they snuck Paco onto the golf course every now and then.

Dean had arranged a meeting with Chief John Marcos on Monday afternoon, so Julia wandered in a little before lunch, just in time to pick up the day pass Sergio had left for her. She tucked it into her clutch and waved at Dean from the hostess stand of the club restaurant.

"I see my friend, thanks."

"Hey!" Dean rose and waved her over. He bent down to kiss her cheek. "I'm meeting John in a few minutes for lunch." He kept his voice low. "Told him it was about a commercial property the police department owns, but I'll tell him I ran into you, and you should be able to steer the conversation around."

"If you feel like I'm being too obvious or forward, give me a sign. I don't want him to start poking into my life after this, and we only met the one time."

"I will."

"Thank you so much for this." She sat down and put her purse in a spare chair. "I didn't see you at the gallery opening."

He shrugged. "It was his third this month. I bowed out and watched a movie with the girls."

"Still on the horror kick?"

"It was *The Birds*. They've seen it like five times now, but they claim it never gets old." He opened his menu, scanning the restaurant. "John just walked in."

"I'll order a drink then." She waved for a waiter. "He won't make me leave if I'm drinking."

The handsome Chief Marcos walked to the table just as the server was leaving with Julia's drink order.

"John." Dean rose and shook the man's hand. "You remember Julia, right? She was just passing by and joined me for a drink."

Julia turned and beamed her thousand-watt smile at John Marcos. "Hi! It's nice to see you again."

"Miss Brooks." He held out his hand to shake. "It looks like you're recovered from your fright. How are you?"

"Doing well."

"Excellent." He took the chair nearest the window, facing the door where he'd walked in. "I never got why you decided to move out to Palm Springs, Miss Brooks."

"Please call me Julia."

Dean said, "Julia dominated the residential market in our territory in LA, so she's here to work her magic in Palm Springs while I focus more on the commercial stuff." He reached for his drink. "Wish we'd given her a better welcome though."

Marcos frowned, then nodded. "Right. The homicide."

'Don't remind me." She reached for the whiskey sour the server had brought her. 'You must be up to your neck in work with that case, right? I know the crime statistics in Palm Springs are low. You probably don't get too many murder cases."

'Not many," Marcos said. 'Unfortunately, random homicides like Mr. Worthy's are the hardest to solve. It appears that he surprised a thief or a vagrant. That person could be halfway to New York by now." The man shook his head and opened the menu. 'It's a shame."

'So you don't think it had anything to do with him personally?" Julia asked. 'You're sure it was random?"

Marcos lifted a shoulder but didn't take his eyes off the menu. 'It's unfortunate, but these kinds of things often remain a mystery. By and large, Palm Springs is a very safe town. Tragedies do happen, but they happen everywhere. I don't think you have anything to worry about."

Julia exchanged a look with Dean, and he gave her an encouraging nod.

'I heard the police found the murder weapon," Julia said. 'A tire iron or something like that?"

Marcos looked up. 'Who'd you hear that from? Sorry, I can't comment on an open case, but that's not accurate. I'd be careful listening to gossip, Miss Brooks."

'Julia." She smiled.

'Right." John Marcos nodded. 'Julia. Just be careful. Lots of rumors tend to fly during times like this."

She leaned forward, resting her chin in her palm and giving Marcos her full attention. 'I'll keep that in mind. I confess, I've had a kind of... morbid curiosity about all of it. Seeing Justin's body was a shock."

'I'm sure it was." He offered her a sympathetic smile. 'But don't worry about that; I really don't think there's a murderer stalking the neighborhood or anything." He turned his attention to Dean. "I heard the repairs to the house were substantial. How's that going?"

Dean motioned to Julia. "On track, right, Julia?"

"I'm happy to say it's going well. I do worry we're going to stumble onto something that might freak out the workmen though."

Marcos waved a hand, still perusing the menu. "I wouldn't be concerned about it."

Just get the french dip. It's a country club; that's what you get for lunch between rounds of golf. Julia was careful to keep her smile steady as Marcos hemmed and hawed.

Finally the server came, took their orders, and left. As expected, John Marcos got the french dip.

"So we don't need to worry about finding any evidence?" Julia sipped her drink. "I'll let the workers know."

"Despite what it shows on television, Julia, it's often quite difficult to determine a murder weapon if it's not a firearm. Mr. Worthy was hit on the back of the head hard enough to fracture his skull, and he died from internal bleeding. Whatever hit him was probably something the vagrant found at the scene." He smiled. "I'm sure you had to deal with your share of the homeless in LA too."

"Yes, but in LA, the homeless population are far more likely to be victims of crimes than criminals." She sipped her whiskey sour. "Is it different here?"

Chief Marcos's smile faltered for a moment, but it held. "Palm Springs is a friendly town. Unfortunately, not everyone belongs here."

What does that mean? Julia narrowed her eyes a little. "Did Justin Worthy belong here?"

"Whether he did or not, Palm Springs loved him. I believe he was particularly fond of the *female* residents." The corner of the chief's mouth curled up.

"I've heard the same thing, which is why it seems so strange that his death wasn't related to that." She toyed with the edge of her glass. "You've questioned Lily's ex, I'm sure."

Chief Marcos smiled. "If you knew Richard Putnam, you'd know how ridiculous that assumption is."

Ah, it made sense now. Richard and the police chief were buddies.

"Dean, why don't you tell me why I should let you sell this piece of property for us while we're waiting for lunch?" He glanced at Julia. "And speaking of Richard, we have a tee time this afternoon. Any desire to join?"

Dean glanced at Julia, who gave him a subtle nod. It couldn't hurt to have Dean eavesdrop a little since Richard and the chief of police were so buddy-buddy.

"Sounds like a plan. Julia, are you sure you don't want to join us for lunch?"

From looking at John Marcos, it was pretty clear the man was set on his theory that a random homeless person had broken into Casa de Lirio and killed Justin.

He'd moved on, but Julia did have the distinct impression that the murder weapon had been a rock or something else at the scene. She'd have to go back and take another look.

"I think I'm going to head out. I have some work to do at the office this afternoon and a few appointments." She rose, and Dean and John Marcos stood with her. "But it was so nice to see you again, Chief Marcos."

"Call me John." He shook her hand. "Nice to see you again too. And again, I'm sorry you had such a shocking introduction to the city. I assure you, you're perfectly safe."

"Thanks." She gave both of them a small wave and left the club dining room, only to run into Lily Putnam crossing the lobby.

"Juliana!" Lily exclaimed. "Did you already join the club?"

Her enthusiastic greeting caught Julia off guard. "Oh, I... It's just Julia. Juliana is Dean and Sergio's daughter. And I'm thinking about it." She wasn't usually a fan of country clubs, but it might be a necessary evil for work. "Dean and Sergio are members and they love it."

Lily gave her a little squinty smile. "Of course. I'm so silly. I'm also on the membership committee for Monte Verde, so if you have any questions at all, just ask me. Then again, I'm sure Dean and Sergio would probably answer any questions you have."

"Always good to get a female perspective though."

Lily pointed at her. "Very true!"

Julia glanced at the bar, which was empty and separate from the dining room. "I was just thinking of getting a drink. Care to join me? I'd love to talk to you about the house. I was thinking about doing an open house, and I'd like your input. I don't want to make it public, but an exclusive event of some kind would be—"

"That's a wonderful idea, we should definitely..." Lily paused, seeming to waver. "I... I'd like to, but I just don't have time right now. So much to do."

"Then we'll meet another time." Julia put a hand on her arm. "Don't worry about it. It was nice to see you. Glad to see you're looking well."

"I'm sleeping better." Lily's eyes softened. "It's been hard, and..." For a moment, she didn't look like a stunning bombshell. She looked tired and old and sad. "I just miss Justin so much."

VIVIAN CALLED WHILE JULIA WAS DRIVING BACK TO Sergio and Dean's.

"Julia." It sounded like Vivian was whispering. "Meet me over at Sunrise Park by the library parking lot."

"I'm supposed to have lunch with— Why are you whispering?"

"Um..." Her voice returned to normal. "I don't know actually. I followed Richard and I'm feeling sneaky?"

"You followed Richard?"

"For psychic reasons! I'm not a stalker."

Julia shook her head. "Okay, I have a little bit of time; I'll meet you there. I'm about ten minutes away."

"Okay."

She turned left and headed across town to Sunrise Park. By the time she arrived, Vivian was outside her car, leaning on the hood and checking her phone.

"Hi." Julia closed her car door and walked toward Vivian. "Why am I here?"

"I wanted company on the stakeout."

"Stakeout?"

Vivian glanced across the street, nodding at the entrance of a senior living facility across from the library. "He's still in there. I decided to follow him after... a thing. Side note: He has really great teeth."

"Focus." Julia leaned on the car next to her friend.

"Right, so I followed him, but he didn't go home. He drove back toward Vista de Lirio, swung by his house, then continued on to this apartment building over by the architecture museum, and guess who he picked up?" Vivian looked over at Julia with a raised eyebrow.

"The blond girl?"

Vivian nodded. "Now that I've had a good look at her, I don't think she's that young. I'd put her late twenties."

"That's still, like, half his ex-wife's age."

"And right around Justin's age too." Vivian shrugged. "Kind of weird to think he'd be into that after talking to him, but there you go. So he picks up the blond girl and then heads over here."

"Interesting." Did Richard have a parent at the retirement home? "How long has he been in there?"

"About thirty minutes so far. I called when I realized he was there for a visit." She looked at Julia. "Mother?"

"He's midsixties, right? He could have one or both parents in senior living."

"That place looks like a swanky resort."

Julia smiled. "That's the idea."

"My parents would kill me if I ever put them in a retirement home."

"My parents put themselves in one," Julia said. "They're in Hilton Head, near my sister and her family. They play golf every day; it's like living at a country club."

"Ahhhh." Vivian looked at her with new eyes. "Is that a little bit of a Southern accent I hear?"

Julia smiled. "It comes out more when I get pissed off. I grew up in the Carolinas, but I came out to California for college and never looked back. I've been here for over thirty years now." Her eyes went wide. "God, I feel old."

"You're not, but I have to tell you, I give it about three years before my parents abandon the cold winters and move down here like my grandparents did. They complain more every year."

"This is why I need to get you into a better house, and that way your parents— Oh!" Julia scooted closer to Vivian. "Is that him?"

Richard Putnam was walking out the front doors of the Desert Oasis Retirement Club, and it was impossible not to see he was troubled.

"Whoever he came to see isn't doing well," Vivian said. "That's a shame."

"Where's the blonde?"

Vivian craned her neck. "I think... there. She was in the office."

"Taking the new flame to meet his mother maybe?" Julia's mind was going wild. "If she's ill, he may not want to take the chance of them not meeting."

The blond woman jogged up to Richard, who held his hand out. She took it, and he wrapped their arms together, tucking the young woman into his side.

She leaned her head toward him and said something they couldn't hear.

"They seem nice." Vivian sounded sad. "He must flirt with everyone."

"Just remind yourself there are plenty of great men in Palm Springs, and most of them aren't possible murderers."

"Good point," Vivian said. "Oh, they're getting in the car."

"Should we follow them?"

Vivian was already opening her car door, so Julia didn't ask again. She slid inside Vivian's car, shut the door, and buckled up as Vivian backed out and sped out of the parking lot after the dark green Mercedes SUV.

They followed the car down Ramon Road, heading toward the checkerboard of strip malls, golf courses, and planned communities in Rancho Mirage.

They turned right off the main road and onto a lush thoroughfare lined with palm trees and rolling lawns. High walls protected most of the residential development, and a stark red wall outlined the familiar boundary of Desert Prep Academy, the swanky school where Sergio and Dean sent the girls.

"Hold up." Julia lifted her hand, and Vivian slowed down, driving past the school as Richard drove in.

"You know this place?"

"It's where my nieces go." She watched as the blond woman got out of the SUV and walked into the main office.

A moment later, Richard's SUV turned left out of the driveway and headed back toward the highway.

"Is Richard Putnam's new girlfriend a teacher at Juliana and Aurelia's school?"

"Maybe," Vivian said. "For that matter, maybe she's a parent."

Julia was dying to figure out who this woman was.

Maybe it was time to ask Michael.

Chapter Nineteen

After Vivian took her back to her car, Julia drove down Palm Canyon Drive, turning in to a small shopping center and finding a place to park so she could meet her actual lunch date. Michael had called her that morning and asked to meet her at a small French bistro for a late lunch.

With Vivian back at her office and Evy—hopefully—finding answers at the library, it felt like the perfect time to take a break and *not* think about murder or ghosts while she had a meal with her favorite sort-of-retired film director. She didn't even want to ask him if he'd met Richard's new girlfriend, she just wanted him to smile at her and act cute.

She walked between two stunning floral beds, marveling that while the rest of the country was deep in the middle of winter, life in Palm Springs was blissfully warm. Flowers burst all around her, and the sun was shining through puffy white clouds.

No wonder the snowbirds love you.

She spotted Michael leaning against a post near a fountain in the courtyard. He was wearing sunglasses, and he appeared to be watching the bird feeder in the garden.

So stinking cute.

Julia walked to him and tapped him on the shoulder. "Hey."

He turned and smiled. He hadn't shaved that morning, and his stubble sparkled silver in the sunlight. "Hey."

"You're never on your phone."

He frowned. "What? Did I miss a text or something?"

"No, I mean every time I see you waiting or just hanging around, you're never on your phone. These days, it's a notable characteristic."

"Oh." The corner of his mouth turned up. "Real life is more interesting, right? Or maybe it's just slower." He shrugged one shoulder. "I've spent a lot of my life looking at screens and through lenses. I think I burned out on it a little."

Julia narrowed her eyes. "Why are you so charming?"

He angled his shoulders toward her. "Why are you so interesting?"

"You're a very non-Hollywood Hollywood person."

"And you're very sarcastic for a real estate agent."

Julia had to smile. "And yet you're still hanging around."

"It's your looks." Michael nodded slowly. "I'm one hundred percent still trying to hit that; then I'll stop being charming and go back to my bastard ways."

"I would have an easier time believing that if you hadn't been ignoring that actress-model-influencer at the gallery opening who very definitely wanted to sleep with you."

The corner of his mouth twitched. "I learned pretty early in my career how to spot people who only want something from me. Maybe..." He hooked his finger through her belt loop. "... that's why I'm still hanging around."

Julia glanced around the courtyard. "I'm going to kiss you now. Right here in front of God and the teenage hostess. Are you prepared for that?"

"It would definitely speed up the whole hit-it-and-quit-it plan." He leaned down, and she could feel his breath on her lips. "Go for it."

"Are you ready though? I'm a very sarcastic kisser."

"If you keep talking about it, you're going to kill the—"

She kissed him. His stubble scratched the edge of her lips, and she nipped the corner of his mouth. He quickly took control, biting her lower lip softly and licking out to tease her mouth. Michael slid his arm around her waist and pulled her closer, pressing their bodies together and holding her.

Right there.

One perfect, shining moment.

Julia could hardly breathe. One hand rested on her hip and the other cradled her face, holding her mouth while their lips met in a slow, luxurious dance.

You could tell a lot about a man by the way he kissed, and Julia already knew that when they slept together, Michael was not going to rush. It would be slow and thorough, and just like this kiss, it would likely wreck her.

He released her and straightened his shoulders, looking down at her with the hint of a smile. "You aren't a sarcastic kisser."

She ran the tip of her tongue over her lower lip and cleared her throat. "The secret is out."

Michael leaned down again and brushed his lips next to her ear. "You're a little spicy though with that bite. But don't worry, I'm not telling." He pressed his lips right below her ear, and she barely kept herself from a full-body shiver.

"Good." She swallowed hard. "Otherwise I'd be forced to publicize that you're not a shallow creep."

"Wow. Way to threaten my reputation." He put an arm around her shoulder. "Come on, Brooks. Feed me or I'm taking another bite out of you."

JULIA SPENT TWO BLISSFUL HOURS NOT THINKING about ghosts at all; then she had to stop by a florist and try to imagine what a sad female ghost might want as an offering.

Her interest had been piqued when Vivian mentioned bringing offerings to the spirits. She started thinking seriously about what a spirit might enjoy and if bringing something to the woman at Casa de Lirio would make a difference.

Flowers seemed obvious, but what else? She picked out a bunch of stargazer lilies with their vivid scent and dramatic bloom.

Casa de Lirio. House of the Lilies. It seemed appropriate.

"What else?" she muttered on her way back to the car.

She opened the door, put the florist box inside, and started the engine. Then she realized she had an inside track. "Justin!"

She had been feeling him all day, but he'd been quiet during lunch with Michael. He was learning and so was she. Julia had realized that she could block him when she was out and running around. In Vista de Lirio? Not so much. But he wasn't as strong away from the neighborhood.

"You rang?" He appeared in the back seat, looking bored. "You're a busy bee today. The police chief, Vivian, Michael the asshole. You even saw Lily."

Julia frowned. "You're right. I'm usually way more of a hermit. But that's not important. What kind of presents should I give a ghost?"

"The souls of your enemies."

"Ha ha." He was joking. Right? "I'm talking about the sad lady at Casa de Lirio. Can you smell these lilies I got?"

"Um, no. I don't actually have a body anymore, so seeing stuff is pretty much the extent of my sensory experience these days. And hearing things, I guess."

"Okay, good to know." So pretty things. Bright things. Something that made sound. "Flowers would be good," she said. "Lots and lots of them."

"I mean..." Justin looked confused. "She lives at Casa de Lirio, so she's surrounded by gardens, but okay."

"Something visually interesting," Julia said, "that isn't flowers. And doesn't plug in because I don't want to leave stuff running while the house is empty." She slapped her leg when she thought of it. "Yes! I'll go to the pool store right now."

"What are you talking about?"

"Just wait and see."

SHE TOOK TWO LARGE BAGS FROM HER CAR AND walked through the garden gate with Justin trailing behind her. This time the gate was locked and Julia felt sure that she was the only living person at Casa de Lirio.

The sun was just starting to go down, so the light show might not be quite as brilliant as it would be the next night, but she was hoping the battery had a little charge. According to what she'd read online, sunset was a good time to make an offering to a ghost.

Justin walked with her, his energy bristling near the site of his death. "So you're trying to get the tall blond lady to talk to you? According to Elton and Mae, she doesn't talk to many people at all."

"Vivian mentioned bringing an offering for the spirits." There was a jumble of things in the bags she was carrying, stuff she'd been collecting ever since Vivian mentioned it, and the last few items she'd picked up that afternoon. "I think I have some ideas that might make her a little friendlier to me."

They walked across the lush green lawn and veered toward the left, going around the house and into the side yard of the estate.

"Like what? Whiskey and cigarettes?"

"Ha ha." She smiled. "Wait and see."

"You never bring offerings to me," Justin said. "And I'm with you all the time."

"I know. We're trying to get rid of you, remember?"

He nodded. "Oh right. You know, if finding my murderer doesn't work, I might have to hang out here and wait for that damn door to open."

"Did you see one right after you died?"

"Maybe?" Justin shook his head. "I was so shocked I wasn't looking. If I'd known I was going to die, maybe I would have been looking for one, but I didn't."

"I have a feeling that may be where ghosts come from," Julia said. "People who were too shocked by their own deaths to move on."

They walked through the palm garden and made their way toward the pool and the cabanas in the backyard. In the distance, the portal offered a slight shimmer, but it was nowhere near as visible as it had been on their second visit.

"It's there all the time," Julia said. "But it doesn't show up all the time."

"That's what I hear." Justin walked over to a lounge chair and stared at the horizon. "The sun is setting."

"Perfect." Julia walked to a table and started unloading the bags.

First she pulled out a candle scented with plumeria. There were potted plumeria in all the alcoves, but most hadn't started to flower yet. She lit the candle and set it in the interior patio where she'd seen the ghost the first time.

Then she set out the stargazer lilies and a rope of beautiful bright marigolds she'd seen someone selling at a roadside stand. Next to them, she set out a bottle of spring water and a cut-crystal glass. She hung a pretty, crystalline wind chime on a potted lemon tree where it immediately began to move from the evening breeze coming off the mountain. It filled the air with delicate music.

Lastly, she brought out a floating solar light fountain. It might have seemed a little cheesy to an interior designer, but fuck it. It was pretty, it made lights flash on the bottom of the pool, and it shot up little jets of water that sparkled in the bright rainbow lights and created a pretty tinkling sound on the surface of the pool.

Julia set it in the water and watched with delight as the light show started in the pool. The sun set along the horizon, and she felt the breeze shift. The delicate sound of the fountain joined the wind chime and the rustling palms; a sense of peace settled over her.

She felt the tension headache drain away. Her breath grew slower and deeper.

"Thank you."

Julia turned and saw the beautiful woman in the white bathing suit standing at the edge of the water, staring at the fountain.

"I'm glad you like it."

"I haven't talked to anyone living in a long time." The woman's voice was surprisingly low and a little husky. "Does it have batteries?"

"No, it runs off the sun." Julia glanced at the horizon. "It probably won't stay on very long tonight, but hopefully tomorrow it will charge all the way."

"I don't feel time the way you do." The ghost stared at the dancing water. "When it is playing, I'll enjoy it. Thank you."

"Can you help me?"

She looked up. "How can I help *you*?"

"Do you know who killed the man in the house?" Julia tried to think like a ghost. "It wasn't very long ago. He's here with us."

"I know who you're talking about; he lived here," she said. "I never did. Not really. But now I do. She wouldn't like that."

"Who wouldn't like it?"

The ghost didn't answer, but she turned around to look at the house. "Is someone else coming to live here?"

"Eventually, yes."

"I hope they have children," the woman said. "Children make me happy. I don't know why."

Interesting. "Did you have children?"

"I don't remember." She walked slowly across the patio until she came to the palm garden. "I like the sounds here too."

"Has anyone unfamiliar been in or around the house?"

The ghost shook her head. "No. But I'm not always here."

"Where do you go?"

The woman looked across the pool and into the distance. "I go away."

Great. That was a heck of a nonanswer.

Maybe it was enough. It was enough for one night. Julia couldn't rush it. The next time she came, hopefully the woman would tell her more. "Thank you," Julia said. "I need to go, but I hope you enjoy the fountain."

The woman was already lost in her own mind. "Fountain," she whispered. "Champagne. Pool. There was a pool. Or maybe it was a shower. Was it a shower? Why can't I remember? The water was so hot—then it wasn't."

Backing away from the ghost, Julia carefully packed up the remains of her offerings, blew out the candle, and stepped toward the front of the house.

Whatever world the quiet woman was in, Julia definitely did not have an invitation. Still...

"Thank you." The whispered words came to her ears. "Thank you for everything."

Chapter Twenty

Vivian called her that night. "I forgot to ask earlier, how did it go with Chief Marcos?"

"He's still very convinced that Justin's death was random and he surprised a thief." Julia was sitting on the patio, enjoying a glass of fresh mango juice Jim had squeezed for her.

She needed a butler. Everyone needed a butler. It was amazing, and if Sergio and Dean thought she was ever leaving their pool house, they were kidding themselves.

"I didn't surprise a thief," Justin said from a lounge chair near the pool where he'd stretched out next to Mae. "Would a thief have unlocked the house and left it open? No. I did that."

"But you don't know why you went over there, so that's still completely unhelpful."

Vivian was still on the phone. "What? What's unhelpful? Are you talking to a ghost?"

"Yes, give me a second." Julia pulled her phone away. "Justin, just be quiet for right now. I'm trying to talk to Vivian. Oh shit! I just realized that I forgot to ask Mick if he knows who the blond woman with Richard is. How could I have forgotten that?"

"Senior moment," Vivian said over the phone.

"Shut your mouth, junior."

Vivian laughed.

"Fine." Justin turned away. "If you're going to ignore me, I'm not going to tell you what Mae told me then."

Mae turned and her perfectly painted red lips made a small O. "You promised!"

"I did not. You assumed."

"Vivian..." Julia sighed. "Maybe it would be better if you came over here for dinner."

"There are plenty of steaks," Jim said quietly. "And I can add to the salad and steam another artichoke if necessary."

A loud, old-fashioned horn sounded from the street, making Julia cringe. "Is that one of the neighbors?"

"No," Jim said. "I believe that's Miss Landa."

"Perfect." Julia spoke into the phone again. "Vivian, just head over to our house after work so you can fill us in and we can fill you in. Justin and Mae are hanging out and Evy just got here. Jim's making dinner."

"Does that obnoxious horn belong to Evy's car? That is truly awful."

"I'm sure that's the intension. No more questions—just come over." She turned off her phone and turned to Evy, who was walking toward them, holding up a large manila folder.

"Do you want to hear what Mae said or not?" Justin said.

"How rude!" Mae sat up and crossed pale arms over her abundant breasts. "Mr. Worthy, you are not living up to your name."

He turned in a flash from abrasive to charming. "Oh, Mae. No one could be worthy of you. That's an impossible standard to live up to."

She closed her eyes, and her lips twitched as if she was fighting a smile. "I think you're just saying that."

"I'm not and you know it." He leaned into her shoulder. "Can I tell her? It's Julia; you trust her, right?"

"It's a secret," Mae said, her blue eyes going wide. "She told me a long time ago. It's why she can't leave."

"Who?" Julia stood as Evy approached with the file. "Hey, Evy. Just talking with the ghosts. Justin and Mae are here."

"Oh good." Evy was out of breath. "Mae's been here awhile, right?"

Julia looked at Mae, who pressed her lips together and put a finger over them in a "don't tell" signal.

"I'm guessing Mae's been here since the... early sixties or so?"

Mae nodded with a smile, her blond curls bouncing in the afternoon sun.

"And she's always been in this neighborhood?"

Mae smiled a little. "It was the place I was happiest. If I was going to stay anywhere, I wanted to always be in the sun and be in a place where people were happy."

Julia smiled. "You're precious, you know that, right? Yes. Mae's always been in Vista de Lirio."

"Perfect, then ask her to tell you what she knows about Carol Stevens."

Mae frowned and shook her head. "I don't know a Carol, honey."

Julia opened the file Evy had set down on the table. "Mae says she doesn't know anyone named Carol. Could she have had a nickname?"

"I'm not sure, but I think one obituary..." Evy rifled through a pile of papers. "Here we go. This was a write-up in the *Times*. And someone..." She ran her finger over the page. "She died in 1994. It was an accident at the house, and I believe they called her..."

"Oh!" Mae said. "Is she talking about Kiki?"

"Kiki Stevens." Evy looked up. "She was a model, and her professional name was Kiki."

"That's who died at Casa de Lirio?" Julia looked between Evy and Mae.

"Yes, that's how I know her," Mae said. "She just goes by Kiki. It's so cute, isn't it?" Mae's smile fell. "Her story is so sad though."

"Okay." Julia sat down and motioned for Evy to join her. "Tell me what you know."

"YOU HAVE TO PICTURE 1994," JULIA TOLD THE TABLE. "Los Angeles, Palm Springs. Take yourself back."

Vivian, Evy, Sergio, and Dean were all sitting around and finishing their wine while Jim cleared dishes and Juliana and Aurelia prepared for bed upstairs.

"I remember the nineties," Sergio said. "Wait, is that a record compilation? Either way, I remember it. Grunge music and heroin chic. I vaguely remember Kiki Stevens, but she was always more runway than print, so not as big in LA. Nice girl though. Shy, if I'm remembering right. People called her stuck-up, but I could tell she was just quiet."

"According to the ghosts, she was right on the verge of being really famous when she died." Julia looked at Vivian. "And she was having an affair with Richard Putnam behind his wife's back."

Sergio's mouth dropped open. "No! I would never have guessed."

Julia frowned. "Are you being sarcastic? I can't tell."

"No, not sarcasm. I'm genuinely surprised by that." Sergio shook his head slowly. "Richard was not the type to sleep around back then, and definitely not with a model."

"Well, according to this ghost, they were in love. Like, *really* in love," Evy said. "But Richard wouldn't leave Lily, Lily didn't know anything about them, and then Kiki died."

'I remember her dying, but I honestly can't remember what happened," Sergio said. 'Was there an accident?"

'She died during a party at Casa de Lirio," Julia said.

Dean's eyebrows went up. 'Really?"

Sergio pursed his lips. 'Richard paid someone to keep *that* out of the papers."

'He almost succeeded," Evy said. 'I found one tiny mention in the local paper and nothing but an obituary in the *LA Times*. The local paper had one item about Kiki Stevens suffering an accidental death at Casa de Lirio, but that was all."

Julia glanced at Mae. 'But since we have *other* sources of information, we know that it wasn't an accident but an overdose of barbiturates. Kiki had a heart attack while she was in Richard and Lily's sauna. Guests found her unconscious the night of the party. An ambulance took her to the hospital, but they weren't able to save her."

'And that's who the ghost is?" Dean asked.

Julia nodded.

'That's horrible," Vivian said. 'That poor woman."

'She was only twenty-eight," Julia said. 'And the bigger story is, according to Mae, Kiki the ghost says that there was no accidental overdose because she didn't take drugs. Ever."

Everyone at the table was dead silent.

Sergio said, 'So… wait, is this ghost saying that Richard murdered her?"

'No, but she is saying that someone did. She may not think it was Richard—I mean, she's still kind of in love with him—but she does say that she never took drugs. That her mother died from alcoholism and that she was always very careful even with that. Mae believes her."

'But does Mae know anything about drugs?"

Julia pursed her lips and nodded. 'I mean, yeah, she's got a pretty good idea about that kind of stuff. And I say if Kiki thinks she was murdered, we believe her. That would fit with her ghost hanging around Casa de Lirio."

"Makes sense to me," Sergio said. "But what does this have to do with Justin's murder?"

"Twenty-eight years ago, a woman who was having an affair with Richard Putnam died under mysterious circumstances," Julia said. "And now a man who was having an affair with Lily Putnam died in the same place. That's an awfully strange coincidence."

"For what it's worth," Vivian said, "I came in contact with Richard this morning and—I hate to say it because I like him—but he's definitely hiding something. I got the same feeling of mixed attraction for me—flattering but distracting—and then reluctance, then guilt, then something else I couldn't identify that was supercomplicated and kind of... affectionate? I don't know, it was a weird one. And then also these very intense flashes of anger." Vivian nodded. "Like, white-hot anger. I had this weird impulse to pull back from him when it hit, almost as if he'd burn me. Hopefully I was able to hide that reaction."

"Did he ask you out?" Evy asked. "Any more plans to see him?"

"Did you not hear the part about me and Julia following him when he was with the blond woman?"

"But you said she might be a teacher at the girl's school."

"That doesn't mean she's not secretly dating Richard." Vivian frowned. "Besides, people tend not to make dates immediately after they've had dental work. There can be drool."

A general "Ohhhh" rose from the table.

"Yeah, that makes sense," Sergio muttered. "If he's not a murderer though, I ship it. And if he's not with the blond woman." He wiggled his eyebrows. "Vivian and Richard. You would sound like a soap opera couple!"

Evy's eyes went wide. "Oh, for sure. A soap opera couple with like... superhot chemistry but tortured romance, and they keep breaking up and every time they do, she buys another toy dog."

Sergio shook his head. "Her poor housekeeper Barbara has, like, seven of them pooping on the Persian rugs now. But Vivian can't seem to stop. It's a compulsion. She needs somewhere to channel her spurned affection."

Vivian was looking at Evy and Sergio like they'd just popped in from another planet. "Are they always like this?"

Dean and Julia exchanged a look. "Mostly yes," she said.

"Yeah," Dean added. "This is actually verging on normal for the two of them."

TWO DAYS LATER, JULIA WAS STARING AT MICHAEL from behind her dark glasses at breakfast.

"You're undressing me with your eyes," Michael whispered. "My plan is working."

She couldn't stop the smile. "I was. Sorry about that."

"Only apologize if you don't plan on following through." He looked up from the menu. "At some point, I mean. They frown on public fornication at Cristo's."

"Well, that spoils my post-mimosa plan," Julia said. "I guess we'll have to go to the gardens then."

"Sorry."

"I'd say you'd have to passionately make out with me pressed against a tree instead, but most of the trees over there are cactus and that could only end badly."

He put down the menu. "More and more, I think we need to go hiking in a very deserted forest, and not for any serial killer reasons."

The corner of her mouth turned up. "And you said I was the spicy one."

"I'm not the one making up scenarios where I have to pull

cactus spikes out of your bare ass," Michael said. "That's all you."

Julia looked up and saw that their server had been waiting for what looked like a few minutes, judging from the appalled expression on her face.

"Eggs Florentine for me." Julia smiled. "Fruit, not potatoes."

"Right. Can I get you a refill on coffee?"

She nodded, and the server sped away.

Michael watched her go. "How long do you think it's going to take for her to realize she didn't get my order?"

"Have mercy on the young ones, Michael." She sipped her ice water. "They like to pretend their elders don't have sex."

A smile made his eyes crinkle in the corners. "Do you ever get the urge to go back?"

"Where?"

"To your youth?"

"No." She shook her head. "God no. I loved my thirties more than my twenties, my forties more than my thirties, and so far my fifties are looking the best yet. Except for the whole psychic medium thing. I could get rid of that."

"Any progress solving Justin's murder?"

Your friend is having an affair with a blond woman young enough to be his daughter.

Lily was probably hiding a priceless diamond and Justin may have found it.

The ghost of a murdered woman is haunting my only real estate listing in town.

"Not really." She shook her head. "I don't know how I feel about aging, I guess, because I don't feel like I'm old enough to age. Does that make sense?"

He smiled, and the corner of his eyes crinkled. "A little."

"Maybe that's why the thing with my heart came as such a shock. Cardiac *events* are things that happen to older people, right?"

"Hey, I didn't expect to die for a few minutes in my early fifties, so I get it."

He did. And why did that make Julia so happy? "I'm sure that someday I'll start feeling decrepit, but as long as I can keep my knees functional, I think I'll be okay." She wrinkled her nose. "I do have to take so many more pills now."

He tapped his chest. "The heart event?"

"Yep. So many pills." She leaned on the table. "You?"

"Want to go back?" He shrugged. "Sometimes. There's a lot I'd do different if I had a second chance, and damn, I wasted so much money." He laughed. "I'm doing just fine, but I wasted so much money on stupid shit."

"Lots of experiences though. That's what I can't give up." She took a deep breath. "Every single thing I've done. Every relationship I ditched, every one that ditched me. The deals I screwed up and the ones that made me money... They all taught me things that made me who I am." She smiled. "And I like who I am."

"Hear, hear." Michael raised his glass just as the server came back to the table. "The huevos rancheros and another coffee for me please."

"Right. Sorry!" she squeaked and ran off.

"To the two of us," Michael said, his glass still raised. "As long as my back doesn't give out on me from the accident and your knees keep holding you up, we're living like royals."

She toasted with her water and took a sip. "I was going to ask you kind of a random question, but—"

"Hold on." Michael pulled his phone from his pocket and put on his reading glasses. "Sorry, I thought I turned this off, just let me..." He frowned.

"What is it?"

"Give me a sec," he muttered as he answered the phone. "Richard?"

Julia held her breath as the silence drew out and Michael's face went from confused to surprised to angry. "Where are you?"

Another few seconds.

"What are they saying? I mean— Yes, of course I'll call. I have his number. I'm just... This is insane, Rich." Michael nodded over and over again. "I'll call right now. ... I know. ... No, don't worry about it, she'll understand."

Julia was thoroughly confused. "What's going on?"

"That was Richard." Michael hung up and immediately began scrolling through his phone. "Someone called in an anonymous tip to the police last night, and they searched his locker at the club." Michael put the phone up to his ear, his face a storm of anger. "They found Justin's Rolex in a drawer. They just picked Richard up and took him down to the police department to answer questions." Someone picked up the phone, and Michael nearly started yelling. "Cy? It's Mick; Richard is in trouble. No, it's not Lily. The police think he murdered her boyfriend."

Chapter Twenty-One

Julia watched the news from Evy's couch—the local stations and even the national ones had picked up the story, and now it was red meat for cable news.

A wealthy film producer.

His used-to-be-famous ex-wife.

A murdered young boyfriend.

Rumors of infidelity.

"Is it wrong that I think less of Rachel Maddow for mentioning this?" Vivian narrowed her eyes. "I mean, she's making a point about the inequality of police investigation and inherent bias in the justice system, but still."

Evy was scrolling through her phone. "It's trending on Twitter. And there's a basketball game on tonight."

"So Justin being murdered by a thief isn't news, but his being murdered by a jealous husband is?"

"A jealous, wealthy husband."

"Who comes from old money," Vivian added. "His family is ridiculously rich."

"This is... pretty much what we thought, right?" Julia couldn't look at the pictures of Richard Putnam walking into the police station in handcuffs with a suit jacket over the cuffs to hide them.

For some reason, the thought made her want to laugh.

Why did they cover the handcuffs? It wasn't as if everyone who saw him didn't know they were there. And why were they handcuffing Richard Putnam anyway if he wasn't under arrest?

"He has to be under arrest," Vivian said. "They wouldn't handcuff him if he wasn't."

"I was just thinking that." Julia stood. "Should we go over to Sergio and Dean's for dinner?"

Vivian looked up. "Why don't we go out?"

"Where?"

"Mati's," Vivian said. "I need olives."

THEY TOOK JULIA'S CAR SINCE IT WAS THE BIGGEST, and Vivian sat in back while Evy directed Julia to a parking lot she swore would be available even on a busy Thursday night.

"I see it," Julia said. "I can't believe this is here." They'd driven down two alleys to find it, but it was only a block from the main drag, which meant it was stumbling distance to Mati's, a Spanish tapas place Vivian had discovered.

"Okay, question for the car: If this is what we were thinking," Evy said, "then why does Richard being arrested not feel right?"

"Okay, it's not just me," Vivian said. "I was wondering if it was just because I'm attracted to the man that I'm doubting this, but I'm not alone. Julia?"

She ignored them as she pulled into a narrow parking spot. "Can we get some wine first? I'm still thinking."

"Okay, but remember, stick to one glass."

They got out of the car and started walking down the alley. "You sound like my cardiologist." Julia's mind was racing because... she was also feeling conflicted about Richard being the killer.

"Is it weird to be fifty-one and have a cardiologist?" Evy said. "I don't even have a regular doctor."

"Evy!"

"Evelyn Landa," Vivian said. "Does your mother know about this?"

"She knows I don't have health insurance, so she probably wouldn't be super surprised I don't have a doctor."

A car appeared at the end of the alley, but the passage was too narrow for a car and three pedestrians to pass. The car stopped, the headlights beaming into their eyes.

"High beams much?" Julia looked down, waiting for the car to back out.

But it didn't.

"Hey!" Evy waved a hand, motioning the car to back up. "Right of way, buddy!" She turned to Vivian. "What's he doing? He just pulled in; he needs to back out."

"We definitely have the right of way."

Julia's eyes went wide when she saw the logo on the hood. "Uh, guys?"

"What?"

Evy waved her arm again. "He could at least lower his high beams."

"Guys!"

The car engine began to rev.

Evy and Vivian stopped.

"What the hell?" Evy cocked her head.

"Run!" Julia grabbed both of them and pulled their arms as the black sedan jumped forward, tires screeching.

"Oh my God!" Vivian screamed as she ran down the alley. "What are they doing?"

"Just run!" They were only half a block down the alley, and thank God none of them were wearing heels.

The BMW roared behind them, but it kept swerving, hitting the sides of the buildings and trash cans as it raced after them. Luckily, the friction seemed to slow it down.

Julia, Evy, and Vivian reached the small parking lot where they'd parked and jumped between the first two cars they could find. Vivian climbed on top of a Honda Accord, and Julia and Evy put a whole pickup truck between them and the BMW.

Luckily, the black car sped away, darting toward the opposite end of the one-way alley without stopping.

"What just happened?" Vivian yelled as the Honda's alarm started to sound.

"I think" —Julia tried to picture the speeding car, but the windows had been tinted and it was dark— "someone just tried to kill us."

THE PALM SPRINGS POLICE DEPARTMENT TOOK THEIR statements, but they seemed more concerned that Vivian had left a scratch on the Honda.

"Look." Vivian shoved a note under the windshield. "This is my phone number and insurance information. I will take care of it; now can you please tell me what you're going to do about a car trying to run down three women?"

"Are you sure the driver saw you?" the young man asked. "It's dark and—"

"I am wearing a white trench coat," Julia said. "Do you really think they didn't see us? He hit the side of the alley several times. Maybe you can get paint samples or something."

The officer frowned. "Do you three listen to a lot of true-crime podcasts?"

"Why? Because we think you're doing a piss-poor job of—"

"Evy!" Julia took her friend by the arm when she saw the

officer's expression. "Maybe we should come down to the station."

"That's not necessary." The man was already putting his notebook away. "I'll file the report, and I have your phone numbers if I get any information for you." He nodded. "You ladies have a nice evening."

"Right." Vivian was fuming. "After someone nearly ran us over. I'm sure it'll be great."

"Ma'am." The patrolman nodded at Julia and walked back to his car.

"So that was not helpful," Julia said. "And I'm still hungry. Mati's?"

"I mean... we have to eat."

"HOW DO YOU NOT HAVE HEALTH INSURANCE?" Vivian asked Evy once they'd reached their table.

"Because the comedian's guild doesn't come with that benefit?" Evy shrugged. "You guys, I'm not out of the ordinary in this town. Remember, I *work* for rich people, and I am friends with other rich people. I do not belong to your elevated economic class."

"Well, I'm paying for dinner," Vivian said.

Evy made a face. "I did not tell you about the health insurance thing because I was angling for free food."

"I know, but I suggested Mati's because I was craving olives instead of going to Sergio and Dean's where we could raid their kitchen for free."

"Good point. You can pay."

Julia was thinking about Richard as they sat down, put in their drink order, and ordered their first round of plates.

"No wine for you?" Evy asked Vivian. "Remember, they have that beautiful albariño you like."

"I can't." Vivian was smiling like a cat who got into the cream.

Julia looked at her. "Why— Ohh!" She clapped her hands. "That's right! This is the week, right?"

Evy frowned. "Week for what?" Her eyes went wide. "Baby week! I forgot all about that!" She looked between Julia and Vivian. "Good Lord, have I only known you girls a couple of weeks now? How is that possible?"

"Agreed, I feel like I've known you both forever," Julia said.

"Same." Vivian's cheeks were a little flushed. "And everything went very well. I went in on Tuesday for my bloodwork and consultation. If everything comes back as expected, we'll be following up during my next regular cycle with the... procedure. I've been on the recommended vitamins for three months now, so I'm feeling very positive."

"You already picked a donor?"

"Yes. I interviewed."

"You can do that?"

Vivian nodded. "Phone interview, but still. He has a great voice. Very soothing."

"Did you pick an Asian?" Evy asked. "Sorry, is that a rude question?"

"If it is, you and my mother are equally rude," Vivian said. "I did. He's Korean. I'm sure my mom would have preferred Chinese, but I felt like this person was the best match for me."

"Amazing." Julia shook her head in disbelief. "So you could be pregnant in a couple of months."

"If everything looks good, then yes."

"I am so excited for you," Julia said. "You're going to make an excellent mother. And I'm already looking for a better house for you. Something away from the retirement golf course and near Sergio and Dean's so you can use them for babysitting."

The server set down their drinks, a plate of olives, and a cheese plate.

"You are very sweet." Vivian immediately reached for the olives. "But I'm not using Sergio and Dean for babysitting. They've already raised their kids. I'm sure they're happy to be past the diaper stage."

"Are you kidding?" Evy snorted. "Sergio is the baby whisperer, and he'll want to hold her forever. The only danger with using him for babysitting is they might not give her back."

"It could be a boy," Vivian said. "I would be excited for either."

A television over the bar switched to the news, and everyone in the restaurant went silent as the story filled the room.

"Noted film producer, financial manager, and local philanthropist Richard Putnam was taken in for questioning tonight related to the murder of Justin Worthy, a local chef. Mr. Worthy was killed weeks ago in an apparent home invasion that left the police with few suspects and fewer leads."

"That's redundant," Julia muttered.

The anchor continued, "Tonight, *shock* in the quiet neighborhood of Vista de Lirio where Richard Putnam once lived with his wife, award-winning soap opera actress Lily Putnam."

Julia frowned. "I didn't know that Lily had won awards."

"Oh yeah," Evy said. "She's got something like half a dozen daytime Emmys."

Interesting...

The TV cut to a picture of Vista de Lirio as a reporter stood on the street. "Ma'am." She flagged down a tiny woman who was walking a three-legged dog. "Ma'am, do you live in the neighborhood?"

The woman didn't alter her haughty expression or even appear to notice the newswoman, but her lip twitched and she responded. "Yes, I live here."

"Oh, that's Genevieve!" Julia said. "Good thing the news lady didn't try to knock on her door." She looked at Evy and Vivian. "Savannah cats."

The newswoman held a microphone up to Genevieve's mouth. "And what is your reaction to Mr. Putnam's arrest?"

"Ridiculous." She sniffed. "Richard Putnam is no more a murderer than I am an actress."

"Oh. I'm sorry, I thought you were an actress," the newswoman said.

"I'm an *artist*." Genevieve sniffed again and waved a distracted hand. "And Richard isn't a murderer. Good day."

"And that is all Genevieve De Winter has to say to you." Evy couldn't stop the smile. "That woman is my hero."

"Hasn't she been married like six times?"

"Five," Evy said. "She claims that all men have a shelf life as muses and she only keeps them around for their inspirational qualities, so when she's no longer inspired, they have to go."

"Well, that's one way of approaching marriage."

Julia took a deep breath and finished half her wine in one gulp. "Ladies, I know that I liked Richard for the murderer—on the surface, he definitely seemed like the obvious choice, but..." She sighed. "He took Justin's watch? And left it in his locker at the country club? That seems stupid, and we know he's not stupid."

"I was thinking the same thing," Vivian said. "And honestly, I still can't figure out a motive for the man. Why would he have cared enough to kill Justin?"

"He really didn't like him," Evy said. "I definitely got that much when I read his mind. I don't know if he'd kill him, but he really hated him. He thought he was obnoxious and using Lily for her money."

"Well, he's not wrong," Vivian muttered. "Didn't we all kind of think Justin and Lily were obnoxious?"

"No comment," Julia said. "He's probably eavesdropping somewhere even though I haven't felt him today. I do know he did not deserve to die."

"Agreed."

"Oh, of course not."

"So why kill him?" Julia leaned forward as yet another reporter asked a stupid question about Richard and the newswoman interviewed a neighbor Julia didn't recognize. "It just doesn't make sense."

"They're going to give him bail, right?" Evy looked between them. "I can't imagine they're going to make him stay in jail."

"All of this seems so fast," Julia said. "First Chief Marcos couldn't be bothered to arrest anyone for Justin's murder, and now they grab the first guy that *could* be a suspect and arrest him. And I thought they were friends."

"Maybe that's why he's going so fast," Vivian said. "He doesn't want it to look like favoritism. You know how parents are always hardest on their own kids and nice to everyone else's?" She looked around. "Just mine?"

"No, you're right. I can see that being part of the motivation," Julia said. "Was Justin wearing his Rolex at the party? I don't remember."

"I don't either, but I'm sure Lily probably told them what Justin was wearing when he dropped her off," Evy said. "The Rolex must have been part of his outfit."

"And Richard took it off his body?" Vivian scrunched up her nose. "Does that seem like something a really rich murderer would do?"

"Maybe," Julia said. "If he wanted to make it *look* like a robbery."

"Oooooh." Evy nodded. "Okay, that's a good point."

"So we know nothing." Julia drained her wine and set the empty glass down. Hard. "We've been poking around and questioning people and communing with ghosts and we still know nothing."

"We know about the secret panel in the kitchen," Evy said. "I don't know if the police have found that yet."

Vivian looked at Julia. "Do you think we should tell them about it? Now that Richard has been arrested?"

"Maybe." Julia stared at the television. "Michael says he's innocent."

"Michael is friends with him," Evy said. "Of course he thinks that."

"That doesn't mean he's wrong."

Chapter Twenty-Two

J ulia woke up on Saturday morning to the most welcome email she'd had in weeks. Someone wanted to look at Casa de Lirio that afternoon, and it was a serious enough inquiry that the office had put it through.

The day after the news of Richard's arrest broke, Steward Brooks had been flooded with calls from people interested in viewing the house, but all of them ended up being reporters or macabre observers. This was the first real sales lead since Julia had moved to Palm Springs, and she jumped on it. Within the hour, she had a meeting scheduled with Patrick and Laurel Van Verden, a financial executive and an interior designer.

Julia jumped out of bed and started to get ready. She'd need to head over to the house to air it out, make sure nothing that looked even vaguely forensic was visible, and hide the offerings she'd left for the ghost.

"Question."

She nearly jumped out of her skin when she heard Justin's voice. "Dammit, you scared me."

"If Richard Putnam is the one who murdered me, and he's

now going to face" —Justin made air quotes with his fingers— "justice, then why am I still here?"

Julia opened her mouth to respond, but she had nothing. "Maybe he needs to admit it or something?"

Justin's eyes bugged out. "Oh great. So because we have the right to remain silent in this country and Richard probably has a smart lawyer, I may never be able to move on to the afterlife?"

"Why do you think I know how this works?" She felt like strangling him. But he was already dead. "I'm just as lost as you are in this whole mess. Why do you think I should know—" A hard knock sounded at the door.

Julia opened it to see Aurelia in a blond wig.

She frowned. "Why?"

"I'm contemplating a shift in hair color."

"It really sets off the black eyeliner. Does your father know you're wearing eyeliner?"

"Which one?"

"The dramatic Brazilian one, your pai. You know who I'm talking about."

Aurelia craned her neck, trying to peer into the pool house. "I assume you were arguing with a ghost."

"Yes. Why?"

"Because there's a police officer on the patio again." She looked up through expertly lined eyes. "You might have to explain yourself."

And you might have to explain how you learned how to do a perfect cat eye at thirteen.

"Tell him I'll be right there. I'm finishing up a phone call."

"Nice cover."

"The wig doesn't go with your skin tone." Julia believed in blunt truth with her nieces. "It washes you out and does nothing for your complexion."

"I know. That's why it appeals to me."

Aurelia turned and skipped away from Julia's door. She shut it and turned to Justin, who was still standing there.

"That kid is really weird."

"And you weren't at thirteen?"

He shrugged. "That was like, my one bad year."

Of course it was. Justin was probably the guy who never even had acne in high school.

"There's a police officer out there," Julia told him. "I'll try to get more answers, okay? Until then?" She pointed at the door. "Out."

Julia finished dressing and walked out to the patio again, only to see the familiar sight of Chief John Marcos sitting on her patio with Dean and Sergio. They were all drinking what looked like screwdrivers, and it gave Julia pause.

Was this an ambush? She knew Dean and Sergio were friends with him, but was this three middle-aged men out to defend the honor of their golf buddy? Was this the good-old-boy network in play? How could anyone expect justice when the power structure in this town was so very narrow?

"Julia!" Sergio smiled. "John had a couple of questions. We told him to come by for a drink."

"Just orange juice for me." Chief Marcos raised his glass with a smile. "I'm on duty."

"Of course." Julia sat down across from him. "What's up?"

"I hate to bring up unpleasant memories, but I was hoping I might ask you for your recollections of the morning you found Mr. Worthy at Casa de Lirio."

She frowned. "When I found Justin? I already told you everything I remember. My memories are probably less reliable now than when I gave my statement."

Marcos leaned forward. "Now why would you say that?"

"Because time has passed. You don't forget things after a while?"

"I don't forget murder victims."

She might have understood that point a little better if said murder victim wasn't still following her around and scaring her out of her wits on random mornings. "I can try to remember, and I'm sure there are some things I will, but if it's a detail—"

"I'm asking because I want to know if it looked like Mr. Worthy's body had been tampered with." Marcos adjusted his seat. "See, I was looking at the photos at the crime scene and there's a pretty big pool of blood from Justin's head wound. It was smeared all over his chest and... Well, you remember they had to replace the tile."

"Mm-hmm." She wondered if she should bring that up at the viewing. *Brand-new tile! We just couldn't get the bloodstains out from the last residents.*

"Now Ms. Putnam—Lily—when she first recounted what Justin had been wearing that night, she didn't mention the watch." Marcos shrugged. "Not a huge oversight, I figured. That's definitely something you might not think about after you just suffered a loss. But then I noticed the crime scene pictures."

"Okay. I'm not sure what your question is."

"My question is, did you notice any signs of the body having been moved? Did it look like his watch had been taken off after he was killed?"

"I can't say that I noticed anything... askew?" Was that even the right word? "He looked like he'd been hit and had fallen to the ground. I noticed the blood. I noticed..." She thought back. "I noticed how pale he was. His eyes were open." She shook her head. "Dean was on the phone, he can tell you. It was obvious he was dead. I didn't notice anything about his clothes, to be honest."

But if Richard had killed Justin, there would have been some evidence, right? His arm would have been moved. There would have been smears of blood maybe. Something.

"I think that's all I needed from you." John Marcos had a

satisfied smile. "Thank you, Miss Brooks. Sergio, Dean." He stood. "I should get back to the office. Nice to see you all."

Julia rose. "Okay." She frowned as the man hurried to his car. "Nice to see you. I guess."

"That was strange," Sergio said.

"Very strange," Dean added, his eyes fixed on the retreating man.

What had just happened?

Had Julia just given John Marcos a reason to release his friend?

Had she just exonerated a murderer?

MICHAEL AND SHE HAD BEEN TEXTING FOR A COUPLE of days, but she was finally able to meet him for a quick brunch before the viewing. She'd already been over to Casa de Lirio, and for the first time, she'd been able to see it as a listing.

No murder.

No ghost.

No iridescent portal to challenge her concept of reality.

Just luxury square footage and mountain views.

"Have you heard of them?" She sat across from Michael in a diner near the airport. "Their name is Van Verden. I was told they're both from Los Angeles, but I haven't heard the name before." She glanced over the brunch menu, which was a combination of old-time staples like waffles and new twists like fried-avocado tacos. "What's your favorite thing here? I haven't been here before."

"The eggs Benedict is good." Michael was staring out the window. "And... um, the tacos are surprisingly good if you're not too hungry."

"What's wrong?" She closed her menu and studied him.

Michael was looking troubled, which was new. Julia felt a

jolt of panic. This was usually where she screwed up in relationships. Men said she wasn't empathetic enough. That she wouldn't listen.

Which wasn't true. She was plenty empathetic, and she was happy to listen to a friend, but she wasn't anyone's mother, and that was a sticking point for a lot of men.

Michael shook his head. "I can't stop thinking about Richard."

"They just took him in for questioning, right? Is he under arrest?"

The server came to the table. "Do you two know what you want?"

"I'll have the avocado tacos," Julia looked at Michael. "You?"

"Um... the chicken and waffles and more coffee." He held up his empty mug. "When you get a chance."

"I'll be right back with it." The smiling server put her pad away and grabbed Michael's mug. "More creamer?"

"No, I'm good, thanks." Michael watched her walk away, his face still burdened by worry. "Technically they have not arrested him. They told him not to leave town. His lawyer says it looks like they're building a case against him, and he won't talk to me." He turned to Julia. "I asked him if he has an alibi, but he clammed up."

Julia took a deep breath. "Do you suspect—?"

"No!" Michael shook his head. "Not even for a minute."

"Michael, are you sure? I mean... I've asked Justin and he can't remember, but to hit Justin on the head like that? It must have been someone pretty strong, and Richard is a tall, strong man. He might have thought Justin was an intruder or something."

"Even then he wouldn't..." He sighed. "Think of one of your oldest friends. A person you know really well. You've been through shit together; that kind of friend."

"Okay." Dean. Maybe it was weird that it was her ex-husband, but it was true. "What do you—?"

"Imagine you were told that friend murdered someone."

Julia tried to imagine the circumstances that might push Dean to murder.

Someone hurting his girls.

Someone threatening his family.

Someone pointing a gun at Sergio.

Sergio and Dean breaking up, Sergio getting a new boyfriend, Dean murdering the boyfriend.

Yeah... that didn't track. "Michael, I know what you're saying—"

"I'm not saying that Rich couldn't be pushed to do something drastic." He held out his hands. "I think everyone has a breaking point. But this? It's just not him, Julia. And it's so hard to explain that to people who don't know him." He took a deep breath and let it out. "Justin's ghost doesn't have *any* memory of who hit him?"

"No. I'm sorry." She reached across and gripped his hand. "It's a horrible situation. And if Richard was responsible—"

"But he's not. I understand why people who don't know him might think this makes sense. But I *do* know him, and I know he didn't kill Justin Worthy."

"Then the truth is going to get out. They can't convict him over a watch," Julia said. "Someone could have planted it."

"I think they must have, but I'm worried about the alibi thing. I think he has one and he's not telling me or the police what it is."

"Why would he do that? An alibi would clear everything—"

"I think he's protecting someone, which is completely something that he *would* do." Michael ran his fingers over her knuckles. "That's why he's not telling. He's the kind of guy that always follows the rules, right? He's going to think that if he didn't do it, the truth will come out and he'll be exonerated."

Julia's mind jumped to the ghost still living at Casa de Lirio. "Did Richard follow the rules with Kiki Stevens?"

Michael frowned. "Kiki?"

"The woman who died at his house almost thirty years ago." Julia gently withdrew her hand. "I was doing some research on the property, and I saw a news article."

"Oh man, I completely forgot about that." Michael frowned. "I wasn't at that party, but I knew her a little. I was out of town when it happened. I thought that was an accident in the sauna or something."

How to phrase this and not reveal she saw all sorts of dead people?

"There were rumors that Kiki wasn't a drug user. That someone spiked a drink or something and that she was killed."

Michael sat back. "I don't remember hearing *that*. And I don't know why anyone would kill her. I guess maybe an ex or something? I don't remember her being with anyone, but I didn't know her that well."

"She and Richard were having an affair." Fuck. How was she going to explain that?

Michael smiled. "Was that in the tabloids?"

The server came back with a steaming cup of coffee and a basket of biscuits for the table.

Michael looked up. "Thank you, miss."

"You're welcome." The girl beamed. "Food should be right out."

"Thanks." Michael waited for her to leave. "Were the papers saying Rich and Kiki had an affair? Was there an alien involved?"

"Ha ha." Julia shrugged. "There were rumors—"

"According to a few magazines, I have three illegitimate children that I'm hiding in Utah, and I'm probably a lizard person." Michael pressed his lips together. "You can't believe that stuff, Jules."

"You don't think it's strange that there have been two

murders at the same house?" she asked. "I have some experience with houses, and most of them have no murders at all."

"It's strange, but it's kind of a legendary house, isn't it? It's had big parties and big personalities drawn there over the years."

And you don't even know about the golden ghost portal.

"It is." She decided to press a little. "Do you remember back then? It would have been 1994."

Michael frowned a little. "I'd just barely gotten to LA. I'd met Richard and Lily then, but I didn't know them. Not really. I guess I knew Lily a little better at that point, but Richard was kind of a mystery."

"How so?"

"He was always very reserved. He clearly loved Lily, but he could be kind of stuffy. There were moments when I could not understand why on earth Lily was with him, but she seemed happy, so I figured it wasn't my business. After I got to know him, I understood what she saw."

"What do you think it was?"

"Loyal." Michael nodded slowly. "Richard Putnam is one of the most loyal and principled people I know. In a business and a place that can stab you in the back the minute you're not at the top, Richard was steady. He didn't play those games."

Julia found herself hoping that Michael's version of Richard Putnam was real because the world needed more people like that.

She reached across and gripped both his hands. "I've seen him around town with a blond woman. A young one. Do you know who it is?"

Michael looked a little cagey. "I've seen her once. I ran into Richard when I was visiting an old friend who lives at the retirement home where his mom is. I saw them, and she kind of darted away before I could meet her."

"Is she his girlfriend? Maybe she's the alibi."

"That's what I'm worried about. But he dodged the question, and I didn't want to press."

"Maybe it's time that you pressed." She squeezed his hands. "Whatever is going on, I believe the truth will come out."

"Because you're psychic?"

She smiled. "Ghosts are surprisingly frustrating in this situation. They are not very good witnesses. Justin still has no idea what he was even doing at the house that night."

"Whatever it was, it had to be sketchy, right?" Michael reached for his coffee. "After all, it wasn't his place. Whatever motive he had to be there, it couldn't have been honest."

Chapter Twenty-Three

"Why was Justin at the house?" Julia ran and whacked the racquetball against the wall. "Oh my God, you're right. This is so satisfying even though I feel like I'm going to die."

Vivian grunted as she lunged for the ball, but she missed. "Your point."

"Was he hiding stuff in the kitchen? What? Was it this crazy Putnam Diamond everyone was talking about?"

"Justin never had the diamond." Vivian served and they exchanged another round of volleys. "And even if he did, why would he have hidden it? Wouldn't he have given it to Lily if he had it? Wouldn't he *remember* if he had it?"

"Maybe." It was Julia's serve, and she made a mess of it. "Ghosts are the worst!"

And still she could feel him hovering nearby. Ignoring her, but still a presence.

Vivian had sweat running down her face. "Once I'm inseminated, I won't be able to do this for a while." She bounced the ball with her racquet and caught her breath. "They want me to keep kind of chill for a few months." She threw the ball up and lobbed an easy serve for Julia.

She returned it. "Then you're going to be able to play again?"

"Maybe."

They played another round and another before their time was up.

Vivian draped a towel around her neck and walked out the door to the hallway between the plexiglass-fronted racquetball courts. "It'll depend on how the baby is doing, I guess."

"Cool." Julia sat down and tried not to die. "I can build up my mad racquetball skills so I can beat you. My cardiologist will be thrilled."

Vivian smiled. "At least you said yes. I tried asking Evy and she just laughed at me."

"Well, Evy doesn't get lectured monthly about building up her cardiovascular health." Julia took a sip of water. "I don't think Richard killed Justin."

Vivian nearly spit out her drink. "That was a segue."

"I know." Julia looked around, but no one was listening to them. Everyone at Vivian's club was either heading into a game or sweating profusely as they headed out of one. "I had brunch with Michael yesterday before the showing."

"How did that go?"

"The showing or the brunch?"

"The showing. I'm assuming the brunch with Michael was nice." Vivian took another drink. "But maybe I shouldn't. He's friends with Richard. What does he think?"

"Him being so sure that Richard didn't do it is making me feel like our instincts about Richard were right."

"Our second instinct?"

"Yeah, the second one." She thought about Chief Marcos's visit too. "And there's no evidence Justin was wearing his watch the night he was killed either."

"How would we know though?"

Julia frowned. "The police were asking about blood patterns, and I guess I don't know enough about them to really be able to tell."

Vivian dropped her voice. "What about Justin?"

"What about him?"

"I guess that I assumed when you saw him that he was wearing the clothes he died in." Vivian frowned. "But is that right? I don't know if there are rules about that."

"Oh my God, I'm an idiot. I didn't even think about that." Julia looked around the near-empty club and hissed, "Justin!"

The ghost appeared with a wrinkled nose. "You're sweaty."

"Yeah, I've been exercising. Don't start." She looked at his wrist. "You're not wearing a watch."

He looked down. "Obviously not."

"He's not wearing a watch," she told Vivian. "But what if it was taken off his body before he actually died? Would it still be on his ghostly... form?"

"Why would I be wearing a watch?" Justin said. "I hate watches. I have a phone for fuck's sake. I don't need a watch *and* a phone. I only have that thing because it was a gift from Lily." He rolled his eyes. "So nineties."

"Your Rolex was found in Richard's locker at the club."

"The last time I had that watch on was at the party," Justin said. "I took it off when we went swimming, and honestly I don't remember what happened to it. I think anyone could have swiped it."

Julia looked at Vivian with wide eyes. "He says he took it off at the party before he went swimming and he didn't see it again. Anyone could have it."

"Not anyone," Vivian said. "Not everyone was at Sunday Dinner last month, remember?"

"Richard." Julia shook her head. "Richard wasn't even there. Someone planted the watch."

On Monday morning, Julia went straight down to the police station with Evy.

"Does this count as fabricating evidence?" Evy sat in the passenger seat, staring at the station. "I really don't want to go to jail. I can't afford it."

"We're not fabricating evidence, we're playing secondhand witness." Julia unbuckled her seat belt. "Justin said the last time he saw the watch, it was on the table by the bar. That's all we're going to tell Chief Marcos."

"And we're telling him about the safe in the kitchen, right?"

"I'll tell him I found it the other day when I was showing the house."

Which had actually been a huge success. She'd heard from the Van Verdens' agent that morning in an email, and the woman had a few more questions that led Julia to think they were thinking about an offer.

"Okay." Evy nodded. "Okay, we can do this."

They walked across the street into the low-slung building that housed Palm Springs's small police department. When she asked for Chief Marcos, she gave her name and said she had information about Justin Worthy's case.

Within minutes, Julia and Evy were sitting in a small room with a coffee machine and a large basket of fruit in the center of the table.

Evy grabbed two oranges and stuffed them in her pockets.

Julia raised an eyebrow. "Really?"

"What? I'm a taxpayer. These are technically my oranges." She started peeling one. "And I'd rather have something to do with my hands when we're talking to police. Traditionally, Landas and law enforcement have had a rocky relationship."

"Miss Brooks." Chief Marcos announced himself as he walked into the room. "Nice to see you again. And Miss Landa.

How can I help you this morning?" He sat at the table and eyed Evy, who continued to peel the orange. "Connie said you have some information about the Worthy case."

"Two things." Julia exchanged a look with Evy. "Evy mentioned to me that she saw Justin's watch at Sunday Dinner."

"I did." Evy stared at the orange. "It would have been the night before he died, I guess. I saw his watch on the back table by the bar."

"At Dean and Sergio's house?"

"People leave their stuff all over," Julia said. "It would have been normal for him to just pile his stuff on a table when he and Lily went swimming."

"I see." Chief Marcos nodded. "Implying that anyone could have grabbed it that night and then planted it in Mr. Putnam's locker."

"I don't really know Richard Putnam," Evy said. "But I figured you should know. He wasn't at the party that night."

Marcos was nodding. "Thank you. I appreciate the information."

"Also," Julia added, "I should tell you that I found what appears to be a secret safe or panel in the kitchen at Casa de Lirio."

His eyebrows went up. "A safe?"

"No lock," Julia clarified. "But it looks like a secret panel. I only discovered it yesterday right before a showing. There's nothing in it, but it was near the place where Justin was killed."

"Interesting." He frowned. "In the kitchen?"

"Yes, at the base of a lower cupboard. Justin could have been looking at it when someone killed him."

"Or he could have been taking something out of it," Marcos said. "Thank you, Miss Brooks. Would you be able to open the house for me today so I can see it?"

She nodded. "Absolutely. I can meet you there around two or three."

"Two o'clock would be ideal."

JULIA TRACKED MICHAEL DOWN WHERE HE'D BEEN house-sitting for friends. It was a house in a luxury development. Large, desert modern, and unbelievably beige. The pool house where Michael was staying matched.

He came to the door, wearing a pair of grey sweats, a black T-shirt, and a pair of glasses that made him look adorably professorial. "Julia?"

"Sorry if I'm intruding," she said. "Sergio gave me your address when I told him I wanted to talk to you."

"No problem." He smiled. "It's a nice surprise."

She sighed. "I wanted to see you. And not in public."

His smile fell. "Everything okay?"

"I realized yesterday morning when Vivian was torturing me at racquetball that Justin had no reason to be at the house and also that I never told you about the safe we found."

"I don't... Richard and Lily had a number of safes. Why is that important?"

"This one was a hidden panel in the kitchen right next to where the murderer bashed Justin on the head," she said. "And we figure Justin must have been in the house to get something out of that safe since he was the one who spent the most time in the kitchen. It makes sense—"

Michael's laughter cut her off.

"What?" Julia frowned. "I'm trying to be open and—"

"And I love that. I love the honesty." He pulled her into the house. "Come in. Is Justin... *with* you right now?"

"No." She waved a hand. "I haven't seen him since this morning."

"It's just that he didn't really cook. I mean, a little. I do think he was trying, but Lily was the chef in the family. She always has been. She's an amazing cook, which was why it was always so amusing to me that she called Justin her personal chef. She didn't need one."

Oh.

Ohhhhh. "So if we found a hidden panel in the kitchen..."

"If there was a secret safe somewhere in the house, especially if it was in the kitchen, it probably belonged to Lily. She loved hiding things. She could be needlessly cagey. About stupid stuff even. It used to drive Richard crazy. She'll hide things for no reason, just to have the drama of a secret."

"Interesting." Why was that important? They still had no evidence that there was anything in the hidden compartment. It could have been nothing.

"Okay." Julia sat on a beige love seat. "In the interest of not keeping secrets needlessly, I should also tell you that I've met Kiki Stevens's ghost and she says she was murdered. And that she and Richard were having an affair."

"Fuck." Michael's eyes went wide. "Really?"

"Yes, really."

"Do ghosts lie?"

"I have no idea, but why would she? What would be the point? She's stuck at Casa de Lirio because she died there and it wasn't natural."

Michael sat down in a very modern, very uncomfortable-looking armchair. "Are you serious?"

"She said she never took drugs. That she didn't even drink much because her mother was an alcoholic. She says someone gave her the drugs."

"Richard?"

She shook her head. "I don't think so, but I don't know what to think at this point. There was no evidence that Lily knew about the affair. Sergio didn't know about it—he doesn't even remember hearing rumors. It seems like Richard and Kiki were the only ones who knew."

"But Lily keeps secrets," Michael said. "She always has."

"Do you want to ask her about it?"

He shook his head. "I don't want to. But maybe I have to."

JULIA MET JOHN MARCOS OUTSIDE CASA DE LIRIO AT two in the afternoon. He drove up in a black Dodge Charger with no other officers with him. He was wearing a pair of black pants and a polo shirt with the department logo on the pocket. "Miss Brooks, I appreciate your meeting me here."

"Please call me Julia." She walked to the gate with the keys. "I hope you don't mind my putting a time limit on this. I got a call from my office that I have another party interested in the house and they want to see it this afternoon. I am very relieved by that."

"What time?"

"About four."

He waved a hand. "Plenty of time for me to take a look at this secret compartment you were talking about." He smiled. "Forensics has already gone over the house."

"Great." She smiled and opened the gate, leading the chief up the walkway and toward the house.

"It's a beautiful place, but I imagine it might be hard to get the right people interested."

"You have that right." Julia chattered as they walked up the pathway to the front. "There was someone who expressed interest right before the murder, but we haven't heard another word since. The showing the other day was the first one in weeks."

Marcos chuckled. "I remember coming this way more than a couple of times when I was still in uniform."

"Oh?"

'Usually noise complaints. The Putnams did love their wild parties."

'I've heard that." She spread her arms. 'I mean, you can see that it's a great house for entertaining."

'It's stunning."

She let him in and walked to the kitchen where she opened the cupboard and popped over the secret compartment. 'As you can see, it's lined, but there's nothing in there now."

He bent down and looked at it. 'Interesting." He took a small black flashlight from his pocket. 'Let me just..."

He poked his head in the cabinet and she heard him laugh a little.

'What is it?

'There's nothing in here now, but whatever was in here before the murder..." He pulled his head back, and there was what looked like a tiny diamond between his fingertips. 'I think it might have been sparkly."

Chapter Twenty-Four

"A diamond?" Evy asked. "How did I miss that?"

"It was tiny," Julia said. "And I don't know if it was a diamond. Chief Marcos took it as evidence, but it could have been a rhinestone or a crystal or something."

They were back on Dean and Sergio's patio on Wednesday morning, but this time Vivian was mixing them drinks since she didn't have appointments until the afternoon.

Julia felt her phone buzzing and took it out.

"Okay." Vivian brought a tray of drinks over to the table. "Delicious Palomas for you two—it's grapefruit juice, so it's healthy—and a virgin Paloma for me."

"Cheers." Evy grabbed her drink and clinked it with Vivian's glass. "Thanks for being the bartender." She lay back in her seat, soaking up the morning sun. "Julia, you should never leave."

"I may not." Even though she had to. She'd been woken this morning by Sergio and Paco, who'd been in some kind of human-alpaca argument she couldn't follow since they were yelling in Portuguese.

Well, Sergio was yelling in Portuguese, Paco hadn't been saying much.

"Hey, Michael texted me earlier. Do you mind if he joins us?"

"Nope." Vivian sipped her grapefruit juice. "Tell him to pick up bagels or something."

"Oh, that sounds good." Evy nodded. "I second the bagel idea."

Julia texted Michael. *You are welcome if you come with an offering of bagels and shmear.*

I can manage that.

He added a couple of emojis, which made Julia think he was in a chipper mood. The last time she'd talked to him the night before, he'd been determined to sit down and have a serious conversation with Richard. Chipper Michael must mean that the conversation went well.

Julia looked at Evy and Vivian. "Has anyone checked the news this morning?"

"Not me."

"No." Vivian shook her head. "Should we put the TV on?" She pointed to the large black screen hanging on the wall next to the patio.

"Maybe." She got up and turned on the television, flipping to a local morning show.

The news ticker at the bottom of the screen told her why Michael was so chipper.

Richard Putnam cleared of suspicion in Worthy killing.

"...sources at the police department confirm that Richard Putnam, the Hollywood producer suspected of murdering Justin Worthy, who was having an affair with Mr. Putnam's estranged wife, has been officially cleared as a suspect following information that establishes what our source calls..." There was a dramatic pause. "...an ironclad alibi."

The blond anchor responded. "Good news for Richard Putnam, but where does that leave the police, Chet?"

"Still searching, Sunny." Another dramatic pause. "As of this morning, there are now *no suspects* in Justin Worthy's murder."

"Well," Vivian said, "I guess that's good for Richard."

"It sounds pretty definitive," Evy said. "I don't think they'd leak that to the news if they had any doubt about his alibi."

"Agreed." Julia heard a long sigh at her right.

Justin was sitting in a wicker chair next to her, banging his ghostly head on the table. "I am going to be here forever."

"If you could tell me why you were at the house that night, it might help."

"I don't remember, okay!" He flung himself back.

Mae hurried over to him. "Justin, honey, come sit in the sun with Elton and me." She winked at Julia. "I'm just sure that Julia and her friends are going to find your killer. They can just... start back at the beginning!"

"Start back at the beginning." Julia sipped her drink and stared at Justin as he and Mae walked to a pair of pool loungers in the shade. Mae was in her white robe and Justin was still in his clothes from the night of his death.

Go back to the beginning.

Julia tried to picture the scene in her mind. Justin bending down to get something from the safe. A blow coming from behind.

How had the killer snuck up on him? The floors were tile; he would have heard anyone walking on it. If he was there doing something he wasn't supposed to, he would have looked up, but there was no indication that he had. He'd been kneeling down, looking into the safe.

"He knew they were there."

Evy looked up from her phone. "What?"

"Justin." Julia looked between Evy and Vivian. "Justin was in the kitchen, bending down and looking into the safe."

Vivian nodded. "That's what the position of the body said, yes."

"On tile."

She nodded again. "Yeah, that whole kitchen is tile. The breakfast room too."

The lights went on for Evy. "How could anyone have surprised him on tile floors? Those things are noisy as hell."

"What if they were wearing socks?" Vivian said. "Or barefoot. I don't wear shoes in my house. It's unhygienic."

Julia's heart sank. "You're right. I was thinking he knew his killer was there, but they could have been barefoot."

She heard the gate moving and realized someone inside must have opened it. Sergio walked out, scratching a stubbly beard. "Michael said he brought bagels." His eyes landed on their drinks. "Oooh, Palomas. Gimme." He reached for Julia's and took a long drink. "Tequila is better than coffee."

"Don't tell your doctor that." She took her drink back and smiled. "Make your own. There's stuff at the bar."

"You're squatting in my pool house and you can't make me a drink?" Sergio sauntered to the bar, giving Julia side eye. "You're ungrateful, all three of you." He washed his hands and motioned toward them, waving his hand in a rough circle. "And what is this now? Are you solving mysteries? Are you the Hardy girls? Sergio's angels?"

Vivian looked over her shoulder with a smile. "Sergio's angels?"

"Actually, I like the sound of that." He pursed his lips. "I'm going to send you on missions now. The first one will be to go to the store and get me some more damn tequila." He held up the bottle. "Because what the hell, ladies?"

Michael walked around the pathway from the garage. "I come bearing gifts of round dough and cream cheese."

Evy clapped. "Bagels!"

Julia's... friend? Boyfriend? Regular date? caught her eye, smiled, and walked over to plant a kiss on her, right in front of God, her friends, and any lingering alpacas. "Hi."

Julia couldn't hold back her smile. "Hi."

Michael set down the bags. "Did you see the news?"

"We did. You must be very relieved."

They hadn't slept together yet, and she was savoring the slowness. It was like getting a bunch of small plates before a big meal. The anticipation was delectable.

"I am very relieved," he said. "I took your advice, and Richard and I talked yesterday. He didn't want to get into the dirty details, but I pushed him and I finally got the whole story."

Vivian perked up. "About Kiki Stevens's death?"

"About the blonde?" Evy asked.

"About his alibi?" Sergio yelled.

Julia's mind was spinning. "Everyone be quiet and let him talk."

Michael squeezed her hand, then reached for an onion bagel and opened a plastic tub of cream cheese. "If someone can make me a drink, I have Richard's permission to tell you all."

"ACCORDING TO RICHARD, KIKI WAS THE LOVE OF HIS life." He spread a lump of cream cheese over an onion bagel. "But as far as he knows, her death was exactly what the coroner said, a heart attack brought on by pills, drinking at the party, and spending way too long in the sauna. The combination of all three was too much. An accident."

"Did you ask him about drugs?" Julia leaned forward. "Because according to her ghost—"

"Remember how you told me ghost's memories can be fuzzy right around their deaths?"

Julia nodded.

"According to Richard, she *had* been using. It was unusual for her, and he was worried. There was a reason, but he didn't understand why until years later."

Vivian jumped on that. "What was the reason?"

"Give me a sec." Michael ate a bite of bagel. "I haven't had breakfast."

"Maury's has the best bagels in the valley." Sergio was smearing cream cheese over half a sesame. "You're a doll to drive all the way out to get them."

"I was in the neighborhood." He wiped his mouth. "So Richard loved Kiki and said he was actually planning to leave Lily, but Lily had just had a miscarriage and they were both a mess. He didn't want to leave her until she'd had time to recover and he had time to think."

"But he stayed with Lily after Kiki died," Vivian said. "Is this revisionist history? Kind of making his affair seem more tragic?"

"It's a fair question." Michael shrugged. "I have no way of knowing for sure, but Richard did say he loved Lily. He never stopped loving Lily, he just loved Kiki more."

"Okay, so if we believe him," Sergio said, "he loved both women, one died, and he stayed with his wife. What does this have to do with his alibi?"

"Because he found out about a year ago, not long after he and Lily finally split, the reason Kiki had been taking pills." This time it was Michael pausing for dramatic effect. "She'd just had a baby. Richard's baby."

Julia's mouth dropped open.

"Oh shit." Vivian sat back. "She was pregnant and he didn't know?"

"According to Richard, Kiki disappeared back east with her family for about four months. She told him her father was having health problems, but she never told him about the baby."

"She was tall," Julia said. "At least six foot."

Sergio frowned. "So?"

Vivian said, "There was a girl in my sorority in college who got pregnant senior year." Vivian shrugged. "Longtime boyfriend, so not really any drama, but she didn't show until her sixth month. She was tall like that. It can happen."

Evy cocked her head. "I confess I'm surprised you were in a sorority."

"Professional social, baby. We drilled teeth during the day and... Well, I'm sure you can imagine the jokes. I'm still in touch with most of those girls." She turned to Michael. "I'm just saying that if Kiki was as tall as Julia says, it's completely believable that she could have hidden a pregnancy for the first half."

"So Richard has a... daughter? Son?" Sergio was shaking his head. "And he never knew. He must have been devastated."

"He was angry when he found out, but what could he do?" Michael sipped his coffee. "Kiki's dead. He finally meets his daughter. Her grandparents raised her, and according to him, it sounds like she had a good life. But it took her years to get the guts up to come out and meet him. What's the point of dwelling on the anger, you know?"

"Ooof." Julia couldn't even imagine. "That girl must have been pretty intimidated. She's the secret daughter of a wealthy, famous movie producer from old money. She probably thought he'd think she was a scam artist or something."

"She's not exactly a girl anymore either. She must be twenty-eight or twenty-nine now. But according to Rich, the scam-artist idea is exactly what made her hesitate to look him up for so many years. She went to college, became a teacher—"

"It's the blonde!" Vivian slapped her forehead. "Of course it's the blond girl. That's who he was with. That's who his alibi is, isn't it? Richard's alibi is his daughter!"

Michael nodded. "The night Justin was killed, Madeline— that's his daughter—had a dinner party with a few friends. She moved out here about eight months ago and has slowly been introducing Richard to her friends and colleagues. There were four other people there who told the police that Richard was there until nearly midnight. They were playing Monopoly, and apparently Richard was creaming them all."

"The medical examiner put Justin's time of death about midnight, right?"

"Or a little after," Sergio said.

Michael continued, "The police don't think there's any way that Richard could have driven from his daughter's house to Casa de Lirio and killed Justin in that amount of time. His alibi clears him."

Vivian sat back. "And he's single."

Michael cocked his head. "Yes, he is. I think he likes you. After he saw you, he didn't complain about going to the dentist nearly as much as he usually does."

"That's very flattering." Vivian's cheeks were a little pink. "So Richard has a daughter."

Sergio smiled. "Madeline. I love that name. What a strange and beautiful thing. He always wanted kids. Did he have any doubts when she introduced herself?"

"I don't think so. According to Richard, Maddy had pictures of Kiki, and she also looks very much like his own mother, whom she's already met."

"At the retirement home," Julia said. "Of course. We followed them there."

Michael turned. "You were following Rich?"

Sergio yelled, "Don't interrogate my angels! They were following orders, Mick."

"I have no idea what you're talking about," Michael said. "Why were you following him?"

"We saw Richard with a blond girl when we were leaving the spa where Justin's ex-girlfriend works, and we thought she was his secret younger girlfriend," Julia said. "We thought she might have been his motive for killing Justin or something."

Michael narrowed his eyes. "Is this a thing the three of you are going to start doing now? Solving mysteries via spa visits?"

Vivian nodded. "Maybe."

"It's not the worst idea I've ever had," Evy said. "That would be buying a haunted ventriloquist's dummy in London that I may never use again because Geoff is still creeping me out."

"Wait, a haunted what?" Michael's eyes went wide.

"I'll explain later." Julia kissed his cheek. "Do you want more coffee?"

"Sergio's angels," Sergio whispered.

"Sergio's...?" Michael shook his head. "Okay, but why would Rich having a girlfriend make him want to kill Justin?"

"He was hiding things and we were nosy." Vivian shrugged. "If he was lying about having a girlfriend, he could be hiding other things too."

Michael stared at her with a furrowed brow. "I guess that makes sense. Kind of. But just so you know, Rich was being discreet with Maddy at *her* request. She didn't want her mother's affair with Rich to be pushed into the spotlight when he was still in the middle of a high-profile divorce."

Julia said, "It would be a lot for her to deal with too, and she's still getting to know her father."

"Exactly. But he *was* hiding one thing."

"What's that?"

Michael smiled. "Remember the interested buyer Dean had for Casa de Lirio before Justin's murder?"

"Yes." Julia sighed. "RIP, interested buyers." Both the Van Verdens and the other party she'd shown the house to had moved on after seeing it in the news. Neither would be putting in a formal offer. Both might have been put off by the news vans parked outside the gate.

"Apparently that's what Rich and Cy were arguing about at the party. Rich had every intention of buying Casa de Lirio in Maddy's name and giving it to her."

Sergio gasped. "Lily would be furious."

"On so many levels," Michael said. "Furious about Madeline's existence. Furious that Rich could buy the house and put it in her name. According to Cy, it wouldn't violate the property settlement for him to do that, but he wanted Rich to keep it quiet until the divorce was final."

Vivian frowned. "Why are people so crazy about real estate here?"

"It's Vista de Lirio." Sergio finished his Paloma. "The sun and the dry air fry your brain a little."

"And we still don't know who killed Justin Worthy," Evy said. "We just know it wasn't Richard Putnam."

Chapter Twenty-Five

That night, Aunt Marie returned.

"Oh my God!" Evy was yelling on the phone. "Get over here quick! She's back!"

Julia was confused. "Who?"

"Aunt Marie! She was staying with her sister in Boulder, but she's back!"

"I'm on my way." Julia looked at Justin, who was staring at the wall in a sullen stupor. "Aunt Marie is back."

He shrugged. "And what does that mean for me? I'm still stuck here."

"Maybe she'll know a way to send you to the other side. Or open that portal at Casa de Lirio. Or... I don't know. Put your soul at rest."

"Yeah, okay. Sure." He stood and waited as Julia got her things together. "Anytime is good for me. Don't rush or anything. I'm just sitting here. Being dead."

Julia didn't say anything but the internal eye roll was strong. *God save me from salty, put-upon ghosts.* Justin couldn't move on fast enough.

By the time they pulled into Evy's driveway, Vivian's car was already there and all the lights were on.

Aunt Marie came out to greet them. 'Precious girl. My niece is in there with her new friend and she's talking about you too, and I can see how happy she is. Thank you, sweetie."

"Thank me for what?" Julia took the old woman's hands and let Marie pull her down to kiss her cheeks. 'For being friends with Evy?"

'She works too much, and she has no sisters. Never has time for anyone but those silly people she meets at parties. That's not the kind of friends you need when things go wrong in your life."

'Oh." Julia couldn't argue with that. 'Well... you know, she's really been great for me too. Her and Vivian."

Marie smiled and wagged a finger at her. 'Come on inside. I knew I was doing a good thing."

'Wait, what?" Julia's heart sank. 'What did you do?"

Marie led her and Justin into the house where Vivian and Evy were whispering like gossips in the kitchen.

'Is the ghost still with you?" Marie yelled. 'I'm getting a Sanka; is the ghost still here?"

'He is." Julia set down her purse and made a *what's going on?* face at her friends, who both shook their heads or shrugged.

'You." Marie turned to Julia. 'You had a brush with the other side of life." She tapped Julia's chest. 'I could feel it when I met you."

Vivian raised a hand. 'I want to point out that all this happened under mild anesthetic, so your memories of it may be—"

'My memories are fine!" Marie dumped two spoonfuls of freeze-dried coffee in a mug that read DON'T GO BACON MY HEART and had a logo from Desi's Diner on the front. 'She's the most obvious one." Marie pointed at Julia. 'But you're all women on the verge."

'The verge?" Evy asked.

"You're changing. Evolving." She pointed at Vivian. "You're going to need empathy in the next few years; I can see it."

Vivian's eyebrows went up. "How did you know—?"

"And you?" Marie looked at Julia. "You were already feeling the ghosts; I just let you make sense of what you were seeing."

"I wasn't seeing ghosts," Julia said. "Not before Justin."

"Think." Marie narrowed her eyes. "You know what I prayed to the Virgin for?"

"What?"

Marie walked over to Julia. "That you all would find the power you needed most." She looked at Evy. "*When* you needed it."

"You're saying that I *needed* the power to read people's thoughts?" Evy said. "Because when I hold Geoff, it doesn't make much sense."

"What does this have to do with that dummy?"

Evy looked confused. "Because that's when I have telepathy!"

Marie waved a hand and stirred her coffee. "That's a crutch, Evelyn Imanuela. You don't need the dummy. You are in control of your power. I don't know why you can't learn this."

"Don't tell me that! I don't want to hear voices all the time!"

"And the empathy?" Vivian shook her head. "I understand what you're saying, but it's too much. I understand needing to be in touch with my feelings, but this is ridiculous."

"You'll learn how to control it with time." Marie took her coffee and walked to the den. "Evelyn, where did you put my sewing machine?"

You'll learn?

Julia stared at Evy. "She's not going to reverse it."

"I asked her." Evy looked defeated. "She says she doesn't even know how."

Vivian sat down on the couch. Hard. "So we're just stuck with these powers?"

"No!" Julia didn't even want to think about that. "What... I mean how...? I can't live the rest of my life seeing ghosts!"

She looked at Justin, who was staring at a wall again. She couldn't imagine how boring it had to be. He was stuck following her around, watching life without being part of it, incapable of resting or finding any kind of peace.

"We need to figure out who killed him." Julia looked at Vivian and Evy. "We'll figure out all the other power stuff later, but we have to figure out who killed Justin first."

Marie slurped when she drank coffee. Julia realized that because the old woman wouldn't leave the murder room. "So this young man was hit over the head?"

"Yes."

"And he's strong," Marie said. "So whoever killed him is strong."

"And a pretty good driver," Evy said. "He's tried to run down Julia three times now."

"Twice." Julia pursed her lips and stared at the suspect board. "Just twice that I'm sure of."

"This person knows you're asking questions about the murder," Marie said. "You need to be careful." She pointed to Richard. "It is not this man. His eyes are kind even if his face is severe."

"Kind people can be pushed to murder," Vivian said, "but you're right. Richard has an alibi."

Evy pointed to Serena, Justin's ex-girlfriend. "Serena was genuinely in love with him. And didn't she say she had an alibi for that night too?"

"The police questioned her, but they dropped it," Julia said. "I don't think she's a suspect."

"That leaves Lily and Justin's friends he was supposed to meet that night."

"Do we even have their names?" Julia asked. "Lily said he was going out to meet them, but has anyone confirmed that?"

"We can ask her this weekend," Evy said. "I'm sure she'll be at Sunday Dinner."

"Has it already been a month?" Vivian asked. "No joke, huh? I can't believe it's been a month."

"Can't believe it's been a month..." Justin imitated her, muttering. "I can! I'm the dead one. It feels like it's been a year!"

"Justin, what friends would you have gone out with last month after Sunday Dinner?"

"Uhhh." He frowned. "Either Graham, Carlos, Chris, or Andrew. Donovan and I aren't speaking lately, so not him." He shrugged. "Ask Lily. I would have told her so she wouldn't get weird. If I didn't, she'd think I was cheating on her."

"Okay, cool," Julia said. "Justin gave me four names. He said he definitely would have told Lily though, so we should ask her."

Marie stood and tapped on Lily's picture. "Who is this one?"

"That's Lily Putnam, Marie." Evy lifted her voice a little. "Lily Putnam? You know, the actress?"

"I don't know her." Marie waved a hand. "I don't know actresses. She has cold eyes."

"She was the victim's girlfriend," Vivian said. "Lily and Justin were together for about a year."

Marie tapped on the picture. "It was her."

Julia and Evy exchanged a look. "Aunt Marie, the police questioned her and we did too. She was really broken up about Justin. Sincerely. She's having a hard time."

Marie shrugged. "So maybe she regrets killing him."

"I listened to her thoughts," Evy said. "There were no hints that she killed Justin."

"Maybe she's banished it from her memory!" Marie tapped

the picture. "Or maybe she hired someone. I don't know, but she has cold eyes."

"She could be a sociopath for all we know," Julia said. "But not all sociopaths are evil. She could have cold eyes and still be innocent of murder."

"We'll question her," Evy said. "How's that, Aunt Marie? Sunday Dinner is coming up this weekend, and we'll ask her more questions then."

"Good." Marie nodded decisively. "Because that one is hiding something. For sure."

THERE WAS JUST SOMETHING MAGICAL ABOUT DESERT nights. Julia walked out of her house wearing long linen pants, a sleeveless silk top, and her favorite sandals. She knew she looked good, and this time at Sunday Dinner, she wasn't going to feel like she was wearing a bedsheet over her underwear. She immediately saw Michael sitting nearby, stationed on the patio and watching the revelers as they filled the yard and the pool.

"Sit with me." He patted the chair next to him. "Tell me what you see."

Julia sat next to him, and he put a warm arm around her shoulders.

She scanned the party, taking in the living and the dead. "You see the band?" It was a new group this week, some ensemble that looked like it had fallen off the back of a Volkswagen camper van. "There are at least two dead rock stars I guarantee you would recognize standing next to them who look like they're critiquing the performance."

"Interesting."

"Want to know which?"

Michael frowned. "I don't think so. I like the idea of ghosts, but knowing their identities would be a little too real. And I kind of like imagining who."

"Fair enough." She continued scanning the grounds. "Mae is hanging with everyone near the pool. That's her usual spot; she looks happy. Justin is with her, and he's glaring at someone."

"Can you see who?"

"No." She looked for Elton and Mrs. G., but she didn't see them. "The visiting ghosts tend to hang along the edges. Looks like they enjoy seeing Morty and Elaine's antics though."

"They're probably seeing a lot more of Morty and Elaine than just antics."

"Judging by how many run away laughing when they duck into the bushes, I think you're right." Julia hooked her fingers with his. "It's not scary. Is that weird?"

"No. Like I said, I like the idea. If there was a place that made me happy, maybe I'd want to hang out there for eternity too."

"Not anytime soon please."

Michael turned to her and smiled. "You too."

Julia looked up. "I'm a little afraid of dying now."

"You weren't before?"

She shook her head. "My life had gotten pretty predictable in LA. I felt disconnected. I guess I didn't care about much. But now..."

Michael smiled. "Now?"

Paco ran past them, a pool towel draped over his back and a bikini top between his teeth. A few seconds later, a nearly naked woman ran after him, trying to cover her breasts with one arm.

"Now my life has gotten distinctly more interesting." Julia turned to him. "I like it."

"I think I'm ready to buy a house." Michael smiled. "Would you like to help?"

Julia couldn't stop the grin. "In Vista de Lirio?"

"Where else?"

"Why?" Did that sound rude? "I mean why now? Why here?"

"Don't get me wrong. I'm still going to travel a lot. I finally signed on to a project that should start shooting next month in the Czech Republic, but..." He shrugged. "I think I like the idea of having my own place."

"A home?"

"Yeah." His voice was slow and sweet. "If it's the right one."

"Hmm." She pursed her lips. "You definitely need to hire me."

"As long as that won't keep me from sleeping with you out of some misguided professional ethic, yes. But if it's a choice between sleeping with you and hiring you, I'll find another real estate agent."

"I don't think I'm going to fire myself for sleeping with a client." She leaned toward him. "But I appreciate the ethical consideration."

Michael bent down and took her mouth in a kiss that quickly turned from slow and lazy to intentional. His hand slid into her hair and held her. His thumb stroked down the silken skin on her neck, his callused thumb sending shivers across her skin.

"So when should I plan on violating professional ethics?" Julia murmured against his mouth. "Did you have a date on your calendar?"

"Maybe when I get back from Prague."

Julia pulled her mouth away. "What?"

Michael laughed. "Okay, good to know you weren't keen to take it *that* slow."

"I am also enjoying the anticipation, but we're in the second half of our lives, Michael. We're not going to live forever."

He put a hand over his heart. "Kick a guy when he just asked you to be his girlfriend, why don't you?"

"Is this you asking me to be your girlfriend?"

"We still do that, right? I don't think I'm old enough to have a lady friend. Or a female companion. Significant other is a mouthful, and partner sounds like business to me."

"So let me get this right." She leaned back and crossed her arms. "You're getting a house here, but you're coming out of retirement, so you'll be working on sets again."

"Yeah. Being completely up front with you, I'm still going to end up traveling a lot. At least five or six months out of the year. But I'm less inclined to rent a place in New York or go couch surfing in Australia between jobs now. I really do want a place here." He smiled. "I'll just plan on working when it gets too hot."

"I didn't sell my place in Malibu either," Julia said. "So that's an option."

"I mean... if you were my girlfriend, that would be an option."

She smiled. "So you're going to be gone half the year?"

"Exactly. I won't be around long enough for you to get sick of me." He played with the edge of her sleeve. "So you want to be my girlfriend, Julia? Or my... lady friend? Please don't say lady friend—I don't think you have enough doilies or cats for that."

"Girlfriend doesn't bother me as long as you're out of the country for a good portion of the year." She stood and tugged him to his feet. "Come on, boyfriend, let's go see who decided to come to Sunday Dinner."

"I don't even get a kiss to seal the deal?"

She rose to her toes and placed a promising kiss on his lips. "Plan on staying here tonight and you'll get a lot more than that."

Chapter Twenty-Six

As they walked through the party, Julia realized something was tickling the back of her mind. She had that feeling she got when she'd seen something or read something important that she couldn't quite remember.

An irritating feeling that got worse after fifty.

She squeezed Michael's hand. "I feel like I've walked into a room and forgotten why I was there."

"I hate that feeling."

"Right?" She strolled past the bar where she picked up a glass of champagne and then headed toward the buffet. Sergio and Dean had hired their favorite taco truck to serve food that night, so chafing dishes of carne asada, pollo asada, and grilled veggies wafted delicious scents between the house and the pool.

The cabanas were full of revelers, and people spread pool towels and beach chairs across the lawn.

"Did the circus come to town?" Michael pointed to a group of people on the lawn who were tumbling.

"Technically, yes. That is an avant-garde dance troupe that incorporates gymnastics into their routines. They're Algerian."

"I filmed a movie in Algeria once." Michael sipped a whiskey on ice. "And I guess now I know they have an avant-garde dance troupe that tumbles."

"Mmm." What was she forgetting? "Hey, is Richard coming tonight?"

"I invited him." He turned to her. "You asked me to, remember?"

"That's what I was forgetting!" She dropped his hand and hustled toward the cabanas where Lily and Justin had been the Sunday Dinner before. Had she shown up?

"Julia?"

She came to a halt on the edge of the cabanas, peeking out from behind a gnarled jacaranda. She felt Michael approach behind her.

"What are we doing?"

"Shhhh!"

"Julia, I can't even hear myself think, the band is so loud. I hardly think subterfuge is necessary."

He was right. She was probably making herself more conspicuous, not less. "Fine."

"What are we doing?" Michael took her hand again. "Are you looking for Richard?"

"No, I'm looking for Lily." She turned to him. "Question, did Richard bring Madeline tonight?"

"Yes. Should he not have? You specifically told me to tell him to—"

"No, that's perfect!" She squeezed his hand and strolled toward the firepit where she could hear Sergio's voice. "I know Sergio and Dean were dying to meet her after all the revelations this week. And this lets me see how Lily reacts."

He grunted. "So that's what this is about. She might be nasty to Maddy. Maybe I should warn—"

"Don't." She patted his shoulder. "It'll be fine. I already

warned Dean and Sergio to keep her with them if she's away from her father; plus she's a grown woman." Richard's secret daughter was twenty-nine years old. She was hardly a delicate flower.

"Julia, what is this all about?"

On the edge of the firepit, Julia stopped and slid her arm around Michael. If anyone was looking, she'd appear to be a woman enjoying the party with her date.

Sergio was letting Genevieve De Winter tell a story about the time she put Jackson Pollock in his place when he tried to seduce her. The tiny woman could tell a hilarious story, but her voice wasn't very loud, so everyone was leaning in.

Sergio was next to Genevieve, and Richard's daughter Maddy was on his left, holding a glass of champagne. She was tall and slender like her mother and had a faint melancholy around her eyes that reminded Julia of Kiki's ghost, but she was smiling and laughing along with everyone else. Her features were a blend of Kiki and Richard, but her coloring was one hundred percent from her mother.

"She's lovely," Julia said. "Have you met her yet?"

"Yeah. Richard brought her to drinks when we met the other night. She's a nice kid. Had a few troubles when she was younger, but it seems like she's making the most of her fresh start out here."

"That's awesome." Julia couldn't imagine growing up without a mother or a father. Without even knowing who her father was.

Speaking of fathers...

Richard was standing across from them, listening to Genevieve and speaking quietly to a man in a bright Hawaiian shirt. They were smiling and appeared to exchange business cards.

And in the distance, Lily Putnam glared at him with daggers in her eyes.

"There." Julia nodded subtly across the patio. "That's what I needed to see."

"What?"

"Lily is by the pool." In fact, Mae wasn't too far from her. "Look at her."

"Fuck, she hates him." Michael sighed. "I was hoping it would mellow out, but—"

"What was Lily and Richard's biggest disappointment as a couple?"

Michael made the connection quickly. "Not having children. And now Richard is a father."

"Yep. And his child is from an affair with a woman while he was married to Lily. You said it yourself, Richard wanted to leave her but didn't because she'd just lost a pregnancy. Can you even imagine how wronged she feels?"

"Fuck." Michael sighed. "Poor Lily."

Julia wasn't too sure about that. "Weeks ago, she said something that stuck with me. She said, 'I will never move on from what that man did to me.' I couldn't get that out of my head."

"The fuck? What Richard did to *her*?"

"It didn't make sense at the time. They'd been married, they broke up. And it seemed like Lily was the one cheating on Richard, not the other way round. What could he have done that was so awful? That would make her hate Richard so much? Then I learned about the affair with Kiki. Then about Madeline, Richard's *daughter*."

"But Lily didn't know about—"

"About his affair with Kiki?" She cocked her head. "Are you sure? I know you think Lily didn't know about the affair or the baby." Julia turned to Michael, keeping Lily in her sight. "But I think Lily knew the whole time. I think she knew everything."

She left Michael talking with Richard and went looking for Evy and Vivian.

Justin appeared when she walked past the pool. "You have to get me out of here."

"Can't you just disappear?" She couldn't find her friends, and they were both supposed to be here. "Fade? You know, that thing you do when I get mad at you."

"No, I can't. It's like I'm being pulled here. I think it's because this is where everything started."

She stopped. "Where what started?"

"The fight with Lily."

Julia blinked. "You never told me you were fighting with Lily that night."

"I just remembered." Justin crossed his arms and sighed. "Will you get your phone out so we can have a conversation please? Otherwise, you're going to realize you look like you're talking to yourself and tell me to go away."

"No phones allowed at Sunday Dinner, remember?"

"Oh bullshit. There's always someone. Last month I saw the little hellion girls sneaking around and taking pictures of me without my shirt."

Julia walked behind a palmetto bush to hide. "Are you saying that Sergio and Dean's daughters have pictures of last month's party?"

"Unless they've deleted them."

Thoughts were flying around Julia's head like a dozen racquetballs all served at once.

Justin and Lily fighting.

Lily's searing hatred of Richard.

The girls had pictures of the party.

I will never move on from what that man did to me! What he's still doing to me. What he forced me to accept in the divorce..."

She looked at Justin. "How much did Lily hate losing the house?"

'She was obsessed with it." Justin rolled his eyes. 'I told her it was just a place, but she was like a maniac when it came to that house. Said it was hers, that she'd earned it or something. I think she was just pissed because she used to be the queen of this stupid neighborhood, living there, and she wasn't anymore."

'No, she wasn't." Julia glanced from behind the palmetto toward the fireplace, one of the dozen bouncing racquetballs coming into focus.

Madeline Putnam was sitting next to Sergio, the unofficial social director of Vista de Lirio, the most exclusive neighborhood in Palm Springs. The young, beautiful daughter of Richard Putnam, whose father would buy Casa de Lirio for her with a snap of his fingers, handing Maddy the house, the view, and the social status that Lily had worked decades to cultivate.

Unless there was something she could give Richard that he wanted more than the house. Something she and Richard had been fighting about in the financial settlement even though it was supposedly missing.

'Lily has the Putnam Diamond," Julia said.

'Of course she does," Justin said. 'That's what we were— Oh!" His face lit up. 'I remember now."

Julia wanted to reach out and hug him. Or maybe smack him. But Justin was incorporeal, which kind of put a damper on both urges. 'What do you remember?"

'That's what we were fighting about that night. She told me she'd hidden the Putnam Diamond somewhere and she was going to give it to Richard in exchange for the house."

'And you wanted to keep the diamond."

'She could have sold the diamond discreetly and still have kept half the money from the house. Who cares that she'd have to buy a new place? We would have had *millions*."

'But the house was more important to her than the money."

'Yes!" He looked furious. 'I was so pissed."

'Is that why you were at the house that night?"

'I still don't remember that. I remember thinking I wanted a drink. That was my main thought. I wanted to get really drunk."

Of course you did.

Julia spotted Evy and Vivian by the pool. 'Okay, stick with me, Justin. I'm going back in."

He shuddered. 'I feel like I'm crawling out of my skin here. Maril— Mae tried to keep me chill, but I couldn't handle it."

"This ends tonight," Julia said. 'We're figuring out the truth, and then hopefully you can move on."

She walked over the lawn, waving at Evy and Vivian; they were two lounge chairs down from Lily, who appeared to be flirting with one of the dancers from Algeria.

'Hey," Evy called. 'We were looking for you. Michael is here?"

Julia raised her voice to make sure Lily could hear. 'Yes! He's talking with Richard right now. Have you met his daughter yet?"

Lily's jaw tightened.

'I haven't. She seems nice though."

'She's a teacher at Aurelia and Juliana's school. Isn't that great?"

A mental racquetball struck her forehead. *The girls had pictures of last month's Sunday Dinner!*

Julia smiled. 'You know, Evy, you should go say hi to Aurelia and Juliana. They were asking about you and Geoff the other day."

Evy frowned. 'Really?"

Julia nodded. 'Should we go find them?" She caught Vivian's eye. 'Maybe Vivian can hold our chairs?" She darted her eyes in Lily's direction.

Vivian caught on. 'No problem. Why don't you ladies go say hi to the kids and I'll keep your place here."

'Sounds good." Evy rose and walked over to Julia.

'Oh look!" Julia steered them toward Lily. 'Lily, it's so great to see you."

Lily glanced at them with a cool expression. 'Sergio's friends. How sweet to see you again, Julia. Any word on the house yet? I really thought Dean would have more offers by this point.'

Bitch. 'Well, it's a very niche property, but the minute we have an offer, your attorney and Richard's will be the first to know,' Julia smiled and waited for Lily to smile back.

Which she did. Eventually. 'Perfect.'

'You know, I had a quick question I wasn't sure if the police asked you or not. I was talking with John Marcos the other day, and he mentioned they were going to try to find Justin's friends that he went out for a drink with the night he died. What did you say their names were?'

Lily looked flustered. 'Um... God, it's been so long.' She closed her eyes as if searching her memory. 'Graham and Donovan, I think. Maybe some others, but I'm honestly not sure.'

'Okay cool,' Julia said. 'I'll pass that along to Dean. They're meeting for a round tomorrow.'

Her face shuttered. 'Of course.' Lily turned back to her dancer friend. 'I hope you'll excuse me...'

Julia and Evy continued toward the house.

'What was that?' Evy asked. 'Lily was thinking in super-confused flashes and so are you.'

'Oh!' She turned to Evy. 'Are you expanding your telepathy? That's great! Right? Maybe it's not great.'

'If I can get some mental discipline, *that* would be great. I'm trying to use some tricks Aunt Marie got from a friend of hers she won't name at all. It's not super clear, but I'm getting a little more control. Are we really going to question the twins?'

'That's great. And yes we are. We're going to the house to ask my nieces to show us the pictures they paparazzi'd last month at Sunday Dinner. They're probably running a thriving blackmail operation, but I just want to see if they caught any of Lily and Justin at the party.'

"Why?"

"Because Justin and Donovan weren't talking lately, but according to Lily, they were going out for drinks the night he died."

"And that means...?"

"Lily killed Justin," Julia said. "And I think I can prove it."

Chapter Twenty-Seven

They found Juliana and Aurelia near Paco's small barn at the back of the estate, which was outfitted with heaters, blankets, and more amenities than most luxury hotel rooms.

Julia and Evy walked around the corner and saw Aurelia hand her sister a phone before she turned to them with a smile.

"Aunt Julia. And Aunt Julia's haunted friend. It's so very nice to see you; how can Juliana, Paco, and I be of assistance?"

"Aren't you supposed to be watching movies?"

"Analu fell asleep."

"So you decided to make a break for it and spy on Sunday Dinner?"

The girls exchanged a look.

"We were just checking on Paco," Aurelia said.

"Cut it," Julia said. "I saw the phone, and honestly I don't care what you have on it, but I need to see the pictures from last month."

Juliana narrowed her eyes. "And what do we get for our cooperation?"

'I won't march over to the party right now and tell your fathers that you're spying on their guests."

Aurelia offered her a measuring look. 'I'm going to need more specificity, Auntie Julia. You won't go right now? Ever? Let's talk numbers."

'Okay..." She considered it. 'Three months. I'll give you three months to wrap up your operation."

The girls exchanged another silent look that spoke volumes.

'Deal." Juliana held out her hand, and Julia took it and shook. 'There's nothing incriminating that we've been able to find." She pulled the phone from her pocket, unlocked it, and handed it to Julia.

'I'm not looking for blackmail material." She scrolled quickly through the thumbnails until she got what looked like Sunday Dinner from the month before.

Evy looked over her shoulder.

'There." Evy pointed. 'Go back, it was below that."

Julia enlarged the pictures and flipped through them carefully. 'I just need to see *her*."

'Lily?"

'Yes." She had a faint memory, but she needed proof. 'Girls, if I find what I'm looking for, I will be taking this phone and handing it over to the police."

'That wasn't in the deal!" Aurelia pouted.

Julia glanced up. 'Murder, kid. There was a murder committed, remember?"

The girls' sighs were extremely tortured. 'Fi-ine."

'There's Justin." Evy pointed at the phone. 'Do you see—?"

'Lily."

Julia stopped and zoomed in on a picture of Lily and Justin sitting by the pool. Justin was feeding his girlfriend grapes, and Lily was laying out, a pool bag swinging from the back of her chaise and her legs stretched in front of her. Her diamond-clad hand rested on her knee.

"There." Julia looked up. "Do you see it?"

"See what?" Evy frowned.

"Her hand."

"Okay, what about it?"

"Or rather, I should say do you see her fingernails?"

Evy looked up with wide eyes. "It wasn't a diamond."

Julia shook her head.

AURELIA AND JULIANA DIRECTED JULIA TO DEAN'S golf cart while Evy texted Vivian to join them.

"All our cars are packed in the front of the driveway," Julia said. "We have to walk or golf cart it."

"Should we call the police?" Evy asked. "We need to look in that hidden compartment again. Or maybe there's another hidden compartment. Maybe there are more rhinestones. Maybe the Putnam Diamond is still there!"

"I highly doubt that the Putnam Diamond is still there," Julia said. "But I'm pretty sure it was hidden there at one point. And we'll call the police if we find something." Julia was dying to know if Lily had any other hiding spots, and she wanted to know *now*. If they called the police, they'd be cut out of the answers.

No way. They were the ones who'd solved this.

"The keys are in the glove compartment." Juliana pointed to the cart. "Sometimes it sticks and you have to jiggle it a little to get it open."

Julia raised an eyebrow. "And you know this how?"

"It's a golf cart, Auntie Jules." Aurelia looked bored. "It doesn't go over twenty miles an hour. Don't be uncool."

"And by uncool, I'm assuming you want your golf cart joyrides to fly under the radar along with your party surveillance?"

Juliana asked, 'How else are we supposed to let Paco terrorize the snobs at the golf club on weekends?"

Julia narrowed her eyes and stared at her namesake. 'You have a point." She knocked her fist against the glove compartment and it popped open. 'Your secret is safe. For now."

'Understood." Juliana and Aurelia stepped back. 'Good luck with the ghosts."

Justin was already sitting in the back seat. 'I'm not sure why we're going over to Casa de Lirio."

'We need to look at that secret compartment again. Justin, did you know where Lily's safe was?"

'Yes. And so did Richard. There's nothing in it now; I checked."

'I thought you said Lily didn't let you see it! When did you check? The night you died?"

'No, she left it open when we were moving her stuff out. Trust me, it was empty."

Julia steered the golf cart between the mass of parked cars. 'Justin said Lily's safe is empty."

'But if she had one hiding spot in the kitchen, she might have had another one." Evy held on to the side as Julia swerved to avoid one of the dogs. 'That's what you're thinking."

'Yep." She spotted Vivian standing near the gate, surrounded by Elton, Mrs. Griffin, and a few other spirits. 'The dead are really out tonight."

'Something feels weird," Justin said. 'I don't know what it is, but if I could itch, I would."

Vivian jumped in the golf cart. 'Where are we going and why?"

'My nieces had pictures of the night Justin was killed."

Vivian looked alarmed. 'They were at Casa de Lirio?"

'No. Here, at Sunday Dinner." She nodded toward Evy. 'Evy, show her."

"Look." Evy shoved the mobile phone in Vivian's face. "Look at her fingernails."

"Oh my God, the rock that policeman found was a rhinestone off Lily's nails!" Vivian clutched the handle on the dashboard of the golf cart. "Can't this thing go faster?"

THEY OPENED THE SECRET COMPARTMENT IN THE kitchen first thing, then systematically started pushing on every other drawer side and cupboard bottom they could find. There were a few more hidden compartments, but all of them were empty.

"Nothing," Evy declared after an hour. "If she was hiding anything in this place, it's gone now."

"It doesn't really make any sense that she'd have kept it here after the house went on the market," Vivian said. "The place is empty, and she's living in another neighborhood."

"But it was here last month when Justin came to poke around." Julia turned to the ghost, who was perched on a countertop. "Wasn't it?"

"What?" He shrugged. "I already told you I don't remember."

"Except you do remember fighting with Lily about the necklace that night."

"Yes, but that wasn't until we got to her place." His eyes went wide. "Oh right. Yeah, that was at her house."

"What started the fight?" Julia asked. "Why did it happen that night?"

He frowned. "I'd heard something at the party. Something about the house."

Julia walked to Justin and held out her hands. "Try remembering. Put yourself back at the party."

Justin closed his eyes. "It was warm, so I got a cold beer.

There was a woman talking behind me, and I didn't recognize her voice. She said something about Richard buying the house after all." He opened his eyes. "She heard a rumor that the buyer Dean was talking to was really Richard's girlfriend. The offer for Casa de Lirio was Richard, except he was using his girlfriend's name."

"And you told Lily when you got home?" Julia asked.

"I guess maybe." He nodded. "That makes sense. Lily already knew that Richard had been around town with a young blonde and... Oh yeah, that was probably his daughter."

Vivian stood between Julia and Justin. "What is he saying?"

"When they got back to Lily's house after the party, Justin told Lily that the offer on Casa de Lirio was really Richard using his girlfriend, but it must have been Maddy."

"Yes." Justin pointed at her. "That was the name. Madeline or Marilyn or something like that. And Lily kind of blew up. That's when she told me about her so-called trump card."

"She told you she had the Putnam Diamond?"

"I think so?" He frowned. "That part is kind of fuzzy, but I knew she'd hidden it. That's why I came here."

"With Lily?"

"Hell no." He cocked his head. "Or wait, did I?"

Echoing Justin's own thoughts, Vivian asked, "If they were at Lily's, how did Justin get here the night he died? I assumed he walked from Sergio and Dean's house, but if he went home with Lily before he came here—"

"I drove him."

They turned to see Lily Putnam enter the kitchen, a gun pointed at Julia.

"You're a terrible real estate agent," she said. "Four weeks and no offers on a prime piece of Palm Springs real estate like this? You need to focus on selling houses, not solving murders."

Chapter Twenty-Eight

"Why?" Julia kept her hands up, backing away from the gun. "Why would you kill Justin?"

Lily rolled her eyes. "I hate playing into clichés, but the man simply knew too much. I couldn't have anyone with that much leverage over me." She shook her head. "I've learned my lesson about that."

"You won't get away with it!" Evy made a face. "You're right; clichés just sound like bad movie writing when you say them out loud."

Lily pointed the gun at Evy. "Then maybe you should shut your mouth."

Evy stuck her hands up. "But really, you won't get away with this. Killing Julia or any of us will only make it more obvious that we were on the right track. We've already told multiple people we suspect you."

It was a bluff. Julia hadn't told anyone she suspected Lily. Still, it might work if they all played along.

"Sergio and Dean know," Vivian said.

"So does Michael O'Connor," Evy said. "He didn't want to

believe us, but he knows we suspected you most. If you kill us now—"

"Hands!" Lily shouted. "I want to see your hands, ladies."

Vivian put her hands up and Evy raised hers higher when Lily pointed the gun at them, but Julia saw the edge of Vivian's phone peeking out from her pocket.

Julia could tell that the idea of Sergio and Dean knowing about her crimes was making Lily panic. She was both encouraged and worried about that. A desperate Lily with a gun was not a safe thing.

"Lily." Julia tried to grab her attention and keep her focus off Vivian and Evy. "Did you try to run me over with your car?"

Lily sniffed. "I have no idea what you're talking about."

"It was Bernardo!" Evy shouted. "Your driver. I heard you thinking it."

Vivian turned to Evy. "Really? And you don't even have Geoff! That's great progress."

"I know." Evy smiled. "I think Aunt Marie was right; it was really just a crutch I was using to block—"

"Will you two shut up?" Lily was pointing the gun back toward them, and her hand was shaking. "You can't hear my thoughts. That's crazy."

"But you were thinking Bernardo." Evy was more subdued and kept her hands up. "Wasn't he your alibi too?"

"Shut up!" Lily said. "All three of you." She kept swinging the gun between Evy, Vivian, and Julia.

The shaking gun was making Julia nervous. She tried to imagine tackling Lily to the ground, but with the way Lily was swinging the gun around, there was no guarantee it wouldn't go off and hit one of her friends.

Lily continued, "Bernardo loves me, and he knows I'm innocent."

"You're going to have a hard time explaining this one." Julia inched toward the stove. "You think he'll believe you when you ask him to alibi you for *another* murder? At some point the man is going to have to question his own loyalty."

"It doesn't matter; I'll figure it out." Lily lifted her chin. "I always have in the past."

"The past?"

Evy glanced at Julia. "She's thinking about Kiki."

"Wow." Vivian waved a hand. "*So* many complicated feelings swirling around about that."

The gun swung back toward them. "Will you shut up?" Lily screamed. "What is wrong with you?"

"I saw her face in your thoughts." Evy squeaked, holding her hands out. "I'm sorry, I can't help it."

"Of course." Julia's arms were getting tired from holding them up. "You killed Kiki too. You found out about Kiki and Richard's affair and decided to get rid of the competition." She really needed to start doing some weight lifting or something.

"Did you know about Maddy?" Vivian asked. "Did you know about Richard and Kiki's daughter?"

"She isn't *his* daughter!" Lily screamed. "The doctors told us. Richard was the one with the problem, not me. *I* should have had children; it was his fault that I didn't." The woman laughed maniacally. "I guess I should be happy that someone is finally taking Richard for a ride. I hope she takes everything from him. Everything!"

Julia felt panic as Lily's control seemed to slip. She glanced at Vivian and Evy, but both of them had their eyes fixed on Lily and the gun.

"Lily, we understand—"

"Bullshit. You understand nothing. Want to know the stupidest thing? I loved him anyway." She pointed at herself. "Even after I found out about that woman, I was faithful. Then *that woman* comes to my own house and tells me I should let my own husband go?" Lily curled her lip. "That they had a future together? They were going to have a family? *Fuck her!*"

Julia's adrenaline was roaring, and she could see Evy starting to panic, but when Vivian spoke, her voice was all compassion.

"That shouldn't have happened to you, Lily." She kept her voice even and soft. "That was wrong."

Lily swung the gun toward Vivian and screamed, "What do you know about it?"

Vivian's voice remained even and soothing. "Kiki and Richard were both wrong. I cannot imagine how horrible that felt. You had every right to be angry."

"I never cheated on him." The gun wavered in Lily's hand. "Not ever, even when the most beautiful men... I was faithful; he wasn't."

"I know." Vivian nodded. "I can see how much you loved him."

"And then that woman comes into his life and he decides... he's just done with me?" Lily's voice grew cold. "That was not the deal."

Wrong or not, Kiki Stevens didn't deserve to die. Julia felt her gut twist; she was desperate to get Lily's attention back on her. Maybe Evy and Vivian could get away and get help. "Did you drug Kiki yourself? Pay someone to do it?"

The handgun stopped shaking when Lily pointed it at Julia. "She was already high—I just helped her along a little bit. Gave her a few extra pills, helped her into the sauna." Lily's shoulders rose. "I didn't lock the door; the woman killed herself."

Justin's ghost moved and stood between Lily and Julia. "I remember now."

"What do you remember, Justin?" Julia kept her eyes fixed on Lily. "Tell me what you remember."

"What kind of sick game are you playing?" Lily snarled. "Shut up about Justin."

"It was her." Justin's voice was pure venom. "Lily killed me. She told me that the Putnam Diamond was here. That we had to go get it so Richard couldn't take the house. I argued with her, tried to make her let this stupid house go, keep half the money and the diamond, but she wouldn't." Justin sounded disgusted. "That's what we were fighting about. We were fighting about Richard buying the goddamn house."

Julia started to hear a thrum in her ears, the warm, vibrating music she remembered from the portal outside coming to life. "Lily, I know you told Justin the diamond was here."

A muscle in her perfectly sculpted jaw twitched. "That's impossible."

"Sergio wasn't exaggerating; I'm psychic. I really do see ghosts."

"And I can read your thoughts," Evy said.

"I can feel how hurt you are," Vivian added. "Please, Lily, let's end this here. You don't want anyone else to get hurt."

Lily laughed. "You're all terrible actresses, and believe me, I can recognize one. It doesn't matter what you say about the house or Justin or anything. You don't have any proof, and Casa de Lirio will be mine by next week."

Julia said, "Lily, I'm not a lawyer, but I am a real estate agent. I know there has to be a way—"

"Yes, after a brutal triple murder" —she waved the gun across the kitchen— "no one will want to touch this place. Richard will be happy to be rid of it if I offer him that ridiculous necklace in trade."

Julia kept her voice even and her eyes on Lily. Her heart was pounding, but she felt oddly calm. After all, she'd lived through worse. She wasn't alone anymore. If she fell, Vivian and Evy were there.

"Justin is here," Julia said. "He's right here with us. He's been with me ever since I found him the morning after you murdered him."

"You're lying."

"You fought about the Putnam Diamond that night." Julia

kept her voice even. "Justin wanted to sell it, and you wanted to trade it for the house."

"I just told you that."

"But you didn't tell us that you fought."

"It doesn't matter." Lily pointed the gun at Julia. "Justin meant nothing to me."

"He wants me to tell you that he loved you," Julia said. "And that he forgives you for killing him."

Chapter Twenty-Nine

"Are you fucking kidding me?" Justin's ghost yelled. "I don't love her, and I definitely don't forgive her for killing me!"

Julia ignored him and kept her voice low and soothing, channeling the profound calm she sensed from the portal and the energy Vivian was pushing toward her. "Justin knows your heart was hurting. He understands why you did what you did."

Evy and Vivian inched closer to Julia.

"No, I fucking do not." Justin's leaned down and screamed in Lily's ear. "I hate you, you old bitch! You hear that? I had my whole life in front of me, and I hate you for stealing it!"

Lily swallowed hard. "I didn't want to kill him."

"Yes, you did!" Justin was nearly jumping in rage. "You fucking did or you wouldn't have invited me to this fucking house to look for a diamond you already had!" He stood up straight. "She has it. It's somewhere in her fucking rental house. Get the police and go search for it."

Even if she did, Julia knew that wouldn't prove anything about Justin's death.

"Lily, I understand why you did what you did." Which was

bullshit, but Julia was struggling to stay calm. "This house *should* belong to you. You're the one who cares about it."

"Yes," Evy added. "This was your home. You made this house what it is."

Vivian slid closer to Julia. "I can feel your energy everywhere, Lily. The house loves you."

Julia moved slowly toward her friends, inching past the giant stainless steel range that dominated the kitchen. Lily moved with her, mirroring her.

"Casa de Lirio is just an investment to Richard." She patted her chest. "I understand the house's *soul*."

"I can tell. There are so many lives here," Julia said. *And so many spirits.*

Something about the portal had to be changing, because Julia could see ghosts in the windows and the doorways. She felt them surrounding her and saw them drifting through the walls and toward the back of the house.

The house itself began to hum. She closed her eyes, a piercing headache starting to form between her ears. "Hurts." She put a hand to her temple and reached out, bracing herself on the range. "Vivian? Evy?"

Vivian stepped forward, her hands raised. Evy was on Vivian's right side, and Julia was on her left. "Lily, how do we work this out so no one else gets hurt? Julia is getting a migraine, and people are going to start looking for us soon. Sergio and Dean expect us to come back to the party."

Lily cocked her head. "You know, I like you three. I wish I'd had friends like you when I lived here."

"We can be friends," Evy said. "Lily, we all want—"

"I wish I didn't have to kill you."

"Wow," Evy muttered. "Very uncool."

"But I do." She lifted the gun and walked closer to Vivian. "Starting with you."

Julia'd had enough. Keeping her eyes down and her fingers

to her temple, she reached for the decorative cast-iron pan the stagers had placed at the back of the stove, grabbed it, and swung her arm in an arc, whacking the gun from Lily's hand and away from her friends.

The actress screamed and clutched her arm as the gun flew through the air; it landed on the tile floor, firing with an explosive CRACK. Glass shattered and sprayed across the kitchen as Evy and Vivian tackled Lily to the ground, and Julia ducked down to avoid the flying shards.

Lily screamed and struggled as Vivian and Evy lay on top of her, twisting to grab her hands and feet.

"Fuck what Justin said." Evy grunted. "This chick is strong!"

"Let me go!"

"It's over, Lily!" Julia tiptoed across the glass-strewn tile and grabbed the gun. She pointed it at the ground and stood next to Lily. "I'm calling the police." Julia took her cell phone from her pocket. "My name is Julia Brooks, and I'm in Vista de Lirio," she told the operator who answered her emergency call. "Lily Putnam just tried to shoot me and my friends."

JULIA SAT ON A CHAISE IN THE BACKYARD, STARING AT the meteor shower that had unexpectedly graced the desert sky. Justin sat on the end of the lounger, his eyes pointed at the lights dancing across the darkness.

"There's something about nights here," Justin said. "I was in LA for a while, but once I moved out here, I never wanted to be anywhere else."

"You can stay if you want." Julia looked at the glowing golden portal that was wide open. Some spirits ran and others crept. Others seemed to linger, unsure of what they should do. "Or you can go. I don't think there's a right or wrong answer."

Justin sat next to her on the end of the chaise, staring. "I don't know what to do."

"I can't tell you." Julia watched as the spirits who looked so solid to her eyes dissolved into a shower of red-gold sparks as they approached the portal. "It doesn't look scary though."

"It looks like you turn into ash." Justin sighed. "But at least I know I *can* go if I want."

"I think it opened for you," Julia said. "But I guess I should tell you that if you decide to stay, I'm okay with it. I know the psychic thing isn't going away or anything like that. Pretty resigned to that now."

Justin turned to look at her. "Really? So if I want to spend the rest of my eternity tagging along with you, you're fine with it?"

Please, God, no.

"Uh..."

The ghost smirked. "It's cool. I know you have a life." He turned back to the portal. "And I don't. Not really. What this is here?" He shrugged. "It's just a shadow of one."

Julia said, "Who knows what's on the other side? It might be awesome."

"I'm not afraid." He stood. "I'm not going to be afraid anymore."

Elton and Mae appeared beside him.

"Hey, kid." Elton patted him on the shoulder. "We'll walk with you if you want."

"Don't you worry, honey." Mae kissed his cheek. "I'll even hold your hand."

Justin turned to her. "Thanks for listening."

"You're welcome."

"And I really hope you don't find any more dead people in houses you have to show."

"Thanks—me too."

"Okay." He turned to Mae. "I guess I'm ready to go."

Mae smiled and took his hand. "You're going to do great; I just know it."

She watched them walk across the lawn and approach the portal. A sound over her shoulder made her turn. Mrs. Griffin appeared, and her eyes looked slightly glassy as Mae and Elton walked Justin Worthy's spirit toward the light.

"What about you, Mrs. G? Any desire to move on?"

Justin hesitated only for a moment; then a bright smile lifted his features and he quickly walked to the portal, disappearing into a radiant cloud of gold as Elton and Mae waved at his dissolving form.

Julia blinked back unexpected tears. "Mrs. G?"

The old woman cleared her throat. "And let Vista de Lirio fall under the supervision of musicians, artists, and ne'er-do-wells?" She puffed out her chest. "Ridiculous."

Chapter Thirty

J ulia woke up to the scent of Michael in her face. She was crushed against his chest, and a line of drool marked his grey shirt. She winced and rolled away to see him smiling at her with a sleepy expression.

"Hey, Blondie. You snore a little bit."

Julia sat up and rubbed her eyes. "This was not the way I imagined our first sleepover going."

"The snoring doesn't bother me. I sleep very soundly since I spent time with the monks."

"I drooled on your shirt."

"Did you?" He looked down, then reached for the edge of his shirt and took it off in one smooth movement. "There. No drool now."

Julia blinked. "Speak for yourself."

It had been a while since she'd had a man in her bed, and the last guy she'd been with had been much younger. Michael was well-muscled and tan, but the hair on his chest was a healthy mix of silver and black. She felt a little thrill run up her spine.

He had scars on his abdomen—probably from his accident —and tattoos across his chest and along his ribs.

A lot of tattoos.

Julia raised her eyebrows. "Spend much time in Thailand?"

He smiled. "You're familiar with Sak Yant?"

"For about three years, I sold houses to a bunch of friends who were all big Muay Thai fighters in LA; they had similar work, and I was always intrigued by it."

"I spent about two years in Thailand a while back; I got the tigers then." He pointed to his chest. "Maybe they're the ones who protected me, huh?"

Julia smiled. "That's not a bad thought."

She lay down next to him and ran her hands up his chest. His skin was warm from the sun coming in her window, and the heat thrilled her. His hands were warm, and his lips, when they took hers, were positively incinerating.

After the cold kiss of near death for the second time in a year, all Julia wanted to feel was heat.

Michael placed his hand at the small of her back and pulled her to him. She could feel the hard line of his body pressed against hers, and it felt delicious and lazy and indulgent.

"Hey, Julia." He didn't stop kissing her neck.

"Hey, Michael."

"Want to fool around?"

She laughed and gripped him around the shoulders. "Don't even think about stopping now."

He ran his hand along her side, cupped her backside for a long squeeze, then hiked her thigh over his hips. "You're pretty flexible."

"Yoga."

Michael didn't rush but thoroughly inspected every inch of bare skin before he took his time exposing another. The strap of her tank top slid to the side, followed by his lips and the rough brush of his knuckles.

"So tell me," he whispered.

"What?"

His fingers skimmed over the top of her breast, raising the sensitive flesh to attention. "Are you going to make me crazy looking for more murderers and criminals with your friends?"

"Possibly."

His teeth closed over her nipple through the satin tank top, and her breath hitched.

"I punched Richard when I found out his ex pulled a gun on you." Michael's tongue slid along the line of skin exposed by her tank and her sleep shorts. "I apologized later; that wasn't very rational."

Julia bit her lip to keep from groaning. "It wasn't part of the plan or anything."

He kissed up her body, taking the tank top with him. "It just kind of happened?"

"I mean..." She could hardly concentrate. "Can we talk about this later?"

"If I asked you very nicely to not look for any more murderers" —his mouth paused just under her belly button; his tongue flicked out, teasing her— "would you stop?"

"Are you trying to sex-blackmail me?" Her eyes crossed when his mouth moved back to her skin.

"Maybe."

She couldn't stop the groan. "Sorry. I can't make any promises."

"I knew you were going to be trouble." He yanked her shorts down with both hands, tossed them over his shoulder, spread her legs, and feasted.

Somewhere between orgasm two and three, Julia might have conceded to limit criminal investigations to misdemeanors, but she couldn't be sure.

Michael crawled up her limp body and took her mouth again, nudging her knees apart so he could enter her. She wrapped her legs around his waist and pulled him closer, gripping his erection with her body.

He groaned and braced himself over her. "You're trouble, but it's worth it."

Julia reached down and squeezed the hard muscles of his ass as he thrust forward. "You talk a lot."

"Can't think." He kissed her again. "Too happy."

"Good." She lost herself in making love to Michael, her part-time boyfriend, who muttered delightfully dirty things when he came.

Julia smiled and let out a long, satisfied sigh when he collapsed on her.

"I'm heavy," he muttered into her shoulder.

"I love it."

She did love it. She loved the weight of him, the solid muscle of his torso and the freckles on his shoulders. She loved the silver hair at his temples and in his half-grown beard. She ran her fingers up and down his spine, as satisfied as the cat who'd eaten the cute, fluffy canary.

"Julia?"

She closed her eyes as the sun angled onto her face. "Yes?"

"Let's take a nap and then do that again."

"I'm game if you are."

He rolled off her, collapsed at her side, and reached for his shirt, which he laid across his chest.

When she frowned at him, he pulled her down, tucked her into his side, and patted her head. "The shirt's for the drool."

Julia laughed, pinched his side, and snuggled closer.

"I APPRECIATE YOU THREE TALKING TO ME AGAIN." John Marcos poured a can of cola over a tall glass of ice. "I was hoping you'd be able to give me a few more details about last night."

"Sure."

"No problem."

"I thought we'd already gone over everything that happened when you questioned us last night." Evy was trying not to look annoyed, and it was kind of working but not really.

Julia bit her lip to keep from laughing.

"Is this really necessary?" She leaned toward Chief Marcos. "Are you trying to see if we change our story?"

"Are you always this suspicious?" Chief Marcos asked.

"Yes." Something clicked in Evy's eyes; she sat back, crossed her hands over her lap, and nodded. "But okay. Go ahead."

"Thanks." His sarcasm was lost on Evy but not Julia and Vivian, who exchanged an amused glance.

The three friends were sitting in their usual spots on Sergio and Dean's back patio as a golden retriever barked in the distance and Paco trotted across the lawn with a bright blue leash in his mouth.

Dean, Sergio, and Michael were in the kitchen, preparing some pasta and steaks for dinner. Michael had already brought his duffel bag into her pool house.

If they were going to make a relationship work, either he or she really needed to find a house. Sharing that small a space could easily kill goodwill.

Chief Marcos frowned at the alpaca, then looked back at his notebook. "So you went over to Casa de Lirio last night because you wanted to search that hiding place in the kitchen again?"

"We wanted to see if there were more," Julia said. "Justin had remembered that he and Lily were fighting about the Putnam Diamond that night, and I thought Lily might have another hiding spot in the house."

"Justin said..." Chief Marcos pressed his lips together. "Justin Worthy's ghost, you mean? Whom you have been seeing since you found his body?"

"Yes, though he walked into the light last night behind Casa de Lirio, so he's not with me anymore." Which was a little weird, to be honest. The pool was alive with Mae's soft singing and Mrs. G's imperious instructions to the animals, but Justin wasn't lounging around and complaining. Elton had retreated to wherever ghosts went when they were bored.

"So you're a medium," Chief Marcos said. "And have you worked with previous police departments?"

She was shocked that he didn't seem shocked. At all. "You're acting like you believe me," she said. "Why?"

"Because I do. You clearly had insight to this case that you weren't getting from the living, Miss Brooks." He looked up. "Or can I still call you Julia?"

"Sure?" She was confused. While Sergio continued to introduce Julia as "his psychic friend" to virtually everyone she met, she'd been expecting more skepticism from the chief of police.

"I've been in law enforcement for about fifteen years," Chief Marcos said. "Trust me, I've seen the fakes, but I can accept that the real deal exists too. I mean, I don't understand it, but I don't understand how my phone works either, and I still use that."

Evy frowned. "Interesting analogy..."

"So you believe me when I tell you that Justin's ghost told me things?"

"We've confirmed your version of events with Lily Putnam, and she claims that she didn't tell you what happened." He shrugged. "So yeah, I buy that Justin was telling you stuff. But that doesn't explain why you went to Casa de Lirio last night. Was it just his memory?"

"Well, his memory and this." She took out the girls' phone. "My nieces had pictures of Sunday Dinner from last month, the night Justin died."

"Pictures?" He reached for the phone. "These are just pictures of Mrs. Putnam and Mr. Worthy. What am I missing?"

"Look at her nails," Vivian said. "That was the clue. Remember the little crystal you found in the hiding spot?"

"Oh right." Chief Marcos nodded. "Lily must have lost one

the night she killed Justin. Good catch." He held up the phone. "I'm going to need to keep this."

"I warned them that might happen," Julia said, "so go for it. Their fathers will be thrilled."

"According to Lily, the night she killed Justin was the same night she took the Putnam Diamond from the hiding spot and put it in her safe."

Vivian huffed out a breath. "Why on earth hadn't she taken it out before then?"

"She said something—before her lawyer came—about Richard getting a court order to see her safe. I think she was paranoid, but it's a moot point now. She kept it at the house because she didn't think anyone would find the hiding spot, and if it wasn't in her safe, she didn't have to worry about Richard's lawyers."

"Wow." Julia shook her head. "What a risk though."

"She's already turned in the diamond. She had moved it to her personal safe, and the Putnam Family lawyers have already filed in court to reclaim it. They're with the Putnam Trust, so it's gone beyond Richard at this point."

"That sounds like serious money," Vivian said. "It's no wonder Lily was paranoid."

"She saw you leaving last night and got suspicious when you didn't come back. She heard rumors that you'd been looking into Justin's death."

"Probably Sergio," Julia said. "He's kind of an open book."

"Possibly. Whatever her intentions were, she held you at gunpoint and threatened your life. Add all that to the murder charges and I don't think we'll be seeing Lily Putnam shopping on Palm Canyon Drive or hosting lunch at the tennis club ever again."

Vivian sat up straight. "Did she say anything about Kiki Stevens? It was on the recording."

"It was." He seemed to debate with himself. "I wish it was a bit clearer; it does help some. But she's holding to her story. According to her, everyone at the party was drinking and doing drugs, so she wasn't responsible for Kiki's inebriation. Lily helped her to the sauna that night and left her there. I don't think we can make any charges stick for that death, especially when it was ruled an accident nearly thirty years ago."

"Damn." Julia shook her head. "That's not the news I wanted for Kiki's daughter."

"You've seen her ghost?" Chief Marcos asked. "Kiki, I mean. I know her daughter is alive and well."

Julia nodded.

"Well, if Maddy Stevens is going to find closure of some kind about her mother, it might have to come from you," he said. "I don't think the justice system is going to be able to give her answers after so many years."

"Thanks for asking anyway," Julia said. "Did you have any other questions?"

"Yeah." John Marcos frowned. "Bernardo Silva nearly ran you over three times. Why on earth didn't you report it to the police?"

"Honestly? I wasn't entirely sure at first if the first two times were just weird accidents or near misses or something. By the time the last one happened in the alley, I thought it was Lily." She shook her head. "We did report it, but I didn't say anything about Lily. I figured no one would take me seriously if I told you a former soap opera actress was trying to kill me because I found her boyfriend's dead body."

"Word of advice, Miss Brooks." John Marcos stood. "I'd start taking your own safety a little more seriously from now on." He looked around. "And wherever you end up, make sure it has more than a guard alpaca for security."

Chapter Thirty-One

There was still tape roping off the house at Casa de Lirio, but Julia smiled as her eyes caught a faint outline standing near the pool, watching the sun set behind the mountains.

She brought out the solar light fountain and gently slid it into the pool next to Kiki Stevens's ghost.

"The truth about your death is out now. Lily confessed, even if she's trying to deny it now. Vivian got a recording of it." Julia looked at the ephemeral blond woman. "The portal opened, but you didn't move on."

Kiki smiled. "Will she go to jail?"

"There's no way of knowing for sure, but probably. She told us she killed Justin, and we can testify to that in court."

Kiki nodded. "Good." She stared at the pool for a few silent moments. "If that woman goes to jail for killing the young man, Casa de Lirio will be off the market." She looked at Julia. "Rich will keep the house. He loves it here. And I might get to see her again. I might get to finally see my daughter."

"Is that why you waited all these years?"

"Seeing him every day was hard, but it kept me going." Kiki

stared at the faint outline of the portal that shimmered among the trees. "I just need to see her once. See my baby happy. I want to see her and her father together. After that, maybe I'll be able to rest."

Julia smiled at Kiki. "I hope it happens soon."

"Me too."

JULIA WALKED BACK TOWARD THE CABANAS WHERE Vivian and Evy were sitting with Sergio and Dean. They'd all walked over to the house at sunset, not willing to let Julia come by herself.

"Kiki's still here."

Dean patted the chaise next to him, and Julia sat down. "We figured that's who you were talking to."

"Michael called a little bit ago," Sergio said. "He was over at Rich's house, and John stopped by. They arrested Bernardo Silva this afternoon."

"Lily's driver?" Dean slid his phone in his front shirt pocket. "What a mess. That man probably had no idea what Lily was getting him into."

"I still can't believe Lily really killed Justin," Sergio said. "John said she told them that she bashed him on the head with a rock, then washed it off and put it back in the garden. They collected some of the stones here last night and are testing them to see if they have skin cells or something." He shuddered.

Vivian frowned. "Is the chief of police supposed to be telling you those kinds of things about an open case?"

Dean muttered, "Probably not."

"But who am I going to tell?" Sergio said. "Besides, everybody already knows by now." He took a deep breath. "I can't lie, I didn't think Pilates gave you that kind of muscle tone. That might be a good class for you, Julia."

"So I can bash people on the head with rocks?"

Sergio held up a hand. "Unlike Lily, I know you will only use your powers for good."

"Lily said Justin threatened to tell Richard everything and ruin her plan," Dean said. "That's why she killed him. Over a *house*."

Vivian added, "I could read Lily's feelings when she was talking about the murder. She might have said she didn't want to kill Justin, but she was *not* sorry. She felt completely justified."

"So she was going to tell Richard she had the Putnam Diamond and promise not to fight him for it if he gave her Casa de Lirio?" Sergio rolled his eyes. "Why not keep the diamond and the profit from half the house?"

Evy said, "That's what Justin wanted."

"You know what?" Julia pictured the look on Lily's face the night of the party as Richard had introduced his daughter to his friends. "It wasn't about the money. It was about getting what she thought Richard owed her."

"Whatever her motives or feelings were, she spilled her guts to John before her lawyer showed up." Dean stood. "She's not going to be able to cry her way out of these criminal charges."

Evy frowned. "Who's her lawyer?"

"Lewis Carey." Sergio stood and walked over to Dean. "I know him. Surprisingly eclectic tie collection."

"Wasn't he the same lawyer Richard hired when he was arrested?" Evy asked.

"Yeah." Dean shrugged. "There aren't that many high-end criminal-defense attorneys who are local. I'm sure she'll trade him in for someone in LA soon enough."

"Stolen diamonds, murdered boyfriends, and secret daughters." Vivian shook her head. "This whole thing sounds like a plot from one of Lily's old soap operas."

"I think even soap fans would have a hard time believing this one," Julia said. "Come on." She rose. "Let's go home."

DEAN AND SERGIO WALKED BACK QUICKLY, BUT JULIA, Evy, and Vivian decided to take their time and enjoy the night air. For several blocks, none of them said anything.

As they got closer to Dean and Sergio's house, Elton, Mrs. G. and Mae joined them, keeping watch over the neighborhood and Julia's new psychic friends.

"I keep thinking about what Lily said," Vivian started. "That she wished she had friends like us when she was living here."

"Do you think having friends keeps you from turning to the dark side?" Evy asked. "I mean, you never hear about serial killers who were part of bridge groups, for example."

"I don't think there would be a murderer in Sergio's Morning Club," Julia said. "But I wouldn't bet my life on it either."

"I'm just saying that murderers don't usually have yoga and wine with the girls or rent houses at the beach for retreat weekends with their college friends. Stuff like that."

"Not unless they plan on killing everyone they invite," Vivian said. "Remember the *Blood-Soaked Escape* podcast?"

"The living are twisted," Elton muttered. "Very twisted."

"That woman invited all her former childhood bullies to an isolated cabin in the woods," Evy said. "I'm not victim-blaming, but there should have been a few more questions asked."

Julia looked at both of them. "I hope you know that I am not going to start listening to true-crime podcasts with you two now that we're psychic friends."

"We're margarita friends too," Vivian said. "And I'll get you a couple of books instead. You seem like the audiobook type."

Julia turned and looked at Casa de Lirio in the distance. She could see the yellow tape fluttering in the wind. "Send them. My only listing is a crime scene for the second time in a month." And if Kiki was right, it might be off the market entirely.

"It'll be okay, honey." Mae smiled at her sympathetically. "This way you can relax and focus on your health."

Mrs. G added, "I am a strong advocate for vigorous exercise at daybreak. It's what allowed me to live as long as I did."

"I'll keep that in mind," Julia muttered.

"What?"

She turned to Evy. "Just talking to the dead."

"Right." Her friend nodded. "So I know your work stuff is kind of messed up, but you now have a hot part-time boyfriend, two amazing new girlfriends, free lodging, and the ability to talk to ghosts. I mean, so far I feel like this move has been a win for you."

Julia smiled. How could she argue with that?

Epilogue

Three months later...

"Are your eyes closed?"

"I told you already, yes."

She guided him under the arching paloverde trees and into the shady entryway where dark green snake plants jumped up to frame the plate glass windows. She stopped walking and dropped his hands. "Okay, open your eyes."

Michael opened his eyes and looked around. He examined the bright yellow double doors, the grey stucco that covered the bungalow, then looked around at the garden inside the high block walls, which were painted a clean white.

The house was a lovingly restored midcentury wonder, and while it wasn't huge on square footage, it had stunning features, a beautiful pool that Julia knew Michael would love, and enough space for Michael to explore gardening if he wanted.

But he hadn't spoken a word.

"What do you think?" She knew he was going to love it, but his silence was unnerving.

He craned his neck to the right. "Is the entire house glass?"

"Just the living portions." She pushed the door open, and the bottom shushed against the smooth flagstone tiles. "It's shaped like an *L*, and the bedrooms go off in this direction." She motioned to the three bedrooms, one of which was set up as an office. "The glass panels surround that branch of the house too but just expose the hallway. Beyond that, obviously, you have privacy walls, and that makes for a beautiful gallery space."

He nodded slowly. "Right. I mentioned that, didn't I?"

"You did."

He looked around the living area. "There's a garden inside the house."

She took his hand again and led him toward the sunken space that occupied the center of the open-plan living and dining area in the house. "This is a mature tropical garden, but if you wanted to change it—"

"Why would I want to change it?" He spun in place, taking in the light, the sweeping view of the mountains, and the graceful paloverde trees that shaded the gravel paths in the yard. "This is amazing."

She broke into a huge smile. "I knew you were going to like it! I started thinking about this place when you told me about the monastery in Hawaii, and it wasn't even on the market yet, but I remembered Dean saying the owners were thinking about moving to the beach. Now, I know the desert isn't the tropics, but the way the glass walls define the space—"

"It feels like you're living outside." He pushed against one thick glass pane. "Are these doors?"

She nodded. "They can slide back when the weather is nice to let the fresh air in, but the last owner put a special UV coating on them to cut back on air-conditioning bills in the summer, and I am told it makes a huge difference."

As did the trees that lined both sides of the glass house, the deep shade covers that spread out like wings, and the crystal-blue pool Michael was looking at in the distance.

"It's designed to make you feel one with the garden," Julia said. "And to take advantage of that clean desert feeling. There's not a ton of square footage. The main bedroom is beautiful and the guest room is nice, but the third bedroom is really more of an office. There is a pad poured along the back wall if you wanted to build a pool house, and that would add some room, but I don't know if that's what— Oh!"

Michael grabbed her around the waist, pulled her into his chest, and kissed her breathless. "I love it. I really love it. I can imagine living here. I can actually see myself living here. I can see my stuff and everything."

She grinned. "The hallway outside the bedrooms would make an amazing place to display your art collection too. You could set up some podiums for the sculptures."

He nodded. "Those are all the bedrooms?"

"Yes." She walked farther into the glass house. "And the kitchen is here." She motioned past the space where a neat kitchen dominated the interior wall. "And on the other side of this wall is the library and entertainment room."

"Julia, I don't even..." He caught her eye. "This is amazing; show me everything."

And this was why she was falling in love with the man.

Michael, in so many ways, was a simple person. If Julia had called him up in Prague and told him she'd found the perfect house for him, he probably would have trusted her judgment and put a down payment in on something, sight unseen.

But he also knew that she delighted in doing what she loved.

"I just have one question." He raised a hand. "Are there any ghosts?"

Her eyes darted to the back wall. "*Inside* the house?"

"I take it there's one outside?"

"It looks like a nice young man, and he's just walking beside the palm trees along the back wall. He might not even be a resident."

Michael opened his mouth, then closed it and nodded. "Okay, so tell me about the library."

She smiled, glad that he'd become fairly nonplussed about the idea of spirits occupying her space.

After all, it was Vista de Lirio. Julia hadn't visited a single house that didn't have someone stopping by occasionally, though obviously the older the house, the more probable that it was ethereally occupied.

Julia happily showed him the library den, the back bathroom, and the interior wine cellar, which were centrally located, along with an area along the back of the house that was surrounded on three sides by glass and the current owners were using as a home gym. Then she showed Michael the three bedrooms in the living wing of the L and the garden in the side yard that was dominated by a massive willow.

He loved it all, and since the price was right smack in the middle of his budget, she texted their contract writer and started making the plans.

"So." He pulled her into an embrace after she put her phone away. "What have you been doing while I was in Prague?"

He'd spent two months on a shoot for an independent film. It was a mystery, but it was also a romance, which he said was the heart of the story. Now he was back in Palm Springs for a month before he'd need to head into Los Angeles for more postproduction fun.

"Work." She swayed back and forth with him. It was nearly summer, and the outdoors would only be pleasant for a few more hours. "I sold two places in the past month, which feels very nice but manageable. Dean is pleased, and the office staff here is really great."

"Good to hear. You looking for your own place yet?"

"Not yet. Thinking about it." They walked along the path beneath the palm trees where the young ghost had been walking earlier. He disappeared as soon as they approached. "Been doing lots of swimming. I decided that's going to be my main exercise since Vivian can't do racquetball anymore."

"And how's she feeling?"

Julia smiled. "Cranky."

"I'm not surprised." He laughed. "My sister had her last kid at forty-two and claimed that it was completely different than being pregnant in her thirties."

"Luckily, Vivian doesn't have anything to compare it to, but I can't remember if I told you that her parents moved out here."

"I don't think so." He raised an eyebrow. "So how's that going?"

"Three generations in one house?" Julia shrugged. "I think she's going to be my next client."

Michael grinned. "Well, I recommend your work." He looked around the manicured yard. "I love it. Feels like home."

"SHHHHHHH." EVY PRESSED HER FINGERS TO HER temples. "Okay, I may need to start drinking more now that Michael is back in the country. You are thinking about him *so* loud."

"Sorry."

"You say that, but the thoughts..." She glared at Julia. "They do not stop."

They were meeting for Thursday-night Palomas on the back patio after the scorching afternoon sun went down. Delicious tequila for Evy and Julia, none for the daintily pregnant Vivian, who'd just barely begun to show.

"I'm not trying to think about Michael. Or sex," Julia said. "I'll hum something in my head if you want me to."

"No, that's what Vivian does, and now I have a series of one-hit wonders from the early aughts seared into my brain." Evy took a sip of her drink. "I just need to work on blocking it."

Julia frowned in sympathy. "I'm sorry."

Evy sighed. "I mean, it's not like you can turn off seeing ghosts, so I can't complain."

Elton looked at Julia. "Why would you want to turn off seeing ghosts?"

"I can't imagine." Julia sipped her drink and decided to avoid the question entirely. "Elton, Mae, and Mrs. G are all here, by the way."

"Good." Vivian shifted in her seat. "I always feel more secure when the alarm system is in place."

Of the three of them, Vivian had been most thrown by their near-brush with death. Evy seemed to take the entire incident at Casa de Lirio in stride and Julia had already had one brush with death, so what was one more? Vivian, on the other hand, was feeling particularly vulnerable, which was understandable in the first trimester of a much-wanted pregnancy.

She'd taken to making sure one or two ghosts were on patrol every time they got together.

"You know, I don't know that ghosts would necessarily sense danger more than a human would," Julia said. "A lot of them are remarkably unobservant."

Evy raised a finger. "Not Elton."

"That's right," Elton said. "In fact, I think I may go check out the perimeter." He glanced at Vivian, then faded away.

"Does he still have a little crush?" Evy whispered.

Vivian put a hand over her eyes. "Please can we not talk about this?"

"I think it's cute!"

"I don't want to think about any man right now," Vivian said. "I have an old man living in my house, and he is not very good about shutting the door when he goes to the bathroom." She shook her head. "This may not be sustainable."

Vivian's parents had taken over the master bedroom in her house because it was the only bedroom on the ground floor and her mother was having issues with her balance they were still trying to figure out.

Which meant that the cozy sanctuary that Vivian had tended since she moved to Palm Springs was no longer her own.

Julia gave it three months before Vivian was calling her for listings. Luckily, she already had a cute Spanish place in mind.

She heard the pedestrian gate open, and Sergio, Dean, and the girls came walking up from the street. Paco was nowhere in sight, but two of Sergio's golden retrievers came running over to greet the family.

"Oh look," Dean said. "Look, honey, it's your angels."

Sergio spread his arms. "Darlings! Make me a drink and I'll join you after I get these monsters headed to bed."

Evy gave him a thumbs-up, and Sergio went inside with the girls while Dean grabbed a beer from the fridge and sat next to Vivian.

"So how are Richard and Maddy?"

Dean smiled. "You know, I think they're doing well. Maddy decided to move into the pool house, and Richard is already redecorating, so the whole house feels really fresh. It's lovely to see them together. You can tell they're eager to make up for lost time."

Once Lily was arrested, she agreed to let Richard buy her out of her half of Casa de Lirio. Her lawyers made it more than clear that she needed cash and not property. Richard was happy to move back into the house he'd never wanted to leave, and he made every appearance of wanting to leave the past behind.

Which wasn't always the easiest when the paparazzi had one field day after another covering Lily's arrest for the murder of Justin Worthy. A beautiful, aging soap opera star killing her young, handsome lover when he threatened to reveal her secrets? It was a made-for-TV movie in the making.

Seriously, there were already two in production.

And to no one's surprise, at least half a dozen murder podcasts had covered the case.

"I'm so happy for him," Vivian said. "What do the girls think about their teacher moving into the neighborhood?"

Dean shrugged. "They're vaguely amused, but since Maddy teaches fifth grade and they never had her as their own teacher, I think existential dilemmas have been avoided." He smiled at Vivian. "Richard asked after you."

She held up a hand. "I'm flattered, but seriously, I do not have the mental energy to juggle another thing even if that means I miss out on dating Vista de Lirio's most eligible bachelor. My parents, this baby, and work have me on my last nerve."

"You just let us know when we can help," Dean said. "With anything. You know we consider you family now." He rose and smiled at all three of them. "After all, you're Sergio's angels."

Evy cracked a laugh, Vivian groaned, and Julia shook her head, but she couldn't keep from smiling. Then she looked around at her friends and realized the desert really was magical.

She'd come to Vista de Lirio a disconnected workaholic, floating through life even while she made it her mission to find other people their home.

And not even a year later, she'd found her family with old friends and new. And if she hadn't quite given up on living in Dean and Sergio's pool house for the foreseeable future, she knew she'd eventually find a place that suited her. For now it didn't matter.

She was home.

Continue reading for a preview of MIRROR OBSCURE, the next Vista de Lirio novel, coming June 2022.

Dr. Vivian Wei is juggling multiple life-changing events when her aging mother witnesses a violent death on the thirteenth tee. The only problem? There doesn't seem to be a crime to go along with the witness. As an empath, Vivian knows her mother is telling the truth, but feelings don't prove a murder. Can Vivian, her mother, and her friends prove a killer is stalking the country club before he claims another victim?

Preview: Mirror Obscure

H er professional name had been Selene Beverly, discreet psychic to the stars and uncanny astrologer, but when she'd introduced herself to Vivian, she used her given name, Maud Peterson.

"Another deep breath in." Maud's soothing voice drifted over the cool morning air. "And out very slowly, letting any negativity—aaaaany friction or resistance—eeeeexit your body." Another deep breath, in and out. "Release it to the universe."

No need for professional names among peers, according to Maud. Vivian was newly empathic. Her friend Julia who was sitting directly in front of her was a medium who was exchanging silent pointed looks with their friend Evy, the telepath of their small supernatural circle.

According to Maud, they all needed practice.

The more experienced touch-telepath happily agreed to join Morning Club two days a week to help Vivian and her friends with their "psychic workouts." At least, that's what Maud called them. She was like a personal trainer, if a personal trainer was more interested in your aura than your muscles, and wore caftans for appointments.

"Another two breaths like that, then we'll start our meditation."

Vivian tried to focus on her breathing and not on the papaya-sized baby in her uterus who had decided to do backflips on her bladder that morning.

I don't have to pee. I don't have to pee. I don't have to—
"Shit."

She whispered it, but when she opened her eyes, every gaze on the lawn that morning was directed toward her. Julia and Evy, Aunt Marie—the one who knew Maud in the first place—and half a dozen other Morning Club neighbors from Vista de Lirio, the weird and wonderful neighborhood that had become Vivian's second home.

"Sorry." Vivian awkwardly hoisted herself to her feet and pointed to her belly. "Need to pee again."

Maud nodded and waved her hands. "As we listen to our bodies and give them what they need—eyes forward please—we focus on centering our spines and connecting with the earth beneath us, the life around us, and the power within us."

Slowly, everyone turned back, closed their eyes, and refocused their attention on Maud's guided meditation. Morning Club was a Vista de Lirio institution. No pregnant lady was going to trip it up.

Sergio Oliveira, their host that morning, shuffled over in a black t-shirt, a pair of grey sweatpants, and house slippers. His shoulder length hair was touseled and thick black stubble marked his jaw.

"What do you need, honey?" He blinked his dark bedroom eyes and yawned a little. "I can't ever sit still long enough for meditation. Can I get you some tea? No Bloody Marys or Mimosa for you these days, but I'll make you a virgin screwdriver if you want." He squinted. "Maybe that's just orange juice. I'll get you an orange juice."

Good lord, he looked like a movie star. It was at least the

hundredth time she'd thought it since Sergio had walked into her dental practice for a cleaning and she'd met the man that had started the string of unlikely events that had landed her where she was, newly psychic and pregnant at forty-two.

Okay, that was unfair. He was really only responsible for the psychic part.

"I'm fine." She brushed her hand over his arm and felt the happy wave of emotion that was Sergio. "I just need to use the bathroom. Again."

He yawned and waved at the house. "You know where it is. I'm going to make you some tea anyway."

"Thanks." Vivian walked to the bathroom in the sprawling 1930s era mansion that Sergio shared with his husband, Dean, their two daughters, and Alula, their live-in nanny.

She sat down and did her business with great relief, then stood, wrestling her yoga pants over her ever-expanding belly, and tried to imagine life in three or four months.

Intellectually, Dr. Vivian Wei knew that her uterus would grow rapidly at this stage of pregnancy to keep track with the swiftly growing baby boy she was carrying. She knew that, she just couldn't imagine it. She was already feeling unwieldy and off balance. Her feet were bigger. Her thick black hair was getting thicker every day, and she felt like sleeping constantly. Thank God she was in excellent shape and health for forty-two, because she could not imagine doing this if she wasn't.

She washed her hands, walked out of the powder room, and toward the sounds of life in the kitchen. Sergio was standing near the electric kettle with Dean, who already dressed in a bright white shirt and linen jacket. Dean may have been a commercial real estate broker, but it was August in Palm Springs. A suit and tie were pure torture.

"Good morning, Vivian." Dean walked over and brushed a kiss on her temple. "How are you feeling?"

"Good, just distracted." She peered out the window at the

group on the lawn. "I have never been very good at sitting meditation."

"Same," Sergio said. "I'll join them in a half hour when tai chi gets going."

"That sounds like a plan." She tried to jump onto one of the half dozen barstools on the other side of the kitchen island before giving up and grabbing a chair in the breakfast nook. "At least the weather is nice."

"For another two hours, and then it's one hundred and eight today." Dean grimaced. "How are you doing?"

"Becoming a better swimmer every day." Vivian smiled. "And thanking the universe my grandparents' development has a pool." It wasn't technically her grandparents' development anymore; it was hers. She'd been living in Palm Springs full time for over a year now, but this was her first full summer. And her first summer pregnant.

What had she been thinking?

Oh right: time was of the essence.

Despite her single status, nothing about Vivian's pregnancy was unplanned. Nothing about her life was unplanned except for the jolt of psychic energy seven months before that had unlocked latent empathic power and turned her world on its head.

She had always known she wanted to be a mother. And she'd always had a plan to become one if she hadn't met the right partner by age forty. She had no qualms about scientific means of conception.

In Vivian's mind, this mindset freed her from the pressure of finding "the right man" for a relationship and fatherhood. There was no time pressure to settle for a subpar relationship when she knew that she could accomplish motherhood on her own. Now, if she met someone, it would be for the right reasons, not because she was on a biological schedule.

Not that she was looking.

With a pregnancy nearing the last trimester, her parents sudden and possibly permanent move to Palm Springs, and the sudden ability to sense emotions when she shook hands with strangers, Vivian knew that any kind of romance was out of the question for the year. Maybe the decade.

At least she had fellow new psychics Julia and Evy to keep her company with the psychic stuff. And Maud. She had Maud.

"Here's your tea." Sergio sat across from her and blinked heavily. "I should probably at least try to meditate, right?" Dean barked a laugh and Sergio turned to him. "At least I try. What do you do for your mental wellbeing?"

Dean didn't even look up from the newspaper. "I kiss you and I golf."

Sergio looked back at Vivian. "See, what am I supposed to say to that?"

"Nothing." She patted his hand. "Come on. I'll finish my tea and we should get out there. If I don't keep practicing the tai chi, I will start tipping onto patients when I look at their molars."

"YOU ARE SO MUCH BETTER AT TAI CHI THAN I AM." Evy wiped the glow of sweat from her forehead. It wasn't from exertion, it was because it was nearing ninety degrees already. "And you're pregnant. I really need to exercise more."

"Yes, you do." Julia took a long drink of the Paloma Sergio had made for her and leaned back in the patio chair. "Ladies, should I start looking for your own place?"

Evy looked around the shaded patio, the crystal blue pool, and the rolling lawn where other members of Morning Club were chatting and sitting with their drinks while the weather was still bearable. "And move away from heaven?"

Vivian smiled. "I have to admit, your setup here is pretty sweet."

Julia was currently living in Dean and Sergio's pool house, and had been for nearly a year. She was family, though, so they refused to let her pay rent. And since Julia was a very successful real estate agent with homes in both Laguna Beach and Malibu, she had plenty of capital if she wanted to buy a house in Palm Springs.

"You're right. And half the time I'm housesitting for Michael anyway," she said. "That is the benefit of having a part time boyfriend."

Michael, Julia's new man, was a director and traveled a lot, so he was barely at his new house in Palm Springs, but at least Julia was enjoying it.

"I'm starting to think you need to start looking for me," Vivian said. "I'm beginning to wonder if my parents will ever leave."

"Oh, I knew it!" Julia smiled. "You *need* to move. Living in Indian Wells is not for you. Why don't your parents stay there, and you find your own place? Here. In Vista de Lirio."

"I thought your dad was helping at the practice?" Evy sipped her Bloody Mary. "Is it a little too much closeness?"

"It is, and he is. My dad is great, and my mom is so excited about the baby. They are definitely helping a lot, but I'm just used to having my own space." She waved a hand. "I'm sure it's just a transitional stage. I'll be grateful they're here when the baby comes. And I never have to cook anymore; that's so nice."

Plus, she didn't have the budget Julia did. Vivian did well, but if she wanted to move, she'd need to sell the house her grandparents had left her, which was a house her parents loved. Her father could golf every day, and her mother had a mahjong club at the Jewish temple full of smack-talking old women, two of whom were fellow retired MDs.

In short: her parents were happy, enjoying the warm weather, and looking forward to spoiling a new grandbaby.

They were never moving.

"I CAN TELL THE MEDITATION CLASS IS WORKING," Joan Wei, MD. was serving dinner and filling Vivian and her dad about her day. "Your color is good."

"This looks delicious, Mom." Her mother was the first generation of her Chinese family born in the US, so she'd learned to cook all the traditional dishes Vivian's dad loved, but also the varied dishes she'd grown up eating in Chicago. Italian, Mexican, and even Slavic dishes like the stuffed cabbage rolls she'd made that evening.

"I hope it's good. It's Marty's recipe and I liked it, but it needed some spice." She spooned a large helping of rice next to the cabbage rolls. "Hopefully, it won't give you heartburn. It's just a little spice."

Vivian's mouth was burning with the first bite, but the flavor was delicious. "It's great." She nodded. "Perfect, Mom." *Tums, here I come.*

"There are more in the pan, so eat."

Despite the heat, it really was a delicious meal. "Dad, how was your round of gold this morning? I hardly saw you at the office."

"It was good, but I'm not betting that Simon fellow again." Allan shook his head. "He's been golfing a lot longer than me."

"You lost to a ninety-year old?" Joan asked.

"I told you." Allan nodded firmly. "Experience."

Vivian looked at her parents with a little bit of exasperation and a lot of love. They'd raised she and her sister to be successful adults, but also raised them with so much love it threatened to make Vivian weepy.

Everything made her weepy lately.

Dammit, she was crying.

Joan's eyes went wide. "Vivian, what's wrong?"

"Nothing!" She smiled. "I was just thinking that this baby is so lucky to have such amazing grandparents." She reached out her hands. "Thank you for being here, Mom. Dad, I'm so glad you two are happy here."

They both reached out to grab her hand, and she felt their love and their worry. Pride and concern from her father, but her mother's emotions were so muddled, Vivian wondered if they were too close to her own.

She wiped her eyes and smiled again. "Let's eat before it gets cold."

"You know, after dinner, we could watch the Desert Classic," Allan said. "I heard they were going to replay it on the Golf Channel."

Great. Awesome. Vivian stuffed the rest of the cabbage roll in her mouth. Just what she wanted to do on a Friday night, watch reruns on the Golf Channel.

VIVIAN WAS SOUND ASLEEP WHEN A MOVEMENT ON her bed jolted her awake.

"Vivian?" Her mother was sitting on the edge of her bed.

"Mom, what are you doing up here?" She'd moved to the upstairs guest room when her parents moved in because her mother's knees bothered her on the stairs. Why had her mother climbed to the second floor? "Is Dad okay?"

"He's fine." She opened her mouth, then closed it.

Vivian sat up and rubbed her eyes. She glanced at the clock and noticed the time. "Mom, what is going on? It's one in the morning; are you okay?"

"No." Her voice came in a whisper.

Vivian really looked at her mother. Her face was pale and she looked... scared? She leaned forward and grabbed her mother's hand.

Terror. Sheer terror.

"Mom, what is going on?"

"I couldn't sleep," Joan started. "I... I have some tea that my mother used and I brought it from home, so I went to make it and when I was waiting for it to steep, I looked out the window in the kitchen. You know there is the thirteenth tee just over the fence line and you can see the golfers when they're teeing up."

"Yeah, Mom, what is going on? Was there someone—"

"He swung the golf club, and I didn't realize what was happening at first, but there was a light from somewhere and then I saw the club and then the man fell down." Her voice dropped to a whisper. "He hit him so many times, Vivian. There was blood and..." She looked up. "I think he's dead. Someone murdered that man."

MIRROR OBSCURE will be available in ebook and paperback June, 2022.

Looking for more?

Whether you're a fan of contemporary fantasy or paranormal women's fiction, Elizabeth Hunter has a series for you!

THE ELEMENTAL MYSTERIES

Discover the series that has millions of vampire fans raving! Immortal book dealer Giovanni Vecchio thought he'd left the bloody world of vampire politics behind when he retired as an assassin, but a chance meeting at a university pulls student librarian Beatrice De Novo into his orbit. Now temptation lurks behind every dark corner as Vecchio's growing attachment to Beatrice competes with a series of clues that could lead to a library lost in time, and a powerful secret that could reshape the immortal world.

THE CAMBIO SPRINGS MYSTERIES

Welcome to the desert town of Cambio Springs where the water is cool, the summers sizzle, and all the residents wear fur, feathers, or snakeskin on full moon nights. In a world of cookie-cutter shifter romance, discover a series that has reviewers raving. Five friends find themselves at a crossroads in life; will the tangled ties of community and shared secrets be their salvation or their end?

THE IRIN CHRONICLES

"A brilliant and addictive romantic fantasy series." Hidden at the crossroads of the world, an ancient race battles to protect humanity, even as it dies from within. A photojournalist tumbles into a world of supernatural guardians protecting humanity from the predatory sons of fallen angels, but will Ava and Malachi's attraction to each other be their salvation or their undoing?

GLIMMER LAKE

Delightfully different paranormal women's fiction! Robin, Val, and Monica were average forty-something moms when a sudden accident leaves all three of them with psychic abilities they never could have predicted! Now all three are seeing things that belong in a fantasy novel, not their small mountain town. Ghosts, visions, omens of doom. These friends need to stick together if they're going to solve the mystery at the heart of Glimmer Lake.

And there's more! Please visit ElizabethHunterWrites.com to sign up for her newsletter or read more about her work.

Acknowledgments

I want to offer a huge thank you to my very faithful and very patient readers, who were supposed to get Double Vision back in February, but patiently waited until now to read this story. I truly hope it was worth the wait!

Many effusive thanks to my publishing team. I send all my love and appreciation to my content editor, Amy Cissell, my line editor, Anne Victory, and my proofreader, Linda. They made this book beautiful, so if there are any typos or messes you found, it's probably because I messed with things after they fixed it.

I could not write and publish the way I do without the expert assistance of my sister and right hand, Genevieve Johnson. I also want to thank my publicity team over at Valentine PR and my agents at Dystel, Goderich, and Bourret.

Further thanks to the wonderful Karen Dimmick at Arcane Covers for her stunning work on this new series. I am absolutely thrilled with her work, and it was a joy to collaborate with her.

And finally, the biggest shoutout to my husband and my son, who are my biggest fans and most constant support. I love you both so much.

It's been a long, strange trip, my friends, but we're making it through. And I hope, like me, you see the light at the end of this tunnel.

—EH
Visalia, California
February 23, 2021

About the Author

ELIZABETH HUNTER is a seven-time *USA Today* and international best-selling author of romance, contemporary fantasy, and paranormal mystery. Based in Central California and Addis Ababa, she travels extensively to write fantasy fiction exploring world mythologies, history, and the universal bonds of love, friendship, and family. She has published over forty works of fiction and sold over a million books worldwide. She is the author of the Glimmer Lake series, Love Stories on 7th and Main, the Elemental Legacy series, the Irin Chronicles, the Cambio Springs Mysteries, and other works of fiction.

Also by Elizabeth Hunter

The Force of Wind

A Fall of Water

The Stars Afire

The Elemental World

Building From Ashes

Waterlocked

Blood and Sand

The Bronze Blade

The Scarlet Deep

A Very Proper Monster

A Stone-Kissed Sea

Valley of the Shadow

The Elemental Legacy

Shadows and Gold

Imitation and Alchemy

Omens and Artifacts

Obsidian's Edge (anthology)

Midnight Labyrinth

Blood Apprentice

The Devil and the Dancer

Night's Reckoning

Dawn Caravan

The Bone Scroll

The Elemental Covenant

Saint's Passage

Martyr's Promise

Paladin's Kiss

(August 2022)

CPSIA information can be obtained
at www.ICGtesting.com
Printed in the USA
LVHW021916030322
712275LV00001B/4